RAVE REVIEWS
FOR *DEADLY DONATION*

"An intriguing first novel, featuring an out-of-the-ordinary protagonist who thinks too much—and not enough." —Rick Blechta, award-winning author of the Pratt & Ellis Mysteries

"*The Donation* stars Rachel Tile, a smart and savvy criminologist who gets drawn into the many layers of intrigue and emotion surrounding the recent murder of her ex-husband, Michael. Diving into the confusing web around the crime and unsure of what she might find along the way, Rachel gathers the spicy facts that will eventually lead to the murderer. All this while seeking a huge donation from some wealthy high-rollers who can help save the program at the university where she teaches. Tepperman has hit a home run with this first book in his new crime series." —Bruce McGregor, author of *GPS Wealth* and *GPS Millionaire*

"A cracking good read! Lorne Tepperman keeps the pages turning as the mysteries and the murders hidden behind the sudden disappearance of a large promised donation to her university are unravelled. Very fun reading—with a fine eye for the dark side of big money at the top." —Lars Osberg, author of *The Age of Increasing Inequality: The Astonishing Rise of Canada's 1%*

"Real estate tycoon gets murdered. But by whom and why? Lots of enemies, most potential murderers. Business associates with axes to grind. Dysfunctional family members, by blood or marriage, that have angry debts. His ex-wife, a criminologist, investigates. It's a well-paced thriller with intriguing labyrinthian complexity. The turns and twists keep you reading page after page after page. Fugue states, Norse legends, shapeshifters, and artistic interpretation all energize the thrill of the read." —Neil Guppy, author of *The Schooled Society*

"If you like 'whodunit' crime fiction in a Canadian (read Toronto) setting, there is much to savour in this densely plotted saga. The narrator, a professor of criminology, applies her classroom knowledge of crime causation to hunt down the perpetrator. As in all good whodunits, the reader is presented with a network of plausible, and deeply flawed, suspects, all of whom—including the narrator—have good reason for wishing the victim dead. For readers familiar with Toronto and its environs, there is further pleasure to be had from recognition of many of the locations and situations that drive the narrative." —Julian Tanner, author of *Teenage Troubles*

"In this dizzying and glorious race through a widow's lively mind, Lorne Tepperman's *The Donation* carries us on a brilliant criminologist's hunt for Canada's most generous man's killer. A powerful and mesmerizing gamble of a book, seen with the wise eye of a master observer!" —Murray Pomerance, author of *A King of Infinite Space*

"This craftily written and fast paced murder mystery has everything: sex, violence, incest, gambling, addiction, marital betrayal, a nasty (and wealthy) victim and a myriad suspects, including the protagonist. Add in Norse mythology and a denouement that is both surprising and inevitable, all set in normally sedate Toronto and pastoral Prince Edward County, and you have a book impossible to put down. *The Donation* is much more than a whodunit. It is a thoughtful meditation on truth, consequences, character and life's meaning." —Michael Adams, author of *Sex in the Snow* and *Fire and Ice*

"Lorne Tepperman, a retired academic, draws on years of experience studying crime, gambling, and family relations in crafting this neo-noir thriller. The thicket of compelling characters he's created is, however, a far cry from any that would be found in a scholarly treatise. Conflicting and overlapping motives, an undertow of corruption and deceit, and clues hidden in plain sight will challenge readers until the final denouement. Given the multi-layered, compelling protagonist Tepperman has fashioned, one suspects this will not be the final mystery Rachel Tile is called upon to untangle." —Rosemary Gartner, co-editor of *The Oxford Handbook of Gender, Sex, and Crime*

Recent Books by Lorne Tepperman

Why You Buy (with Megan Markus)
Canada's Place: A Global Perspective (with Maria Finnsdottir)
Consumer Society (with Nicole Meredith)

DEADLY DONATION

Lorne Tepperman

Rock's Mills Press
Rock's Mills, Ontario • Oakville, Ontario
2024

Published by
Rock's Mills Press
www.rocksmillspress.com

For retail, library and bulk orders, please contact the publisher at
customer.service@rocksmillspress.com.

Prologue

Statistically, there was nothing remarkable about this murder. On average, one or two people get murdered every week in Toronto. This victim was just one of the week's quota.

And it was homicide in the usual way—death by gunshot. Nothing remarkable there either.

The police found his corpse where they often find homicide victims—in the victim's own home. It wasn't a domestic dispute. They thought the victim was alone in the family home when he met his end. But the home itself was far from ordinary. It was one of Toronto's largest, most expensive mansions. No surprise there: the victim was one of Toronto's, actually one of Canada's, richest people. Had it been a robbery gone wrong, the crook could have made off with extremely valuable stuff. Yet nothing was stolen.

Another odd feature: there were no signs of forced entry and the security system was disabled the night of the murder. So, the killer could have just walked in, invited or not.

The condition of the corpse was puzzling too. Only two bullets were needed to kill the victim and both found their mark. That's how professional hitmen kill—neatly and efficiently. But the forensic pathologist found another injury too, not made by a bullet. It was the kind of mark amateurs leave behind when they lose their temper.

The most puzzling feature of this murder was the way people reacted. Some people said the victim was Canada's most generous philanthropist. Nobody gave away more money than he did, the on-air talking heads all said. And many members of the manda-

rin class treated the murder like a great national tragedy. Prominent people hailed the victim as a great giver and benefactor. But in the business community, most of the people who knew him best were indifferent. Secretly, some of them were even pleased. They may have even been thinking, "That SOB finally screwed over the wrong person and got what he deserved."

I should have let the police sort it out. But I just couldn't leave the case alone, because I had known Michael. Although, it turns out, I hadn't known him as well as I thought I did. And I hadn't known him nearly as well as I should have. So, I guess that's on me.

I was driving home when I heard about Michael's death the first time. A CBC announcer broke into the traffic report to say Michael Coale had been murdered in his Toronto mansion. The housekeeper had found his body after getting back from her day off. There had been no witnesses to the crime, as his wife had been on a Caribbean vacation, his stepson at a friend's house, and his stepdaughter at her apartment studying for a test. The police didn't have any suspects yet but claimed to have some promising leads. They said they'd provide more information later that afternoon.

Michael Coale. My ex. At one time, I'd hated him with a passion. Now he was just a bad memory, someone I used to know. Someone I thought I knew.

But Michael's murder was a huge news story in Canada, so big that it knocked what normally would have been the day's top story into second place. Suddenly, no one—except for a few diehard fans—was talking about that hockey game last night. Nick Dempster, the NHL's leading scorer, had been playing his last game before retiring in his prime. There'd be no Stanley Cup for Nick or the Leafs this year, and that turned the game into a must-see for Toronto's unshakeable hockey fans.

Daniel—my hockey-fan husband—couldn't stop talking about Nick's untimely retirement. In fact, Daniel was inconsolable.

Personally, I didn't care about Nick Dempster any more than I cared about Michael, though I had no reason to hate the hockey player. It was all just another band of high-decibel noise.

The news story that interested me most had been knocked into third place (or maybe tenth, for all I knew). "Ontario to sell off the Science Centre. Lands to be used for upscale condo development." Of course, this was nothing new. Ontario was "open for business." Over the years, in the interest of cutting taxes while raising revenues, the provincial government had privatized Highway 407, allowed a private spa to take over much of Ontario Place, and six years ago had agreed to a global consortium of private investors taking over Strachan University—*my* university. The new owners quickly moved to cut the arts and humanities faculties and beef up applied studies, including criminology. They had also raised tuition fees and sent administrators and faculty members on fundraising missions around the world. After all, as a private institution, we had to pay our own way, with no recourse to public funds.

A lot of our budget now came from those higher tuition fees—especially those paid by international students. They now made up eighty percent of our enrolment and paid $150,000 a year for the pleasure of attending Strachan. Other revenue came from selling off parts of the campus deemed "surplus," and the rest from donations: gifts, bequests, and endowments. As Director of the School of Criminology, I had learned a lot about fundraising over the past year.

But today, everyone was talking about Michael's murder. My phone rang. It was my sister Megan. "Did you hear the news?" she asked breathlessly. "Someone murdered Michael." I imagined her saying this with a scary-face look, mouth wide open.

"Yeah, I heard," I said. But I had nothing more to say about it.

Suddenly I wasn't feeling so good. I apologized and said I had to go, saying I was stuck in traffic. I promised to call her back.

My heart was pounding. I couldn't breathe and my hands had started to shake. Sweat was dripping down my face, hindering my vision. Afraid of crashing the car, I pulled off Yonge onto a residential side street and stopped. After pausing to catch my breath, I slid over to the passenger door, got out, and bent over the curb. My lunch had tasted better going down, that's for sure.

Anita had told me to expect this kind of thing now and then, despite the medication she had prescribed. "It will take you a while for the panic attacks to stop," she'd said. I'd been having such attacks, off and on, for fifteen years—but far more often in the last six months.

Feeling slightly calmer, I eased back onto Yonge Street. I could have watched a foreign movie with subtitles while navigating this glacial flow of traffic. But happily, I wasn't far from home now. I'd make it home, no matter what.

It had been another perfect day in the life of Rachel Tile, I thought sarcastically. When I woke up this morning, I couldn't remember anything about last night—what I'd done or where I'd been. In the last few months, I'd been having these blackouts pretty regularly. For reasons I didn't understand and couldn't explain, I had started drinking way too much; but the blackouts were something new and, to be honest, they scared me.

My capable, but also very judgmental, mom would be appalled if she knew about my booze-induced blackouts. When I was young, she had successfully scared me away from alcohol, using the fear of fat alone. (She showed me photos of women who had packed on the pounds, allegedly because of drinking too much or too often. Who was I to say she was wrong?)

A loud honk interrupted my reverie. I started driving again.

I got a second call about Michael while I was in my driveway, still in the car trying to catch my breath. It was from an ex-student, one of the most talented criminology students I had ever taught. Roxy Duncan had become a constable for the Toronto police and I considered her a good friend. "Hi Rachel" she said. "I'm guessing you've heard about Michael Coale?"

"Yes. I heard it on the car radio."

"I just wanted to say I'm sorry for your loss."

"No need. Michael hasn't been a part of my life for many years." To myself, I thought, "If you knew him, I doubt you'd be calling his death a loss. He was a pretty horrible person."

Oops, it seems I said that out loud. That made her chuckle.

"Whatever; anyway, I was at the Coale mansion today," Roxy added. "The department has assigned a lot of us to this case. And wow, I've never seen such opulence."

"I'll have to take your word for it, Roxy, since I've never been there. And Michael made a lot less money back when I was married to him. Our house never would have wowed anyone. But, you know, I might get a peek at their mansion yet."

"How come?"

"Michael told some folks he might donate more money to our university. And when my dean got wind of it, he told me to make sure Criminology reels it in. Fundraising is a big part of my job now; and if I know Dean Grabol, he's not going to let Michael off the hook just because he's dead. Michael's going to sign that darn check wherever he is—and between you and me, I'm guessing that's Hell. So, I may have to take my begging bowl to the Coale mansion and see all that opulence for myself."

"Ewww. I don't envy you that job, Rachel."

"No, I'm not looking forward to it. Anyway, thanks for calling, Roxy. And thanks for thinking of me." We said our goodbyes.

2

Finally out of my car and inside my house, I called out to Josh. When he came downstairs, I broke the news about his dad as gently as I could. I wasn't sure how he'd take it. He and Michael had rarely talked to each other in the last fifteen years.

At first, Josh seemed stunned and said nothing. He just stared into space for a bit, rubbing his chin. Then he shook his head slowly.

"I'm sorry to hear that," he finally muttered. "How are you taking it, Mom?"

"I'm shocked. Aren't you?"

"Of course. I mean—yes and no. I can hardly believe he's gone. But getting murdered? He had such a knack for making enemies. I never got why he had to be like that."

Yeah, that makes two of us, I thought. Michael loved pushing people's buttons—getting them riled up—and the funny thing is, he didn't care at all. He enjoyed having enemies. If he had kept a record of all his enemies, it would have run to many volumes.

Fresh out of things to say, Josh rummaged in the snack cupboard for potato chips. Finding them, he opened a bag and started shoveling chips into his mouth like paper shredder devouring old receipts.

He'd never get an apology for Michael's lousy parenting. And I'd never get an apology for our lousy marriage.

But I didn't have time to brood about this before Michael's sister Jennifer showed up at my door. She and I had been best friends forever; in fact, I'd met Michael through Jen.

"You heard about Michael's death, right?" she asked. "It was all over the news today."

"Yup, I heard. Do you know anything more than they're saying on the radio?"

She shook her head. "Not much. It's still early. The cops are pretty interested in the security system being out of commission; they think it's suspicious. And poor Beth thinks the police investigation will be no picnic." Beth was Michael's second wife and now his widow.

"I hear the cops can be pretty blunt and tactless. Beth says they're like, 'Sorry for your loss, Ma'am. Now, how bad *was* your marriage and do you have an alibi for the time of the murder'?"

"That's awful, but I'm sure it only felt that way," I said, aiming to defend Roxy and her fellow officers. Though Roxy would have been plenty tactful, I bet. "Beth's nerves must be raw."

"What really upset her is they wanted to grill her son Will, who's an emotional wreck. You know that kid has to be a suspect because he and Michael fought all the time—*all* the time."

"The poor guy!" I said. My heart was starting to pound like crazy again. I hoped Jen would leave soon—like, right away. I didn't want to faint in front of her, but she lingered, idly looking around the room as she talked to me.

"Speaking of which, how's Josh taking it?" she asked, not noticing my hands had started to tremble again. Behind my back, I clutched my right hand with my left to keep it steady. Please go, I thought. Dear god, please go.

"He says he's okay. But who knows?" I mumbled.

Just then, my husband Daniel got home. Oh no, I thought, imagining how this was going to unfold. Daniel would want to chat and joke around. He always wanted to chat and joke around.

"I heard about your brother's death," he said to Jen, scrunching up his face like he had smelled something bad. "How are you holding up?"

"I'm okay," she said. "But after I heard, I felt like I needed a hug from my favourite criminologist. So…"

"Yes, yes. Of course," I said, turning to give my best friend a hug, actually grateful to have something to do with my hands. I hoped she couldn't smell the vomit wafting off my face.

Then, without goodbyes, just a simple, "Gotta go," Jen got back into her car and left. That was Jennifer, for you: always on a mission. Since I'd known her, she'd been a woman on a mission, though I could rarely guess what any day's mission might be.

I sighed with relief but still felt like I might faint. Daniel didn't give me the opportunity.

"You're home early," Daniel said, looking at me with his head tilted to the side.

He could see I wasn't right. "Did you skip lunch again today? You look like a ghost. Let me get you something. A nice ham and cheese on French bread, with mayo and a pickle?" Daniel's head was already in the blissful kingdom of not-work. He didn't care about Michael's death at all, that was plain.

I shook my head. "No sandwich, Daniel. I just have to lie down."

Eager to cheer me, he exclaimed, "I heard the weirdest story this afternoon. About a guy in Florida—a 'Florida man'—who over twenty-two years, married and divorced six sisters all from the same family. And he divorced each one for the same reason: emotional incompatibility. What do you think of that?" he asked me, chuckling.

"I need to lie down, Daniel," I whispered, shifting from one foot to another, ready to explode. When was Daniel going to get the message? I wondered.

Daniel clutched his hands to his chest in mock horror. "Shall I call 911, honey? And pack you a bag for the hospital?"

"I'm not joking, Daniel," I mumbled. "I really need some alone time." My heart was pounding so loudly I was sure Daniel could hear it, and maybe the people next door too.

"Climb into bed and I'll bring you tea and cookies. The sugar will make you feel better. Then nap. I'll make us dinner tonight: the special pasta you like. We can watch that funny new show on Netflix—that one with the woman who dreams she's died and gone to heaven. It's called something like *Heavens To Betsy*, I think."

I started to hyperventilate, gasping audibly. Sweat was dripping off me in sheets and I figured my face was beet-red by now, but Daniel hadn't noticed. I'd say something rude if I didn't get out of there right away, so I rushed upstairs. Shutting—almost slamming—the bedroom door, I passed out the moment my body hit the bed and slept until five-thirty.

As usual, I had strange dreams. In one, I lay on an operating table with masked people—doctors, I hope—peering at my naked body. In another, I ran to catch a train, afraid I'd miss it; but over and over, I kept missing it anyway.

Then there was a third dream. I was standing in front of a huge audience at the annual meeting of the American Society of Criminology, receiving the Edwin H. Sutherland Award for best theoretical monograph of the year. They had loved my book, *Versions of Guilt in Criminological Theory*, published by Harvard University Press only eight months earlier. But suddenly, in my dream, the book I was holding exploded with a bang and the audience disappeared. I shook with fear when I woke up.

Finally awake, I took a long, hot shower and began to feel normal again. My heartbeat slowed as I forced myself to stop thinking about things that would make it go nuts again. Slightly rested, I could finally imagine spending time with Daniel—sweet, reliable Daniel—and his long, jokey stories, tasty pasta sauce, and funny TV shows. I'm lucky to have him, I told myself for the thousandth time. I guess I believed it.

We'd been married nearly fifteen years now, and if it hadn't been pure bliss, it had been good. It had been much easier than life with Michael, that's for sure.

Daniel was always relaxed and maybe that's because he'd grown up rich. He once told me he'd even owned a Maserati when he was a teenager. But Daniel didn't talk much about his childhood or his first marriage. His first wife had died shortly after their daughter Ellie was born. So, Daniel and I had raised Ellie together, and today she was a university student. We lived pretty well, all things considered. Daniel had inherited a trucking company from his parents which he and his older brother Peter ran together. Daniel dealt with all the personnel issues and marketing, which he could handle (mostly) from home.

Coming downstairs after my nap, I smelled Daniel's special pasta sauce simmering in the kitchen. It contained "secret" ingredients that I guessed might include bay leaf, paprika, roasted red peppers, soy sauce, tabasco, and two dozen garlic cloves. Surprisingly, the mixture worked. It tasted subtler than it sounds.

"I smell special pasta sauce," I called out as I came down the stairs. "Will we dine on Daniel's Pasta Delight this evening?"

Daniel kept his eyes on the pot he was stirring and laughed. "Yes, my love. Your nostrils are working at 100 percent effectiveness. Dinner will be ready in fifteen minutes. Although fifteen minutes may turn into three hours if I keep looking at your beautiful face."

I had to laugh. I probably still looked like death warmed over, but he'd never say so. I went to the wine cupboard, found a bottle of Oregon pinot noir, and poured myself a big glass. "Vino?" I asked.

Anita wouldn't have approved. She'd told me directly not to mix alcohol with the pills I was taking, but I needed an alcohol buzz to take the edge off my nerves, medication or no medication.

"Of course," he said. "A person cannot eat pasta without vino—nor even stir it without vino. Didn't a famous chef once say, 'A meal without wine is called breakfast'? Oh yes, and Ernest Hemingway also said, 'My only regret in life is that I did not drink more wine'."

We took our food out to the back patio to enjoy the balmy evening. Finally, with half a plate of pasta and salad inside me, I was ready to start talking.

"I bet Michael was having an affair with someone. He was always doing that, you know. Maybe he was even having sex with a client's wife. So, maybe a jealous husband killed him. It sounds primitive but it's possible, right? Or maybe his wife Beth killed him. She'd probably inherit all his money, right?"

"Anything's possible, sweetheart, but Beth has money of her own. Maybe she just got sick of Michael's arrogant manner. I'd kill that jerk for his personality alone."

We hadn't gotten far in solving this crime, but Daniel's interest was fading fast, so we cleaned up the dishes and started watching TV—that ridiculous Betsy show.

Finally, after an hour of passive TV viewing, we headed up to bed. Daniel kissed me gently on the cheek and turned over, fast asleep in just under ten seconds. But I couldn't put Michael's murder out of my mind, so I put on a bathrobe and headed into my home office. I scribbled notes—random ideas that came to me—as I thought about Michael's murder, and finally went back to bed around four.

In the days that followed, I endlessly reviewed, revised, and extended those notes: notes on theories about murder that I had studied. I felt certain they would finally help me identify the murderer. In the end, they did.

3

Michael's funeral was a few days later, on a sunny Sunday, and for Josh's sake, we had to go. But frankly, that funeral was a mess.

The day started out well enough. We'd been having gentle autumn days and scorching summers for most of the last ten years, so this was nothing new. I just loved this kind of weather.

When Daniel, Josh, and I got to the funeral chapel, the place was already packed. Michael's coffin was on view, covered with wreaths of flowers. An usher gave Daniel and me seats near the back and handed us programs. Josh went to sit up front with Beth and her children.

Scanning the room, I saw a few of Michael's creepy relatives—cousins, aunts and uncles—sitting in front of us, and when they turned around I smiled and waved. Some smiled back, while others pretended they didn't know me. That family was all about money: who had it and who didn't. They'd never thought I was good enough for their precious Michael.

I don't think they had much use for Jen either, once she had gone into the arts instead of business. I pitied Jen for growing up in that family, surrounded by a constant discussion of money. All they thought about was how to get it, how to keep it, what to buy with it, how to invest it, and so on. No wonder Michael became such a shallow creep. The mystery is how Jen turned out so well.

All at once, we heard live music from behind a screen: a violin and piano duo. An MC in a well-cut morning coat strode to the front of the room and in a resonant baritone voice, asked us to stand. Two beefy men wheeled Michael's casket up the centre aisle to the front of the room. The MC asked everyone to sit down again and we did.

Then he asked Jennifer to say a few words. She was dressed dramatically, as usual: this time, in a high-necked black silk pantsuit with a Nehru collar. A long braid of blond hair hung down her back, nearly touching her waist. A tiny pillbox hat sat on her head, spilling a black veil on to the upper part of her face.

Jen seemed nervous, unused to public speaking. From a sheet of paper in trembling hands, she read out a poem by Khalil Gibran, of all people. The piece, a century old, went like this:

> Even as the holy and the righteous
> Cannot rise beyond the highest
> Which is in each one of you,
> So the wicked and the weak
> Cannot fall lower than the lowest
> Which is in you also.
> And as a single leaf turns not yellow
> But with the silent knowledge of the whole tree,
> So the wrongdoer cannot do wrong
> Without the hidden will of you all.
> Like a procession you walk together
> Towards your god-self.
> You are the way and the wayfarers.
> And when one of you falls down
> He falls for those behind him,
> A caution against the stumbling stone.

I puzzled over what the piece was saying to her. It sound-ed accusatory. Maybe the poem was about karma or cosmic justice, or our unity in the face of death. Anyhow, it sounded serious.

After that, Matt Carling, Jen's husband, came up to the po-dium and talked about how much he'd enjoyed working with Michael at Westlake Holdings. Matt was the CFO there, Mi-chael's second-in-command. He called Michael "a born lead-er" and praised Michael for giving so much money to philan-thropic causes. Matt, for his part, was intensely forgettable—a born nobody; at least, that's what I'd always thought, though I'd never even hinted at it to Jen. I couldn't understand why my talented best friend had married him.

Then the MC called on Michael's stepchildren to say a few words. Melissa, at eighteen already beautiful and poised, walked slowly to the podium, wiping her eyes. She wore an elegant black silk dress with a full skirt, and carried a bouquet of white flowers. As she began, she choked up and had to clear her throat. Michael had been a wonderful father who loved his kids and made sure they had the best of everything, she said. That wasn't the Michael I had known.

After Melissa returned to her seat, the unseen piano-and-vi-olin duo played a fragment of a well-known sonata. Beethoven, I guessed, though it could have been Schubert.

As the music ended, Michael's stepson Will ambled up to the podium. He was obviously stoned and people whispered about this to one another. Dressed in black slacks, a gray shirt and black suede jacket, Will looked like he'd slept in his clothes. For more than one night. He hadn't shaved for the funeral and his long blonde hair was uncombed and greasy. He looked hy-gienically challenged, like a street person. I wasn't the only one shocked by his appearance. People who looked like him usually loitered on sidewalks, with tin cups and printed messages in front of them.

Will's speech—short and awful—went something like, "I'll always miss Dad and can't stop thinking about the last time we spoke." He began to sob. "We were arguing. My mother said I had to pull up my socks and do better at school. I was failing three subjects. Dad said he never imagined a son of his would turn out so badly. I said I hated them both and never wanted to see them again." By now Will was crying so hard he could hardly speak. Snot was streaming out of his nose. "Dad, I'm so sorry," he whispered. "I screwed up—I know that. I didn't deserve to be your son. You were too good for me."

Melissa came up to the podium and led her sobbing brother back to his seat, pausing repeatedly as he bent over to wipe his nose on his suede jacket sleeve.

Behind the screen, the piano-violin duo started up again: this time, a familiar hymn melody decorated with classical flourishes. I knew I had heard it before—a kind of Muzak for funerals.

When the music ended, my son Josh strode to the podium. He hadn't planned to speak but Melissa had insisted he say a few words. Michael was his biological dad, Josh said, but Daniel and I had brought him up. He'd tried to build a relationship with Michael, but Michael could never see him as his son. Josh said he'd always regret that. Now, they'd never break through that barrier. Without any fanfare, Josh thanked the audience and returned to his seat. It wasn't a glowing tribute to the deceased, but it was at least an honest expression of Josh's loss.

A soprano now joined the musicians behind the screen, and together they performed a medley of sad but triumphant African American songs.

When the musicians finished their latest foray, a young

blond woman came up to the podium and introduced herself as Trish McCormack—Michael's personal assistant. Without any doubt, she was the most beautiful woman I'd ever seen in real life. She put Barbie dolls to shame, and frankly I was stunned by her appearance. Trish thanked everyone for coming and assured them that Michael had been a genius. She'd learned a lot from working with him, she said. And she too mentioned Michael's fabled philanthropy.

When Trish finished talking, the vocalist sang "Amazing Grace," an anthem to the liberation of oppressed people everywhere. Nothing could have been less suitable, I thought. Yet many in the audience looked distressed and a few even started to cry. Meanwhile, Beth, who hadn't said a word, just sat back and enjoyed the music. There was no wailing, snuffling, or twisting of handkerchiefs by Michael's wife.

When the music ended, the MC announced a helicopter would fly Michael's body to the airport, and from there by private jet to an expensive cryogenic and cloning facility south of the border. There was a small chance Michael—well, a version of Michael—could one day be cloned back into life. The deceased had left instructions in his will to, at least, try this. Three men in black suits wheeled his coffin out of the room and into the waiting helicopter.

Then Beth and her children, plus Josh, left the room through a side door. The MC invited everyone to follow them into the Memory Room, where we could offer our condolences.

After twenty minutes in a slow-moving lineup, Daniel and I came face to face with the mourning family. We shook hands with Beth, Melissa, Will, and finally Josh. Nearby, Trish McCormack watched us closely, making sure everything went off without a hitch. I didn't see Jen anywhere. I guess she didn't want to mingle with her relatives any more than I did.

4

Daniel and I said good-bye to one of the friendlier Coale cousins and started to leave, but bumped into Jen just as we were exiting. She had come back into the hall with a bag she must have retrieved from her car.

"Good. You're still here," Jen said to me, sternly. "We need to talk."

Daniel said, "I'll fetch the car," and continued to the parking lot.

"I need to talk to you about the police investigation. They're leaving us in the dark, and we were hoping—Beth and I—that you could find out more about what they're up to. They seem to be getting a lot of their information from Trish McCormack and we think Trish isn't a reliable source of information."

"I can't snoop on the police," I said. "And why would the police tell me anything?"

"But you've got that friend in the department—Roxy, isn't it? She might tell you things off the record, as a friend. She'd know you're not a suspect and can be trusted. We also hoped you might do a little investigating yourself, for us. Beth thought there might be something in Michael's diaries about his enemies." She hefted the bag she was holding and held it out to me. "Michael must have planned to write his autobiography one day. So, he filled all these volumes with his views about the people he mistreated. Who knows? Maybe one of them isn't on the police radar yet."

I protested, "Those should go to the police, Jen. They should be part of the official investigation."

"I know," she said, "but Beth doesn't want the police pawing through her family's personal business. She especially wants to avoid any of Michael's words leaking to the press and that's why she wanted you to look at them first: to identify anything we might need to censor. We can pass them on to the police if you find anything useful."

"And beside that, I haven't cared about Michael—alive or dead—since he abandoned me and Josh fifteen years ago. So why should I do this now?" I protested.

"Do it for me," Jen said. "I need to understand what happened. And you're my friend, so naturally you'll want to help me. Besides, Michael was Josh's father, so this would be a favour to Josh too."

Jen's reasoning was absurd. But as she went on, I realized I had two other reasons for looking into Michael's murder. The first was simple curiosity. I wanted to know what had happened to my former (horrible) husband and Josh's dad. The second reason was less admirable. My dean expected me to get that $20 million Michael had thought about giving Criminology and maybe—just maybe—that donation was still in play. Looking into Michael's murder as a favour to the Coale family might score me brownie points with Beth, while going after the $20 million might get me some information about Michael's murder. The two activities—fundraising and investigation—were two sides of the same coin. At least, that's what I told myself that day, and for weeks afterward.

Honestly, I didn't like asking Beth for a big donation that her dead husband may—or may not—have intended to give Criminology. But I had no choice. The dean had been starving Criminology of funds for the last three years. If I didn't come through with a huge donation—well, a lot of things would happen. We wouldn't be able to draw top students to our school with hefty fellowships. Then, after a year or two, our top faculty members would start taking jobs in better-funded criminology programs around the world. And soon, we'd have to close down our Criminology program in all but name. I couldn't let all that happen on my watch; it would be the destruction of everything I had worked for in the last fifteen years. So I had to raise big bucks any way I could.

As I said, not admirable, but my dean was riding me hard. This was a large part of the reason for my panic attacks these days and my heavier-than-usual use of alcohol.

"Let me think this over," I said to Jen. "I want to help you, and, to be honest, I've wondered about Michael's murder myself. But I'm not making any promises." Yet, truth be told, I was only being coy. I was already hooked on the mystery of who had killed Michael. So that's on me.

I didn't say much to Daniel during the drive home but I'd found the funeral depressing. While Daniel droned on—some ridiculous story about a crash diet his mother had tried once—I glanced at the bag of diaries I'd tossed into the back seat and let my mind drift. I'd read the diaries mostly to humour Jen. I owed her that much, and the diaries just might make interesting reading.

That said, I wouldn't have much time to read the diaries in the foreseeable future. I was scheduled to give a guest lecture in Philadelphia three days from now, receive an award at the University of California ten days later, and fly to Oxford for an expert seminar in about a month. So, where was I going to find time to read a shopping bag full of handwritten ruminations?

Worse still, I didn't expect to find anything important in those diaries. I certainly didn't expect to find any clues about who killed Michael, but I was wrong there. I was even wrong to think Jen had pulled me into Michael's murder mystery the day of his funeral, when she gave me his diaries.

In fact, I was already tangled up in the mystery. And that's because of what had happened the last time I saw Michael alive, just days before his murder.

I remember that day very clearly. The occasion was a fundraising event the university called "A&S Donors Day." Most of us called it "The Meet Market." Major donors had come out to watch academics talk the talk and walk the walk. If we impressed them enough, they might give us the money we wanted. "Major donors"—the people invited to this event—had already given the university more than five hundred thousand dollars each, or were likely to do so. Yes, they were big dogs, alright!

How hard could this be? I wondered. I just had to remember what my parents had taught me: knowing and doing is everything. Find out what you need to know and learn it. Then find out what needs to be done and do it perfectly. So I put on my best clothes—my navy blue suit, my best pale blue striped blouse, my best low-heel black shoes, and an elegant gold and diamond pin—and went hunting for dollars.

My boss, Dean Sandor Grabol, had asked me to pitch a proposal for the School of Criminology. "Someone," who turned out to be Michael, wanted to give the university $20 million and his money might go to Criminology for a program on global crime.

Even the near-mythical figure of Wyn Campbell-Carter, head of fundraising for the university, was attending this gala event. Wyn was gigantic, at nearly six and a half feet tall, and he was dressed in one of those fabled Tom Ford suits that sold for upwards of twelve thousand dollars. As the university's third highest paid employee, Wyn could afford to dress that way. In fact, he had to dress that way if he was going to talk wealthy donors out of millions of dollars. Reportedly, he had raised half a billion dollars for the university in the past five years.

Sandor welcomed everyone, then talked about what the university needed and how major donations could break down the "barriers to knowledge." Even as we spoke, our alumni were pledging millions of dollars to their old school, he said. As an example, he mentioned a deal in the works with alumni in Saudi Arabia. The university was close to landing a $40 million endowed chair that would go a long way to bridging the cultural divide between Islamic culture and western culture.

He also thanked Michael Coale—"one of our premiere donors"—for coming out today, saying he felt sure Mr. Coale, an illustrious graduate of our university, would find lots of research "worth supporting." He hailed Michael as the "Canadian titan" of today's real estate market. He didn't mention the recent tenement fires at properties Michael owned in Vancouver, Montreal, and Halifax, or the housing code violations in Manhattan, Mexico City, and Kolkata. Just an oversight, I guess.

As one of four unit heads invited to pitch the Meet Market that day, I would propose a program for the study of global crime. I'd have twenty minutes to present my School's plan orally and twenty minutes to answer questions. After making my pitch, I'd mingle with the donors at a cocktail party and answer their questions. It sounded easy and important. I was excited to think about it, and believe me, I spent a lot of time thinking about it.

I'd taken two weeks to prepare my proposal and had started even before Michael was identified as the mystery donor who needed impressing. So, yes, I felt ready. And to make a long story short, I did a super job. I told them about some of the recent research literature on drug smuggling, human trafficking, internet fraud, gun running, and sex tourism. I made a solid presentation, then answered a few friendly questions. At the cocktail party afterward I chatted comfortably about my presentation with a half dozen prospective donors.

As we chatted, Jen roamed around the room with her camera, snapping photos of the people present. I didn't expect to see her there but celebrity photos were her thing and this event was a treasure trove of important faces. As usual, Jen had dressed uniquely. Her long blond hair was tied back with a red Madras kerchief, and she wore a beige cashmere turtleneck that accented her figure. She may have intended this to signal "I am a beautiful woman!" and "I am also a serious person." On her feet were brown, calf-length Doc Martens, the kind that people wear on motorcycles and tough terrain.

So, Jen looked like a war correspondent in a combat zone. She was there to photograph scholars as they battled for dollars.

Meanwhile Michael, as a prized donor, strutted around the room enjoying the admiration of Dean Grabol and the lesser donors. Two years earlier, he'd given $130 million to the university's School of Business, earning him the right to name their new wing "The Michael Coale Centre for Business Innovation." I have to say this for Michael: he was always full of surprises. His new interest in criminology surprised me, since Michael had never shown an interest in criminology before. But Sandor hogged Michael's attention, introducing him to other directors, principals, and department heads, so I never got a chance to ask him about that.

I only got a moment to say hello and tell Michael I hoped we could chat later about my proposal. He hugged me and whispered in my ear, "But not here."

I'd been dreading that moment of contact because I couldn't predict what Michael might do. Would he be friendly or indifferent, or embarrassing in some way I couldn't even imagine?

5

I won't keep you in suspense: Michael gave me a quick hug before we parted. He may have also slipped a piece of paper into my pocket, but I'm probably just imagining that.

Mere minutes later, I met Yevgeny Tretnikoff—Gene as he preferred to be called—at the food and drinks table. The university had put on a beautiful spread. In the centre of the table was a large bowl containing what I imagined was caviar. Reaching across the table, I spooned up some, covered a cracker with the small black eggs, and took a bite. The taste was incredible—beyond belief.

"This is good caviar, but it isn't the best," said a man who had suddenly appeared beside me. "It may even be vegan caviar made from tofu. The best comes from fish in the Black Sea." He spoke with a thick accent I couldn't identify—maybe, Russian. And he spoke slowly and carefully, accenting some of his words more strongly than I was used to. "This is GOOD caviar, but it isn't the BEST. The BEST comes from FISH in the BLACK Sea."

I turned to look at him, then asked if he knew a lot about caviar. "I've eaten a LARGE share of caviar in my time. For me, it's one of life's GREAT pleasures. And it's best eaten with CHAMPAGNE and followed with fresh fruit. Shall we GET some fruit?"

He spoke loudly, as though addressing troops before sending them into battle. A few people, overhearing him, turned their heads towards us but that didn't faze him a bit. If anything, it encouraged him. He smiled and waved at them while educating me about the food. Then he watched me eat the caviar, his lips slightly parted.

Aged somewhere between forty-five and fifty-five, the stranger was my own height and built like a weight lifter, with a deep tan, closely cropped beard, and gold-framed glasses. He wore designer jeans, an expensive tan suede jacket, and a blue open-necked dress shirt, like a model in *GQ*.

"I should introduce myself and thank you for this education in caviar," I said. "I'm Rachel Tile. I don't know if you were here for my presentation."

"Oh, yes" he said. "You were persuasive. I wanted to write you a CHECK right away." He smiled and so did I.

He removed a small silver case from his jacket pocket and from the case, took a white embossed card. It contained Cyrillic letters and under them, English letters reading:

Yevgeny I. Tretnikoff

London • New York • Moscow

Antiquities and Investments

I pocketed the card and asked him which of the many fruits on display he recommended.

"It's a matter of taste. I prefer POMEGRANATES, for their tartness and colour. However, blackberries or blueberries are also suitable," he said. Again, he sounded like he was lecturing troops on the wisdom of making good recreational choices while on furlough. "And whatever you DO, remember to use a CONDOM and wash your HANDS afterward," he might have been saying. People were staring at us again, and he still didn't care.

Lacking pomegranates and blackberries to top off the caviar, we spooned blueberries on to small dishes and started eating them with our fingers, licking our fingers as we went. I saw him watching me with what seemed like slightly disguised delight.

"A VONDERFUL combination. We must get MORE caviar to go with these berries," he exclaimed. He turned and moved briskly back to the buffet table. We loaded up more crackers with caviar, then moved to the side of the room to feast on caviar and fruit. Meanwhile, I had started to feel slightly self-conscious about the way Gene kept looking at me. He was plainly interested, and not in an academic way. Still, it felt pretty good to be looked at that way.

"What brings you to Canada?" I asked him. "I don't think we're famous for our caviar and antiquities, at least not yet."

"I have an interest in the new gambling casino in Picton, the Calypso. You may have heard of it. And I expect to build other properties in Prince Edward County: a hotel, a concert hall, a spa, some condos, maybe a clinic. That area is ripe for development. But I don't want to bore you with that. What are *you* working on right now? Are you studying international crime?" he asked me.

"Afraid not. I'm writing a second book about rage. When I first became a criminologist, I wrote about theories of guilt, and lately I've been working on theories of rage," I said, laughing. I didn't want to sound self-important.

"Well and GOOD. Those are important topics. Now, I'd like to learn more about your plans for that program on international crime you discussed today. So let me invite you to my office, where we can talk about that at greater length." Or, as he said it, "So let me INVITE you to my OFFICE, where we can talk about this at GREATER LENGTH."

We agreed to meet the following Thursday. Then, almost immediately after Gene left, someone else came over to say hello. He wore a magnificent gray suit with a striped, white shirt and patterned tie.

Unlike Gene, the new guy was tall enough that I had to crane my neck to see his handsome face. Though young-looking, he wasn't young; yet he moved gracefully, like a squash player. Even his face was lively, and he had surprisingly large hands, like a concert pianist's.

"Professor Tile, I loved your presentation today. I learned a lot. I've never studied criminology, but your talk made me think it's a topic I need to learn more about." He spoke with a slight English accent.

"My name is Bradley Wong and I own a pharmaceutical company. We do most of our business in the Global South, where criminal gangs are a huge problem. They steal our product, interrupt our supply chains, and threaten our workers. They make it nearly impossible for us to deliver our product on time and in the needed quantity."

He spoke quickly and my ear had trouble switching from Gene's Russian accent to Bradley's English one. But his face did most of the work. I needn't have heard a word to know that he was welcoming me and trying to draw me in.

"My colleague Sarah Broadfoot could tell you useful things about criminal gangs," I said. "She's studied gangs in South and Central America. I'll put you in touch with her if you want."

"That would be brilliant," he replied. "I want to hear lots more about the program you're proposing. Could you come by my office next week? Here's my business card if you're interested," he said. His card showed an office address at the MaRS building, a science research centre ten minutes away from my office.

We shook hands—my hand felt like a pebble in his—and he returned to the drinks table for a refill. I took this opportunity to leave, exhausted from my presentation and the face-to-face conversations.

Outside, the day was still balmy and the sun was only starting to set. The air was smoggy again today, as it so often was these days, and I had a brief wheezing spell. I was gasping, actually. As usual, I'd forgotten my asthma puffer, but after a few minutes, I was breathing easily again.

Looking back on it now, I realize I was experiencing an ignorance-is-bliss moment. I had no idea then what kind of men I'd just met. They may have seen me as a way to get to Michael, given his supposed interest in donating money to our school. Or as an attractive, available woman at a boring event they had decided to attend. This gave me more questions to ponder as I headed home.

6

Dressing for work the next morning, I hummed to myself and thought about my time with Michael during "the old days." I also wondered why I married him.

I'd thought about that question a thousand times and there's no simple answer. I have to say he was impressive: very smart and very engaging, at least at the beginning. But when our marriage ended, I was depressed for months. I couldn't work on my dissertation—could hardly eat or sleep. It was a bad part of my life, that's for sure.

After Josh was born, I had to care for my new baby and finish my degree, despite all the stress and nightmares. Yet, bit by bit I came back to life. And in 2007, I moved back to Toronto to take a teaching job. Soon after, I met Daniel, dated him, and married him. Daniel was just about the complete opposite of Michael, so I figured everything would turn out better. It did, and here I am today, forty years old, with children, a husband, and a good job. But thinking about Michael again.

Michael remarried too. While living in California, he married Beth, who already had two children—Melissa and Will—from an earlier marriage. Beth was the daughter of a second-rate Hollywood actress. She had the beauty and schmoozing skills Michael needed in a wife, for business reasons.

Then, in 2017 Michael came back to Toronto, with his family in tow. The media said it was for business reasons, but I bet it was for legal ones. I'd expected to run into him sooner or later at Jen's house, but never did. Before that brief encounter at the Meet Market, I hadn't seen Michael for fifteen years. He looked about the same and maybe I did too.

I was just a kid when I first met Michael. Barely seventeen, I'd just started university and, like lots of students, I was making new friends. Jen Coale was just one of them. One October evening, I came over to Jen's house to "study"—really, to kill time before a test—and that was when I first met Jen's big brother. Michael was in third year, an economics student.

At Jen's home that first evening, so many years ago, we chatted on the back porch. We laughed a lot and made a lot of noise, but it didn't matter at all. Jen's home was a chaotic mess. Her parents—permissive bordering on negligent—were nothing like mine and I got the impression they traveled a lot and drank a lot. They just weren't around much. Looking back on this now, as a criminologist, I can realize that was a toxic environment.

That first evening, Michael watched us for a while and laughed at our "pretend-studying."

A week later, Jen fixed me up with Michael on a date. We went to a movie—something brainy. An indie film maybe. A week or two after that, we went out for a walk. The evening was frosty, with a biting wind and blowing snowflakes, but we kept holding hands, walking and talking.

Soon, Michael and I were seeing each other every weekend, and sometimes in between. We started having sex wherever and whenever we could find a private spot. Sometimes even in out-of-the-way, not so private spots at school. We couldn't keep our hands off each other. We were hooked on each other, or so I thought.

Here's what Michael wrote in his diary about our first meeting:

October 14, 1997
One of Jen's school friends came over tonight and she's hot. Rachel Tile: I couldn't stop staring at her and wondering what she'd look like in a bathing suit, in her underwear, or in nothing at all. I'm going to find out. But I can't seem too eager. She's shy and I don't want to scare her off. I'm going to make Rachel Tile my special project this fall. I'm already off to a promising start. I invested a few bucks in some stupid hippie group she's raising funds for and now I'm in.

I didn't mind being Michael's "special project" back then. In fact, I was flattered. But what's his game now? What exactly does he want? I wondered as I dressed for school the morning after that Meet Market get-together.

That was going to be my first question the next time I saw Michael. But there was to be no next time, because Michael got murdered before we could meet.

* * *

I was scheduled to meet Yevgeny (Gene) Tretnikoff at his office a week after the Meet Market and knew I had to learn something about him beforehand. I Googled the man, but couldn't find out much. So I asked my graduate research assistant Connie—"Clever Connie" was how I thought of her—to search the Internet for more information. Around noon, Connie phoned me with her report.

"Yevgeny Tretnikoff was born in Moscow, studied engineering at the University of Moscow, then served in the Russian army. He quickly rose to the rank of major-general in charge of special operations units. After leaving the army, he formed a private security firm, founded a company that deals in antiquities, and built gambling casinos in Macao, Singapore, Brisbane, Birmingham, Lagos, and Picton, here in Ontario. He's married, and has one daughter, Irina."

She also sent me an article from the *Hong Kong Times* about Gene Tretnikoff's activities before coming to Canada. It had appeared on the first page of the local news section on June 15, 2013:

Investor Yevgeny Tretnikoff has announced plans to build what will be the biggest gambling casino in the city when completed. With space for more than 3,000 gamblers in more than 25 rooms (or "gambling studios," as Mr. Tretnikoff calls them), the ten-story casino will be one of the largest gambling venues in the world. Mr. Tretnikoff's other casinos, in Dubai, Mexico City, and Mumbai, are also large but pale in comparison with the new one. The new casino will also feature six gourmet restaurants, a luxurious spa, a hotel that can hold three hundred guests at $5,000 a night (or more), and a full-floor shopping centre. Mr. Tretnikoff has already rented space in the shopping area to many of the most famous brands in the world, including Gucci, Burberry, and Maserati.

The builder is awaiting a go-ahead from the planning commission. However, the police commissioner opposes Mr. Tretnikoff's application, as have several local business groups. They denounce the intrusion of what they call "foreign criminal elements" into their community. Mr. Tretnikoff's many-tentacled business syndicate extends into several fields, such as antiquities dealing, import and export, and arms dealing. His companies have been investigated for possible smuggling, money laundering, racketeering and several acts of violence. But a company spokesperson reports that Mr. Tretnikoff has never been convicted of any crime.

"What's your assessment of this guy, Connie?" I asked her after reading the material.

"I don't know," she said. "He sounds shady, maybe even dangerous, Professor Tile: someone you ought to steer clear of. And what's with that 'many-tentacled' stuff—it sounds super creepy."

I had to agree, the image was grotesque but perhaps oddly fitting. Then I remembered Michael's diaries. I'd scarcely started looking through them yet. Maybe I'd find out something about Mr. Tretnikov in there. I'd dig into them as soon as I got a chance.

7

I agreed with Connie's assessment of Gene Tretnikov but couldn't avoid the guy. After all, he might give my School a lot of money. So, just before 4 o'clock, I took an elevator to the third floor of the Bank of Commerce Building. In the northwest corner, I found Suite 318 and knocked on the door.

Gene (as I would come to call him) opened the door, smiled, and welcomed me into his private office.

Inside a large dimly lit room, dark wooden bookcases were stuffed full of old, leather-bound books, the way they might have been in a gentleman's library, circa 1924. Another part of the room looked like a private art salon, with early twentieth century paintings—if not originals, then magnificent reproductions—covering most of the walls.

Then, hanging on the wall nearest Gene's desk, I saw a black and white photo portrait of a young girl—aged twelve or thirteen—in a simple black frame. The girl, serene and innocent, looked down at an open book in her hands. "My DAUGHTER, Irina," Gene said proudly, seeing me stare at the picture. The picture was signed "Janus", as Jen Coale liked to sign her photos. Small world, I thought.

"Please make yourself comfortable," Gene proclaimed, holding out his hands in welcome. And for the next ten or fifteen minutes, he showed me the art work on his walls and said a few words about the pieces he liked best. Mostly, he left me to look at whatever caught my eye. When I was done, I turned and smiled at him.

"Mr. Tretnikoff—Gene—thanks again for your invitation, and for taking so much trouble." I pointed to the table covered with delicacies. "I hope we can do justice to this magnificent spread."

We sat down and made ourselves comfortable on deeply

padded, leather-bound sofas. But my mind kept returning to what Connie had told me about him. Was he hitting on me, I wondered?

"Is your wife here with you, Gene?" I asked him, casually.

"No, she stayed on in London, where we have a home. I came to Toronto to keep my daughter Irina company during her first year at your university, and to help her settle in. When I return to London, Irina will stay on here. We haven't worked out the details yet. Now, your turn. I'd like to know you better."

"There's not much to know about me. I've been teaching at here for most of the last fifteen years and occasionally, writing books."

"But that's not the WHOLE story, Rachel. You won scholarships and prizes as an undergraduate student in philosophy. You went to Harvard University on a scholarship and got your doctorate there studying the philosophical bases of criminology. While there, you married Michael Coale, who was studying at MIT. When he left for a job in Silicon Valley, you stayed behind a year, then joined him in California while you wrote your dissertation. After Josh was born, you stayed home with the baby while Michael conquered the business world. Then, Michael proposed a move to New York and you and Josh followed him. But after a year in New York, you divorced Michael, returned to Toronto, and took a job at your university. Michael stayed in the US for another decade. He married Beth and started a new family; then, he moved back to Toronto too. Am I correct?"

I was surprised by the thoroughness of Gene's information—also a little creeped out by the thought he'd gathered it all. "Yes, you're right on all counts," I said.

Why was this guy trying so hard to impress me, I wondered again? I knew what I was after, but what was he after?

"I've been curious about you too," I said. "How did you get started in antiquities? Do you have a deep interest in ancient art?"

He smiled. "I have a deep interest in present-day hard currencies. During my time in the military, I discovered that wars unearth hidden treasures. This is especially true in the Middle East, where many civilizations have lived and died. Wars in Lebanon, Syria, Iraq, Iran, and Afghanistan uncovered a treasure trove of ancient objects that collectors are eager to buy. I've acquired many of these objects and made them available to buyers. I hire people to find them, then other people to appraise and certify them. My job is to find out what collectors will pay and what they want, then get it for them at a price that suits both of us. That's how our economy works, you know."

"Some might say you're robbing those countries of their historic artwork," I said.

"Yes, they might say that. But I've done all the paperwork and broken no laws."

I knew that, in many countries, you could easily bribe the right officials to sign off on such export items, but I wasn't going to challenge Gene on this. Looking around the room, I asked, "Did you grow up surrounded by this kind of art and culture?"

"No, the opposite. I grew up in a desperately poor family, wanting more than anything to acquire wealth and art and culture. In fact, I wanted ALL the pleasures of a wealthy life. So I became a fighter and a winner, like you. And now I have all the things I ever wanted." Standing now, Gene poured two glasses of champagne and prepared plates of caviar, crackers, and fruit for both of us. We ate in silence for a few minutes, nodding and smiling.

"You're right," I told him. "Caviar *is* better with champagne and pomegranates. And Russian caviar *is* better than any other kind, so far as I can tell."

When he'd finished eating, Gene nodded and smiled. "RACHEL, you're a busy scholar, so let me ask you what you need. Maybe I can provide it."

"I need money for that program on global crime we discussed last week. You showed an interest, and our school needs money to start the program. We can give you naming rights to a building or chair as gratitude for a large enough donation. The publicity value of such a…"

"Let me interrupt you, Rachel. I don't want my name on anything. There is a time for spotlights and a time for shadows. Surely your father taught you that."

"My father!? You know my father?"

"I certainly know his reputation. The talented Jack Tile. Hit a bumpy patch? Made a mess? 'Call Jack to Tile it over!' One reason I wanted this meeting was to learn more about the celebrated Jack Tile's celebrated daughter."

He'd rattled me. But I recovered enough to move on by asking, "So, who did you want to partner with on this donation?"

"I was thinking of your former husband, Michael Coale. He and I had a deal in the works. As part of that, I'd support his donation so he could get his name on something prestigious. But before that, I would need to know the status of Michael's donation," Gene said.

I shook my head. "I'm sorry but I can't tell you. Information of that sort is confidential."

This didn't please Gene but he only paused for a moment to think of a reply. "Well, once you know where Michael's donation stands, get back to me and we'll discuss this further.

Gene bowed slightly and I turned to leave. No doubt about it, Gene was the most confident, commanding person I'd ever met. By doing his homework, he'd stayed a step ahead of me through the whole meeting and I didn't like that feeling.

I knew now that I'd have to connect with Michael if I wanted any money from Gene. So the next morning I called Westlake Holdings, where a secretary passed me over to Trish McCormack. Trish said Michael was traveling on business for the next few weeks, and would only be in the office for brief periods. He'd asked her not to book any appointments for him while he was away.

I left my name and asked her to have Michael call me when he got a chance. I expected a return call but never got one. Later, I'd find out why.

8

The next day began with a lovely autumn morning. But it was already seven-thirty when I woke and I had to rush to make my nine o'clock lecture. When I slid into the lecture hall the digital wall clock showed 8:59. Sweat was streaming down my face and I was panting.

"Hi everyone, and thanks for coming out this fine morning," I managed to say. "Still, this is a horrible time of day for a lecture, so I'll try to make it worth your while. The title of my lecture today is 'Who's to Blame?'"

I felt comfortable in front of them, relaxed and open. Here I was, as always, a tall, slender woman with unwashed ginger hair worn in a ponytail. I was dressed in my usual, casual way: tailored slacks, a tailored shirt, and (today) a bottle-green quarter-zip sweater. Everything I wore signalled "What you see is what you get." If some people thought I dressed like a slob, I wasn't going to fret about it.

I started by showing them a thirty-second clip of an ad they'd all seen dozens of times before, usually referred to as the "Feeling lucky?" advertisement. Someone who sounded like Bob Marley was singing a catchy reggae tune, backed up by three female vocalists, a guitar, drums, and thumping bass. The lyrics were simple enough:

Lucky? Yeah!
Feeling lucky today? Yeah!
Lucky, lucky, lucky!
You'll get lucky today!

As this tune repeated in the background, knots of handsome men (aged twenty-five to fifty-five) and beautiful women (aged eighteen to thirty-five) crowded around roulette wheels, slot machines, and blackjack tables. They were all smiling or laughing (or both). Some of them were thrilled about (seemingly) winning large pots of money, and many others hugged or touched one another in eager anticipation. Sexual excitement filled the casino—as it turns out, the Calypso, the casino Gene Tretnikov owned in Picton.

Everyone was going to get lucky today! Catching the enthusiasm, many of my students sang along, mouthing the lyrics soundlessly or making the well-known hand gestures of the people on the screen. "Lucky, lucky, lucky!"

Then, I lectured the students about gambling and asked them to consider who we should blame for gambling addiction, a problem that afflicted two to three percent of the adult population. Should we blame the addicts who couldn't control their gambling urges and, often, lost everything they owned. Or should we blame the businesses that profit from their addiction, the governments that promote gambling, and the cultural tropes that glorify "getting lucky"? After an hour of lecturing and a short break, I opened the floor to discussion, then gave them a brief writing assignment to turn in when they left the classroom.

The more I thought about gambling, the more I hated it. For me, gambling epitomized the stupidity and crassness of our consumer society. I think I got that message across this morning, though maybe not.

Out on St. George Street, what seemed like thousands of students rushed around me as I made way from the lecture hall to my office. A phone message on my desk said Dean Grabol wanted to see me as soon as possible. I called his secretary to schedule a meeting.

He would want a progress report on my fundraising, and that presented a problem, since I had no real progress to report. As of today, I had yet to get one thin dime from anyone I'd met at the Meet Market.

I could probably stall the dean for a while, giving him temporary grounds for optimism. But I'd need a plan and that would take some relaxed thinking. I figured my new BFF, Al K. Hall, would help me figure out how to spin the impatient dean. But it might be another few hours before I got a chance to visit the esteemed Mr. Hall in the flesh, so to speak; so I practiced a bit of deep breathing instead. And I worked on my theories about murder, revising and upgrading the notes I had made a few nights earlier.

That night, I dreamed about murder. In my dreams, I witnessed Michael Coale's murder: two gunshots in the darkened home I had never seen. The killer wore a mask and a long trench coat, so I couldn't see his features. Was he taller or shorter than Michael. Then I "looked around" the room where he had been shot and saw Michael standing behind a huge mahogany desk. The room looked a little like Gene Tretnikoff's office, but without the fine art. The walls in this imagined home office were covered with pictures of Michael.

When I phoned Michael's office after breakfast that morning, I half-expected Trish McCormack to apologize for not getting back to me. Instead, she acted like I was the one being unreasonable. "Mr. Coale said he was surprised to have you contact his office again," she said. As if Michael hadn't suggested we should talk! What the heck was going on? Was this a Michael problem or a Trish problem? Because it sure as heck wasn't a Rachel problem. I'd remember all this later, when Jen told me she didn't trust Trish.

Then, I prepared for my appointment with Bradley Wong. The day before, Clever Connie had e-mailed me some information about Bradley Wong's life:

Born in Singapore, Bradley Wong studied chemistry and life sciences at National University of Singapore, graduating *summa cum laude.* Got his PhD in biochemistry at Oxford University; did postdoctoral research at California Institute of Technology; then headed a laboratory at Pfizer Pharmaceuticals. Served in advisory and managerial positions at the World Health Organization and the US National Institute of Health. Formed and runs Jupiter Pharmaceuticals. Received several honorary doctorates; also awards from United Nations and World Health Organization. He is married with one child. His father-in-law is said to have connections with organized crime in Singapore, Malaysia, and Hong Kong.

Organized crime again—another Tretnikoff?—I wondered.

But the reference to crime only applied to Bradley's father-in-law, not Bradley himself.

A search of scholarly publications showed Bradley was the real thing, academically speaking. He'd published dozens of research articles before 2008, and as a young scientist, he'd published articles in journals that even I knew were prestigious: *Nature, Science, Scientific American*, and the like. He'd also published specialized articles about infectious diseases in the Global South. They reported experimental efforts to develop drugs and vaccines that were cheap to make, easy to deliver, and needed little or no refrigeration.

But once Bradley had started working for the World Health Organization and the National Institutes of Health, there were more articles *about* him than there were *by* him. The articles published after 2020 were all in business magazines. They mainly discussed Jupiter Pharmaceuticals: the company's funding, stock value, quarterly sales, and plans for expansion. They predicted that, under Bradley Wong's leadership, the company would achieve worldwide prominence in the war against infectious diseases.

A few mentioned the discussions between Wong and Michael Coale, predicting that Coale would invest as much as $1.2 billion towards expanding Jupiter's production in Mexico. But the last article I read, in *Forbes*, revealed that Michael and Bradley had failed to sign an agreement. Coale's company, Westlake Holdings, had decided not to invest in Jupiter after all. The article did not speculate on reasons for this decision. I felt sorry for Wong's setback but thought that, surely, a smart guy like him would find a way to set things straight. And I was curious to hear what he'd say about his dealings with Michael.

I paused to marvel at the architecture of the MaRS building. All steel and glass, MaRS was home to some of the world's most innovative industrial research. Then, with only minutes to spare, I took an elevator up to Bradley Wong's floor and followed a small sign to a door with his name on it. I knocked and the secretary invited me in.

9

Bradley Wong was seated behind a large, cluttered desk, and on a couch near the desk sat an older man in a smart, double-breasted business suit. On one wall of the vast, brightly lit room, I saw a poster-sized black and white photograph. It showed Bradley in the central foyer of the MaRS building with his back to one of its massive windows. In the lower lefthand corner of the photo, you could make out the unshaven face of a disheveled middle-aged man peering into the building. You could also read the curiosity, surprise, and envy on his face.

Unexpectedly, Bradley stood and smiled, interrupting my scrutiny of the room. "Welcome, Professor Tile. I'm glad to see you again. This is my associate Juan-Carlo Guzman. We all call him J-C, and you should call me Bradley."

"Thank you, Bradley. Nice to meet you, Mr. Guzman. J-C. I've brought a book you both might find interesting. It's by my colleague Sarah Broadfoot—I told you about her when we met two weeks ago—titled *Rulers, Rebels, and Robbers: Drugs and Politics in the Colombian Jungle*."

Bradley seemed thrilled to receive this. "Thank you. We'll both read this with great interest. And on another occasion, I hope we can meet Professor Broadfoot." He handed the book to J-C, who scanned the back cover and flipped through the pages.

"I see you admire good photography, as I do," Wong said.

"The picture you were looking at is by one of our local artists, Jen Carling. It captures all the contradictions of our neighbourhood: a place of knowledge and wealth, but also ignorance and dire poverty," Wong said.

The picture was weird—almost nightmarish. I thought about saying this to Bradley but didn't know how he'd take it.

"Thanks for giving me this time for a meeting. I'm sure your schedule is busy."

"I always have time to chat with an interesting person." He smiled again and invited me to sit in the room's most comfortable-looking chair.

"I'm here to discuss the program I'm developing on international crime. You'd mentioned an interest in it when we last met. I believe you heard about it through Michael Coale as well?"

"Yes," Bradley replied. "Michael mentioned it when we were working on a major deal a few months ago. Unfortunately, the deal didn't work out."

Then J-C interjected, "Professor Tile, you will scarcely believe what was at stake. Jupiter is very close to perfecting a line of medicines that will reduce the incidence of major infectious diseases by at least fifty percent. In my native Mexico, I saw the effect of these diseases firsthand. They destroyed families, weakened communities, and ruined the national economy. Millions died unnecessarily, because people lacked the medications they needed."

He stopped to catch his breath before continuing.

"With Michael Coale's investment, we could have saved these millions of lives. Our firm was prepared—is prepared—to sell our life-saving medications at a mere 10 percent above production cost. But Jupiter needed at least a billion dollars to achieve this goal. We asked Michael Coale to see the humanitarian value of this investment. As well, Jupiter promised Michael a 10 percent return, but Michael wanted a 30 percent return. This rate of return would have made our drugs unaffordable for the people who needed them, so the prospect of a deal died, then and there."

By now, J-C was vibrating with nervous energy. His eyes were bulging and his skin had taken on a menacing red tinge.

Bradley, sensing my discomfort, jumped in. "J-C is a passionate man, Professor Tile, and more than that, a man for whom moral behaviour is supremely important. Actions that stand in the way of realizing our goal, like those of Michael Coale, distress him deeply."

"Have you found anyone to replace Michael Coale?" I asked Bradley.

"We're still looking for investors to provide the money we need at a rate we can afford. I'm optimistic we'll get there but we've been set back at least a year by Mr. Coale's callous behaviour. As many as twenty thousand more Latin Americans will die who might have been saved by our medicine."

"Thank you for your honesty, Bradley. I hope you find a new investor soon."

"So you see our predicament, Professor Tile. The things your Program will study are relevant to us—Latin American crime gangs, governmental corruption, and such. But for the moment, we have neither the cash nor the time to discuss a donation. Please get back to us about your program in a few weeks, when our financial situation is clearer."

Sensing we were done for the day, I stood and smiled. "I'm grateful to both of you for giving me your time." The two men stood, and Bradley asked his assistant to see me down to the bank of elevators.

Another "maybe" on the donation and two more members

of the Michael-Coale-is-an-asshole club. I was struck by how business makes strange bed fellows. Trying to picture selfish Michael in the same room with humanitarian Bradley was weird enough. But seeing the rational scientist, Bradley, with that tightly wound J-C Guzman was even weirder.

Out of curiosity, I resolved to do a little post-interview research on Guzman. I'd dip into Michael's diaries for more information and also ask Clever Connie to see what she could find out about Bradley Wong's angry assistant. As a criminologist, I knew I needed as much information as possible about people with a motive to kill Michael—especially, people with hot tempers.

Back at my office, I emailed Connie and asked her to see what she could find about Juan-Carlo Guzman. Within an hour, she phoned me back to tell me that, according to the Internet, "Juan-Carlo Guzman" may be the alias for someone named Manuel Mendoza. Connie said, "If that's right, Guzman was an officer in the Mexican secret police in the 1990s, when innocent people—students, unionists, and other citizens—were 'being disappeared.'"

I took a moment to reflect, then said "If Guzman is Mendoza, then he knows how to kill people and may have killed plenty of them in the past. But is he still killing people? That's what I need to know, if I'm going to have any dealings with his boss. Maybe he's gone straight since starting to work for Bradley Wong."

"I don't think you should proceed with this," Connie said. "But if you do, please talk to Javier Murri about J-C. Javier's a doctoral student in political science, and he's involved with the International Society for Mexican Expatriates. Maybe he can find out about J-C through the expatriate community."

"Thanks, Connie. You're a gem," I said and hung up.

An hour later, Connie sent me an email with contact information for Javier Murri. It also contained material from the report of a Commission to Study Missing and Disappeared People, published in 1995 and translated into English in 1996. The report read as follows:

Fifteen witnesses—five men and ten women—testified they had been interrogated by Sergeant Manuel Mendoza after a nighttime arrest by the National Police. During the interrogation, all were tortured for periods lasting up to five hours and none was permitted to have a lawyer present. Eight said they were raped during the interrogation. All were questioned about their role in opposing the government. Twelve of the detainees were released the next morning, after being instructed not to tell anyone about their experience. Three were detained in a local prison-stadium where they were subjected to further questioning and torture, one for as long as four months.

Though Sergeant Mendoza was not the only police officer present, witnesses agreed he was in charge of the interrogations. He also employed the most brutal methods, including the use of lit cigarettes and cigars, electrical cables, waterboarding, suffocation, and rape. Throughout the interrogation, witnesses were degraded, threatened, and beaten. Several said they doubted they would get out of there alive.

The report sickeningly described the tortures these prisoners endured. Below the text were pictures of a twenty-two-year-old Manuel Mendoza—known to me as J-C Guzman—and his two assistants, one slightly younger and the other slightly older.

When I got Javier Murri on the phone, he confirmed that Guzman and Mendoza were likely the same person. "The man we're talking about has come to Mexico City three or four times in the last two years to meet officials in the Health Ministry. He now represents a pharmaceutical company based outside the country, perhaps in Canada. My contacts didn't mention the name Jupiter but that would fit."

"Just one more question, Javier, and I'll let you go. Do you know whether this man still engages in criminal or violent activities today?"

"From the way people still talk about him, Mendoza was nastier than Freddy Krueger. You know who I mean? The *Nightmare on Elm Street* guy? Do monsters like that ever reform?"

"I couldn't say," I admitted. "But thanks for looking into this. You've helped me a lot, Javier."

"Good luck, Rachel. And stay safe. Keep away from Freddy Krueger, if you can."

Now I was scared stiff. Back home that evening, my buddy Al K. Hall tried his best to calm my nerves but it was no go. Freddy Krueger haunted my dreams all night, though he spoke with a Spanish accent.

I wish I could tell you I never saw Guzman again. But I can't; he wasn't done with me yet. Little did I know that I was destined to piss him off.

10

I slept restlessly that night, with many nightmares: clowns, murder scenes, Freddy Krueger—that kind of stuff. It took me the whole morning to calm down. Then, still a little groggy,

I headed down to King Street for a scheduled two o'clock appointment with Matt Carling. The day was so beautiful I walked there from school. I have to admit I kept looking over my shoulder—scanning the surroundings—for signs of menace.

When I got there, a young woman in a dark suit appeared in the reception area. It was Trish McCormack and she looked just as she had at the funeral, well put together and dazzling the world with her smile. "Hello, Professor Tile, I'm Trish McCormack. I wanted to give you my condolences in person and say how much we miss Mr. Coale."

I saw an opportunity and seized it. "Thank you, Ms. McCormack. I was hoping to talk to you about a piece of business that Michael's death left unfinished. Could we talk when you have a few free moments?"

"Of course. If it's just a brief chat you need, why don't you pop by my office when you're done with Mr. Carling?" And then she pointed out Matt's office.

"Lovely to see you again, Rachel. It's been ages. Can I offer you a tea or coffee?" Matt asked enthusiastically from over in the corner, where he had bent over to tie his shoe laces. Standing up again, Matt was just as handsome, confident, and well dressed as I remembered him. Today, he was wearing a charcoal gray business suit, a light gray shirt, and a patterned tie in blue and green.

"Thanks for seeing me, Matt." With a slight nod towards the Maple Leaf emblem on the wall I said, "It's a shame about Nick Dempster, isn't it? My husband Daniel is despairing about the Leafs' chances this season."

"Yes, Nick's irreplaceable. The Leafs will almost certainly sink into last place without Nick around next season," Matt said, smiling but starting to shift from one foot to the other.

"I know you're busy, so I'll get right down to business. The dean has told me that Michael had planned to donate a large sum to a program for the study of global crime. But he died before the donation was complete. Did he talk to you about this?"

"No, Michael never mentioned anything about that. Maybe he hadn't made a final decision on the matter. Or maybe he didn't plan to involve Westlake Holdings in the donation, so there was no need to discuss it with me."

"Two of Michael's business associates—Bradley Wong and Gene Tretnikov—have also shown an interest in donating to this program, and I've spoken to each of them. Like the dean, they'd also heard about Michael's plan to donate this money. Does that surprise you at all?" I asked.

"A little, I guess. I have no idea why they would've heard about this and I hadn't. But Michael spent a fair bit of time with them in the last few months."

Abruptly, Matt looked at his watch. "Is there anything else I can help you with, Rachel?"

I wanted to ask if anyone at Westlake might know more about the company's charitable donations. But I sensed Matt was giving me the bum's rush. It would be a tactical error to make him give me a definitive "no" on a contribution to our School. So I shook my head to show I didn't have any more questions, and smiled.

"Oops. I almost forgot. Before I leave, I need a quick word with Trish McCormack. Could you please direct me to her office?" So Matt pointed to a door just down the hall and went back into his office to sit behind a perfectly organized desk.

11

Trish looked up from her desk, smiled when she saw me, and said "Hello again, Professor Tile. Please come in and have a seat." As I sat down, she closed the door behind me.

What to say about Trish? Her looks are every woman's dream. Trish is a little taller than me, has perfect features, unblemished skin, shiny hair, and a beautiful smile. She's sexy but doesn't look like she's trying to look sexy. She dresses in stylish expensive clothes but wears them in a casual, relaxed way. She's perfectly accessorized and wears only one or two pieces of jewelry at a time: say, a gemstone ring and an unusual pin or necklace. Everything about Trish is understated and yet, somehow, she looks like a movie star. I hoped I wasn't staring at her. She made me feel like a bag lady.

"I wonder if you know anything about Michael Coale's plan to give $20 million to a program of research on global crime. My boss, Dean Grabol, says Michael approached him with this idea. But Michael died before anything was finalized. Do you know if Michael had written down anything about this plan."

Trish looked uncomfortable. "That was just one of Michael's little brainstorms. He had a million of them. A lot them didn't go anywhere."

"I don't get it," I said. "Michael spoke to my dean about this. He even talked about it to Gene Tretnikoff and Bradley Wong. And then he came to the Donor's Day event where I pitched the proposal. We spoke. We were even supposed to have a follow-up meeting when he got back from his out of town trip."

Trish smiled and nodded her head. "I'll be honest with you, Rachel. Michael was never out of town for more than a day in the weeks before he died. And he told me to make sure none of your calls got through to him. He didn't want to talk to you."

"What?! He suggested we meet. I was just following his lead."

"But that's the thing, Rachel. He seemed to think you *weren't* following his lead. Your calls just exasperated him."

"What? Why?"

"I don't know. I assumed you knew."

When she saw how perplexed I was, Trish added "Michael was—he would call it—a great kidder. One day, a few months ago, Michael was laughing so loudly I could hear him all the way down the hall. He was gasping for breath, he was laughing so hard. Fundraisers had been bugging him every month or two with requests for money, and Michael was irritated. So he invented a little strategy to get everyone out of his hair for a while. He announced he had twenty million to give away but couldn't decide whether he wanted to give it to medical research or a project on international crime in the School of Criminology. Michael told the fundraisers, 'Don't bug me about this. I want to see proposals presented at the Donor's Day events before deciding who'll get my money. If anyone.' He reserved the right to be unimpressed by everybody's presentations."

"You mean, Michael never intended to donate the money at all?" I asked her. "He had us running around like rats in a maze just for a laugh?"

"I think so. You should let your dean know that was always a distinct possibility."

"Tell me one more thing. Medicine and crime? Of all the topics Michael might have picked, why did he pick those two?"

Again, Trish looked at me uncomfortably. "I have two theories about that. One is that he wanted to mess with you. It could have been Michael's way of saying, 'Dance for me, Rachel. I'm rich, so jump through hoops for me.' That's theory number one."

"Okay," I said gritting my teeth. "And theory number two?"

"Theory number two is that he was messing with Mr. Tretnikoff and Mr. Wong. The last thing Tretnikoff wants to see is a spotlight cast on international crime. And the last thing Wong wants to see is Michael's money benefiting one of Jupiter's competitors. Michael liked making them both nervous. He even got them to consider contributing to his donation."

"Wow. What a prick! Sorry. I was at the funeral. I know you admired Michael as a boss."

"I admired his business intelligence and learned a lot from it. But one thing he taught me is that being a prick and being a good businessman are not mutually exclusive. Michael used to say that being ruthless is sometimes necessary. So don't get me wrong. I was never under any illusion about Michael's morals. But I can't be telling you anything new, right Rachel? You were married to the guy."

"And yet somehow Michael was known as Canada's biggest philanthropist."

"Yes. Funny, huh? For Michael, philanthropy was just a hobby—a game, really. Some rich people buy sports teams and compete with each other for trophies. Michael preferred competing for haloes and praise. He turned charity into a pissing contest. And his greatest pleasure was leveraging some business deal to make his own charitable contribution look bigger. He loved bundling up other people's gifts with his own."

"The point is, Michael's little scheme worked," I said. "He had me rushing around like a rat in a maze. And both Mr. Tretnikoff and Mr. Wong *were* curious—maybe even nervous—about Michael's donation plans. What's more, everyone *is* interested in learning if Westlake or the Coale family will follow through with one of these choices. So, Michael had a good laugh on everyone."

I excused myself and went to the washroom, where I downed a small bottle of vodka. You know, the kind you see in mini-bars. Feeling slightly fortified, I came back to hear the rest of this horrible story from the most beautiful woman on earth.

When I sat down again, she resumed talking. "You know, you might still get a donation out of the Coale family, if you push for it. But Westlake's funds are likely frozen until the board chooses a new CEO. I'm not sure Matt Carling even has the authority to approve major spending at this moment."

With the vodka in my brain now, I was careful to speak slowly and calmly.

"I just realized that, with Michael dead, Matt could move into the top position at Westlake and maybe Bradley Wong could make a deal with Matt. Is that right?"

"Probably."

"Will you benefit too if Matt gets the top job?" I may have smiled salaciously when I asked this. I hope I didn't.

She shrugged. "I don't think Matt likes me much: definitely, not as much as Michael liked me."

"Why not?" I asked.

"For two main reasons. First, Michael often used me as his messenger. If Michael had bad news for Matt, I had to deliver it, then deal with Matt's reaction."

"And the second reason?"

Trish hesitated. "This is sensitive, but as Michael's ex, you're already familiar with Michael's sex drive. Michael and I sometimes played romantic games. None of this got in the way of my work, but Matt didn't like it. It was unprofessional, he said. Michael's previous personal assistant, Susan Baccardi, had left the job after just two years, alleging sexual harassment by Michael. Susan wanted a large settlement before she would sign a non-disclosure agreement, and Matt didn't want that happening again."

"Did Matt have any reason to think you'd do the same thing as Susan?" I asked.

"No. I liked Michael and didn't have a problem with his impulses. They didn't affect my job or my marriage. Or Michael's either, from what I understand. But Matt may have felt powerless in the sexual dynamics here."

"So, in the end, who do *you* think killed Michael?" I'm afraid I slurred that sentence, and may have smiled salaciously again. God, I hope not.

"Your guess is as good as mine, Rachel. If Michael's murder had anything to do with business, I suppose Bradley and J-C are major suspects. They stood to gain the most from Michael's death. Tretnikoff is a wild card—really hard to judge. I don't think he uses violence if he doesn't have to. And then there's Matt but he's…you know, Matt. But I'm not saying any of them killed Michael, you understand?"

All at once, we heard shouting down the hall at the reception desk; someone was demanding to speak to "the person in charge." Trish hurried out of the room to see what was going on and I followed. An angry looking man of about forty, big, with a lot of tattoos and facial hair, was pacing impatiently in front of the reception desk.

"Excuse me, what is the problem here, and who are you?" Trish asked the man, politely but firmly.

"I'm Joe Dubash. I installed Michael Coale's household security cameras eight months ago, but he never paid me for the service. I've sent him six notices, phoned his office twice, been to his house, and been here before and all I get is the run around. If I'm paid today, I'll go back to his house and turn on the cameras again. But if I don't get my money today, I'm going to rip those suckers off the walls altogether. It's your call, but I'm done waiting."

"I don't know anything about this, Mr. Dubash, but I'm sure we can settle the problem without any more noise and trouble. Please come into my office and we'll sort this out," said Trish.

Just as he started to follow Trish down the hallway, Dubash noticed me and said "Oh. You. Say, did the police talk to you about me, yet?"

Without skipping a beat I answered, "No, they haven't." Trish gave me a surprised and quizzical look. But all I said to her was "It looks like you've got to deal with this. Thanks for your time, Trish."

I turned and bolted before she asked me a question I couldn't answer, taking the stairs so I wouldn't have to wait for an elevator. I wanted to get away from there as quickly as possible, because I had no memory of ever having seen Dubash before. I had no idea who that guy was. But I had a feeling it wouldn't be good for me to know him.

12

Coming home from Westlake, I spent forty-five minutes trying to recall where I might have seen Dubash before, or at least where he might have seen me. But I knew the exercise was doomed to fail. Blackouts never give back the memories they steal—at least, that's what the research tells me.

I was relieved when, shortly after getting home, I found an entertaining text message from my sister-in-law Mary, Daniel's brother's wife. It promised me a pleasant diversion.

The message said, "I tried to phone you last night, but as usual you didn't pick up. We're having a party tomorrow to celebrate our wedding anniversary. A small party—just you and Daniel, Ellie and her boyfriend, me and Peter. We'll have dinner and wine so come around 6:30. Let me know that you can make it, and don't bring a gift."

I'd check with Daniel who would say yes and probably bring a gift. So I texted Mary and told her we'd be there. I loved visiting her and Peter, though we didn't see them often. They were an island of normality in what was rapidly becoming a sea of craziness. Mary and Peter always said what they thought and showed a real interest in how other people were doing.

There was also a text reminding me I had promised to visit my parents this week. That wouldn't be quite as much fun as the party at Peter and Mary's. I knew I wouldn't be quite as relaxed at my parents' place. Still, I had to go and maybe I'd even dress up for them—make it a special occasion.

I thought I'd wear the same suit to Mom and Dad's as I wore to the Meet Market, so I checked my closet to see if it needed dry cleaning, and it did. Then, when I checked the pockets I found a folded slip of paper with an address and a date on it. It was for an address on Michael's street. It was also for the date Michael got murdered. And no doubt about it, the handwriting was Michael's!

Michael must have slipped this into my pocket when he hugged me at the Meet Market. He had secretly invited me to his house. But I hadn't gone, had I? I don't think I would have gone. But maybe I did go and that's where I saw Dubash. And then maybe Michael told me there was no donation to be had—it was all just a joke. Maybe he even made fun of me.

Or maybe I went there, saw Dubash, Michael told him to screw off, then put the moves on me and I told Michael I wouldn't have sex with him anymore. And he said, "Well then, Rachel, I'm going to have to give my $20 million to the

Department of Immunology after all." And maybe he capped it by saying, "You were always a cold bitch, Rachel, and you shouldn't play so hard to get. You're not as hot as you used to be." Then, maybe I saw a gun on his desk—wait a minute, what's a gun doing on his desk? But I saw a gun on his desk, picked it up, and shot him twice. Then I wiped my fingerprints off the gun and the doorknob and left the house. Maybe all that happened.

I started having a panic attack and almost passed out, but then my phone rang. It was Roxy and I didn't pick up. I was afraid she was phoning to ask me about Dubash. But an hour later, when I checked my voice mail, I heard her said, "Hey Rachel. I just had a couple of quick questions about your rage theory. And about violence during blackouts. Call me when you get a chance."

I had no intention of returning this call before I figured out what I was going to say. So I went to visit my parents instead.

I hadn't seen my parents for a month and, as usual, I came alone. They didn't have much use for Daniel and the feeling was mutual. Daniel aside, I wanted a distraction from thinking about work and Michael's murder and getting the donation. I wanted to get away from all that, but it didn't work out quite as I had hoped.

My dad isn't a tall man but he's what people might call "robust." He has a broad chest and big shoulders—about the same dimensions as Gene Tretnikoff, though he lacks Gene's elegance. And he speaks in a quieter, more measured way. Unlike Gene, he doesn't exaggerate or use superlatives. He would never insist that Black Sea caviar is superior to all other kinds of caviar, for instance. He would let the diner draw her own conclusion from the evidence. "Your honour, the evidence speaks for itself. Trust your taste buds. Black Sea caviar rests its case," he might have said.

My mom, the child psychologist Tanya Tile, is also unique. Consider her take on raising children, for example. Probably just about every parent in North America has read her books—thumbed them to pieces if they've raised more than one kid. Her most famous book, *Best in Class: Perfecting Your Child, One Step at a Time*, has already gone through eight editions.

Her main message is in the title of her most famous book. You can raise your child to be *perfect*, however you define that term. But perfect parenting takes patience, insight, and dedication to doing the job right, one step at a time. Figure out how you want your child to behave, model the behaviour, get your child to copy you, and reward the behaviour now and then (but not all the time.) Continue this pattern until you get the "perfect" result you want.

It was Mom who also introduced North Americans to the Japanese idea of *amae*—the creation of dependency feelings in a child through close sleeping arrangements. The Japanese *think* this creates "interdependence" between parents and children, but I *know* it gives parents a lot more control, through the threatened withdrawal of affection. No wonder the Japanese are so committed to rituals and following the rules. Amae!!

Both Megan and I got close attention from my mother when we were growing up. And me in particular, I'd say. I was her pet science project, her beta model, her test dummy. I was the child on whom she'd developed her famous theory. And I probably developed my interest in theory from her—apples don't fall far from the tree, as they say.

But her theorizing also came at a cost. Even today, I carry a heavy load of guilt at never having achieved the perfection my parents wanted. Of course, we never discuss that. In the Tile family, things must stay pleasant. For Jack and Tanya, life is a performance art, where you show off the interesting things you're doing and learning, but never the things you're feeling. If something makes you mad or sad, do something about it. Leave the scene. Take revenge. Tile it over. But don't talk about it.

13

When I got there, Mom and Dad were in the back garden. It was an English garden, if you know what I mean, and the flowers were running amok. But that didn't bother my parents. A small portable TV was broadcasting CNN with the sound turned off and they both had drinks in front of them.

"Thanks for coming by, Rachel. It's an age since we last saw you. Can I fix you a cold drink?" Mom asked. "We're having gin and tonics."

I told her I'd take a scotch on the rocks, and she went inside to fix it for me.

Dad looked like a middle-aged white version of Tiger Woods, dressed in white golf shoes, maroon slacks, and a canary yellow polo shirt. "Been out on the links?" I asked him.

"Yup, just got back a few minutes ago. A perfect day for golfing," he said, smiling at me. He sighed and took a big swallow of his G and T, glancing idly at the TV and then back at me.

"I suppose you and Josh were at Michael's funeral a few weeks ago," he said. "A terrible husband, of course, but a savvy businessman. The news guys say no murder weapon has been found yet, is that right?"

"Right. And I don't know if they will *ever* find it."

I remembered that Dad knew a little about guns. When I was growing up, he kept one in the house for protection. He might still have it, for all I knew. But I wasn't interested enough to ask about it.

Mom came out with a drink for me and a plate of cheese and crackers. "Here's something to nibble on," she said and sat down.

"Have you done anything wonderful this week, Rachel?" she asked me, with a smile on her face. Mom wanted her smile to communicate that she was just kidding, but I'm sure she was serious. She wanted me to have done something wonderful she could boast about, or at least, feel great about.

I thought for a moment, then said "Well, I've been working on my new book about rage. I'm teaching my very popular introductory class of seven hundred students. And oh yes, I'm in the middle of raising twenty million dollars for my criminology school, but otherwise, nothing special."

"That's nice, Rachel. What will you do with all that money, if you don't mind my asking?"

"We could use the interest from it to hire new faculty members or give our graduate students more financial support, among other things."

"I imagine that will get you a nice raise as well," she said. "Or don't things work that way around the university anymore?"

"Yes, I'll probably get a bump in pay. But you know, the dean expects us to do this kind of thing. It comes with the job of director."

"Well, just so you're pleasing the Big Guy, that's what matters," Mom announced, again smiling but still serious. I knew she still wanted me to spend my life pleasing Big Guys and Big Gals.

"What have you two been up to since I last saw you?" I asked.

Mom answered, "We had the loveliest time last weekend. We took a little trip down to Picton—do you know the Royal Hotel there? It's gorgeous and we stayed for two nights. The rest of the time we walked, bicycled, went antiquing, ate and drank and killed time. And smooched a little too, didn't we Jack?"

Dad smiled. "Yes, Tanya, that is an accurate description of everything we did, including the smooching. Seriously though, it's a beautiful part of the province."

"Why did you take this little trip?" I asked.

"Actually, smooching aside, your mother and I went to have dinner with a former cabinet minister who will remain nameless, the Mayor of Picton, and the MPP for Prince Edward County, and their wives. The food at the Royal was outstanding," my father said.

"And why did you visit those people in particular?" I asked.

"A client wanted me to explore the possibility of getting permission to develop properties in and around Picton. He wants to build condos, a hotel, a spa, and maybe even a private clinic."

"I'm sure I know your client's name, Dad. Want to bet twenty bucks on that?" I asked, smiling.

"Sure, and make it fifty, but I won't tell you the right name if you guess wrong. Or I should say, *when* you guess wrong."

"Take out your wallet, because your client is Yevgeny Tretnikoff, otherwise known as Gene Tretnikoff."

My dad shook his head in wonderment, took out his wallet, and handed me a fifty-dollar bill. He had a broad smile on his face. "How did you know that, Pumpkin? I don't think you picked that name out of a hat."

By now, Mom was howling with laughter and spilling small amounts of her G and T on the patio floor. I bet she just about peed her pants.

"I met Gene Tretnikoff a month ago," I said to Dad, "and he told me what you just did. But he didn't say you were working for him."

"Gene just wants me to smooth the way with local politicians and civic leaders, to minimize local resistance. You can never tell when someone might get in the way of progress, even when the community stands to make a fortune from development."

"Are you in on this deal financially?"

"Gene and his associates are putting up the money and forming a corporation to oversee the investment. Gene asked me to serve as chairman of the board and sign relevant documents for the corporation. In effect, I'm the face of that organization, and I get shares in the company for doing that. So that's why I dined with local dignitaries in Picton last weekend."

"Why didn't Gene do this stuff himself? He's a good talker."

"The funders wanted someone who's known and trusted in Ontario to front the organization, so that's where I come in. Honest Jack Tile, that's me. And you know honey, that's why artificial intelligence will never rule the world. People will always want to make deals with other people—to look them in the eye, have a drink with them, share a joke, and shake their hand. That's what I give my clients: the personal touch."

"And what about the plans themselves? Are you satisfied with the likely effect on the residents? And what about the effect of drawing larger numbers of people to the Calypso?"

Then, ridiculously I have to admit, I did a brief imitation of the "Feeling Lucky Today?" song, complete with hand and body movements. My mother cracked up at this, but not my father. He grimaced and took another sip of his drink.

"We've considered all those things, Rachel. Sandbanks Beach is already running at full capacity, and can't take any more people. But growth in the area will lead to the development of new beaches and even more tourism. As for the town itself, Picton isn't a small farming community any more. For the last twenty-five years, people have been flooding in from Toronto, Ottawa, and Montreal. They want urban comforts, and we plan to provide them. As for the casino, it's already a going concern. Gene owns a chunk of the action and he'd love to see more people coming out to gamble. With this development, the gamblers will have places to stay, eat, and relax. Think of a mini–Las Vegas on the shores of Lake Ontario. That's what we're trying to create."

I was horrified by this plan and Dad's role in it. Then, unable to stop myself, I asked him one more question. "Studies by respected researchers have shown that building a casino draws crime and addiction into an otherwise peaceful community. Do you want to be a part of those changes in Picton?"

Dad's face reddened. "Let me give you my thoughts about that, and then change the topic. First, the Calypso has already come to town. Second, the effects of a casino on local life are chances, not certainties. Third, in our legal system, people are personally responsible for staying out of trouble, whether casinos exist or not. I just lost fifty dollars on a bet but you don't hear me whining, do you? That's because I'm responsible for my own choices and I gamble responsibly. Most people do. Fourth, I've played a role in many other property developments and have never analyzed the ethics of the investors or their plans. That's not my job as a lawyer. My job is to simplify any activity that's allowed by the law, and that's exactly what I'm doing."

Then Dad stood up and marched into the house, looking away from me. I was stunned. I felt a surge of panic and for a moment, thought I'd faint; but I recovered before my mother noticed anything. Not that she was any good at noticing such things, in my own experience.

"Your father doesn't like being challenged on law and morality, honey. Especially not now. The Calypso has become *quite* controversial," Mom said. "Give him a call later this week. I'm sure you can smooth it out together."

"Bye, Mom. I'll see you another time," I muttered.

"Keep being perfect, sweetheart," she said, smiling. Then she stood up and did the first line of "Feeling Lucky Today?" complete with hand and body movements, shouted "Ta-da," and waited for my reaction.

I gave her a thumbs-up and left for home.

It felt odd to worry about my dad's involvement with the Calypso. I had never lectured Gene Tretnikoff about the dangers of gambling and he was even more involved with the Calypso than Dad was. But my father's involvement was more personal. In the end, I didn't care how Gene made a living, but I cared how my father did.

Going to my parents place to escape my worries hadn't worked out very well but I still hoped to get some pleasant R and R at Mary and Peter's anniversary party the next day. However, that wasn't going to work out much better.

14

The next day, after delightful afternoon sex and a hot shower together, Daniel and I headed out to Peter and Mary's house in Woodbridge. Daniel had photoshopped a framed reproduction of the famous painting "American Gothic," with Peter and Mary's faces replacing those of the aged "Gothic" farm couple. "They'll love it," Daniel said. He was rarely wrong about these things.

Arriving at their home, I brought out the bag containing our gift, an anniversary card, and a bottle of red wine. Mary opened the door before we could even ring the bell. Smiling broadly, she gave us each a hug and a kiss. "You two look wonderful," she said, eyeing us in mock surprise. "Is there a new food or vitamin you can recommend? If so, I'll run out and buy it."

Remembering the afternoon sex, I giggled and Daniel smirked. "Nope," he said. "Just ordinary clean living."

Peter greeted us wearing a ridiculous party hat. "You've got to kiss the anniversary boy," he said to me. I smooched his cheek. Daniel gave Peter a hug, then handed him the bag containing the gift, the wine bottle, and the card. "Happy anniversary, you two. I hope you enjoy another thousand years of married health and happiness."

Mary laughed. "It only feels like a thousand years. And the first hundred are the hardest."

In the backyard, we found Daniel's daughter Ellie sitting in an easy chair on the back patio. Standing beside her was an unfamiliar man. He was muscular and very tall—maybe six-five or six-six—with broad shoulders. He towered over Ellie, who was about my height. The guy was dressed in an expensive dark blue suit, white shirt, tie, and shiny black shoes with tassels. With black hair that was neat and slicked back, Mr. Boyfriend looked like a fit, prosperous businessman in his mid-to-late twenties.

For her part, Ellie had on a sexy red dress that showed off all her curves. She looked fabulous and seemed thrilled to be with this guy. She was also sporting a new tattoo on the side of her neck: a small heart with an arrow through it. I wasn't keen about tattoos and, as far as I knew, this was Ellie's first. I planned to keep my mouth shut about it.

Peter gave me a glass of red wine and I polished it off in two and a half gulps. When I handed it back to him for a refill, he laughed and said I must be thirsty.

"I see you have a new tattoo, Ellie. It looks nice. What led you to get it?" I asked her, not able to stay away from the topic.

"Oh, I fell in love, so it seemed like a good idea. This is the guy I fell in love with: Bobby Gupta. Bobby, this is my father Daniel and his wife—my stepmother—Rachel Tile."

Bobby shook my hand and said, "A pleasure to meet you. And for the record, I got the same tattoo, on my shoulder." He turned to smile at Daniel, shook his hand, and exclaimed, "Nice to see you again, Daniel."

"How do you two know each other?" I asked, looking at Bobby in surprise.

"We met at the Calypso—that casino in Picton—a few months ago. Since then, we've bumped into each other a few times," said Bobby, smiling at Daniel. "In fact, we saw each other there just yesterday. How come Josh didn't come tonight?" Bobby asked, looking at Daniel.

"Some kind of heavy date he had on the books," said Daniel.

I'd been hearing about Bobby for a few months, but every time I suggested meeting him, Ellie would claim he was too busy to come around. "I'm glad you guys are finally meeting," Ellie said now.

Bobby kept patting his hair, as though wanting to make sure it was all in place; also, tucking his shirt into his pants and picking bits of invisible lint off his trousers. Was he always so self-conscious about making a good impression? Or just nervous about meeting his girlfriend's stepmother for the first time. I wondered what she had told him about me.

"I'm crazy about this girl," Bobby said. "I even named my boat after her, *Queen Ellie*, in gold letters eight inches high on the upper deck." Ellie grinned at him, and Daniel nodded approvingly.

"What do you do, Bobby?" I asked him. "Ellie isn't the best news source in the world. Nor, it seems, is my husband."

"I work for a businessman. I drive him around, take messages to his associates, collect debts, and make payments when necessary. Other times, I work a few business deals on my own."

"Your boss must trust you," I said. "What's his name?"

"Yevgeny Tretnikoff, but he goes by the name Gene Tretnikoff. You wouldn't have heard of him. He keeps a low profile."

"You mentioned meeting Daniel and Josh at the Calypso a few times. Do you work there or spend your leisure time there?"

"A little of both, I guess."

Ellie chimed in. "Bobby, that's enough business talk for now. Dad, what have you been up to? I haven't talked to you and Mom for ages. It's my fault. I've been busy studying, also falling in love." Again, she grinned at Bobby.

"I've got no news," said Daniel, smiling. "I keep on trucking. Other than that, I lounge around in my pajamas and now and then visit Bobby at the Calypso. Plus, I make luxurious meals for my beautiful wife." He grinned at me.

"I'm glad to hear you're enjoying the good life. Mom, what have you been up to?"

"Still teaching and writing. And trying to raise money for a new program that will study international crime networks."

"Do you know a lot about that topic?" Bobby asked.

"Nothing whatever. But my dean asked me to raise money to get this program going, and I can't refuse him. And while trying to raise this money, I met your Mr. Tretnikoff. He showed an interest in our program," I said, smugly. Bobby looked surprised, then smiled.

After half an hour of chit-chat, Mary invited us into the dining room. The rest of the evening passed pleasantly, without any more talk about criminology. And as Daniel and I were leaving, Bobby shook my hand again. "Good luck with that project of yours." Then Bobby returned to the couch and kissed Ellie's hand.

In the car on the way home, I told Daniel "I don't like that Bobby guy, do you? He's too smooth. I don't trust him. By the way, you might have mentioned you'd met him."

Daniel was defensive. "I barely know him. We've just had a few beers. To me, he seems like a regular guy who doesn't put on airs. He works hard. As to whether he intends to marry Ellie or just name boats after her, I can't say."

"Have you met Tretnikoff too," I asked?

"Nope, but I've heard about him from Bobby. I don't know how much time he spends around the Calypso."

"How much time do *you* spend there? And what do you do there?"

"I drink beer, play poker, a few hands of blackjack now and then, and watch the serious players. You can't imagine how much money changes hands in that place. And how unlucky some people are. A few of those guys should be chained up and kept under house arrest. They think they know how to play cards, but they sure don't."

"Do you ever win?" I asked.

"I lose more often than I win, but I have good wins now and then. Yesterday I won four hundred dollars and gave it all to Josh, for the date he's on tonight. It made me feel fantastic!"

We got home and Daniel went upstairs while I stayed downstairs and sipped a scotch. Replaying the evening in my head, I couldn't stop thinking about Tretnikoff, Bobby, and the Calypso.

Then, just to take my mind off Daniel's foolishness, I finally looked through Michael's diaries to see if I could find anything there about gambling. I hadn't spent much time on the diaries since Jen had turned them over to me. Good thing I thought of checking them: what I found was surprising, to say the least.

September 8, 2022

I had a visit from Josh last week. He wants me to lend him money to pay off his gambling debts, of all things. It seems his idiot stepfather Daniel Rosso helped my son to do some illegal gambling at the Calypso which, predictably, led to him losing lots of money. Russo inherited a ton of money and it's his fault Josh is in this bind. They're probably trying to hide the gambling losses from Rachel. She'd flip if she knew, my Rachel. Anyway, Daniel can screw off, I'm not in the business of making personal loans to foolish wimpy husbands who are afraid of their wives. I told Josh he'd have to find the money somewhere else. I wasn't going to bail him out.

So, Daniel was helping Josh to break the law by gambling underage with fake ID, and, maybe, to even acquire a gambling addiction! I was furious. I wanted to wake up Daniel and shout at him for a while. In the end, I resolved to settle this matter with Daniel at a later, calmer time.

But my anger didn't go away and when I finally fell asleep, I had a nightmare. It was set in a casino where a multi-tentacled creature—some kind of octopus with a top hat on—spun a roulette wheel, causing me to lose one bet after another until I had lost all my money and all my clothes. In a flash of anger, I flipped over the roulette table, detonating a bomb that blew up the whole casino, me included. In the last scene of my dream, a bomb levelled the whole town of Picton.

15

Daniel had already left the house by the time I got up the next morning. As I drank a second cup of coffee, Jen phoned and just the sound of her voice made me feel guilty. Her brother had been murdered and she had asked for my help. But I had gotten busy and hadn't checked in with her, to see how she was holding up. And after all, I had promised—well, sort of promised—to find out who had killed Michael.

"Hi," I said. "Sorry, I haven't had a minute free in the last two weeks and I've turned into a bundle of nerves. So I'm going for a run this afternoon—Sunnybrook Park and thereabouts—and wondered if you'd like to jog with me. Then we could go for something to eat," I suggested.

"Sounds good, but I've got a four-thirty tennis date with Martha Crawford at the Granite Club. Come on along and I'll ask Martha to find a fourth player. Then we could get something to eat afterward."

I hadn't played much tennis in the last ten years, but I didn't mind giving it a try. "I'll meet you at four-fifteen in the dressing room, okay?"

"Excellent. And please bring a proper tennis outfit. The

Club is stuffy about dress codes—it's like visiting the Vatican."

I said I'd dig up my white tennis skirt, if I could find it. Then I remembered an occasion in the ancient past when Jen and I'd gone to play at the Glendon College tennis courts with Michael and another boy—who was Jen seeing then? I do remember the other guy daring Jen to take off her top and play in her bra, which of course, she did. Not long after that, someone from the college ran down to the court, insisting she put her top back on. I was mortified but Jen laughed it off.

I rummaged around the closet for my gym bag and tennis outfit and found my racquet in the basement. Meanwhile, a text message arrived from Jen saying, "Martha's son Robert will be the fourth player. This will be fun!!!"

Getting myself ready in the Granite Club change room, I saw the full range of human anatomy. The women there were tall and short, fat and slender, young and old, dark and light, toned and flabby. A real cross-section of the fabulously wealthy.

That said, Jen looked beautiful with her clothes off. She'd stayed in shape through good eating, sleeping, resting, and vacationing, not to mention exercising, tanning, manicuring, shaving, et cetera. Jen also *knew* she looked terrific. She carried herself confidently, clothed or naked.

"Okay, let's get out there and give them what-for," she exclaimed. "We shall fight them on the beaches, we shall fight them on the landing grounds, we shall fight them in the fields and in the streets, and we shall fight them on the tennis courts; and we shall never surrender."

Metaphors (or should that be similes) flew out of her mouth like angry bees out of a hive.

Outside, a pleasant breeze was blowing but it wouldn't hinder our game and the temperature was perfect: not too hot and not too cold. At courtside, we met a woman in her mid-fifties and a man in his early thirties. "Martha, this is my friend Rachel Tile," Jen said. "Rachel, this is Martha Crawford and her son Robert."

Martha was a slender, young-looking fifty-five-year old, with dark, beautifully cut hair and a stylish but traditional tennis outfit. About my height, Martha wore Gucci sunglasses and held what looked like a Wilson Blade SW 104 Autograph v7 tennis racquet. That's the same brand Serena Williams used to win all those championships in the early 2000s. Maybe it was the same racquet, for all I knew.

"Hello," said Martha. "It's nice to meet you. By the way, Robert goes by his father's name, Delamont, not mine, Crawford."

Robert was a handsome man, even elegant. As I'd soon discover, he was also smart, funny, and eager to please. And because he was comfortable with himself, Robert was comfortable with others. His tennis outfit was stylish but traditional, and even his racquet, though visibly old and much used, had been well-maintained.

Robert took my hand and grasped it firmly. As we shook hands, he stared into my eyes for about three seconds too long for me to miss his interest. An electric current flowed between us and I felt excited. But after breathing deeply three times, I calmed down, panic averted. Meanwhile, Robert watched me with amusement on his face.

"We can chat after the game," said Jen, "so let's get started. We only have the court for forty-five minutes."

Jen and Martha were well-matched, that was clear, but Robert was far better than the rest of us: a composed and skillful player. He played a strategic game, slow and smooth. In fact, he never broke a sweat and walked through the rallies. Meanwhile, the rest of us ran around the court like chickens with our heads cut off. I was the worst of us, making a few good returns but missing simple volleys in ways that earned me groans from Jen and laughter from Martha.

For his part, Robert never tried to make the rest of us look bad. In fact, he tried to help us improve. On one occasion, he suggested I grip my racquet higher up the handle. I tried that and instantly started to play better. I smiled at Robert through the rest of the game, though Jen and I were demolished by his play. Sweat streamed off my face when we finished.

"What do you say to a cool drink after we change?" asked Martha. "Meet in the clubhouse in fifteen minutes? That should be possible if Jen doesn't take a half-hour shower like she usually does."

Jen smiled. "Okay," she said. "But just a short drink. Rachel and I have dinner plans, so let's not turn this into a major event."

When we got to the clubhouse, Robert was already at a table for four, nursing what looked like a gin and tonic with a piece of lime floating in it. "Ladies, I'd given you up for lost. Forgive me for starting to drink without you. I suppose Martha couldn't get Jen out of the shower."

"No, smarty-pants," muttered his mother, smirking. "Rachel was talking my head off in the change room and I couldn't get her to budge. However, we're here now, so stop complaining."

We ordered drinks and Jen started eating cashews out of a bowl on the table. As usual, she was dressed eccentrically, wearing a cheap H&M dress that looked vintage—like what a low-income housewife might have worn in the 1950s. I suppose she was making a statement about the club's snobbishness.

"That was quite a tennis game you played today, Robert. Are you a big sports fan?" I asked.

"Now and then, I play tennis doubles for fun. But I prefer individual sports like singles tennis or golf. And I never watch team sports if I can help it—don't know why, I just never got interested."

"I hear from your mother that you have a degree from Harvard and you're an investment banker," I said.

"That's right. I make money for people who scarcely deserve it, while surviving on bread and water myself. What do you do for a living?"

"I teach criminology at a local university and write books. Oh yes, and raise money for my School."

"I did a little work in criminology myself, years ago. I wrote my senior thesis on money laundering in the Caribbean. It was later published as part of a book."

"Wait a minute," I said. "Are you the Delamont who co-authored *Safe Haven: An Essay on Secret Banking* with Reginald Kellogg in 2015?" I asked him in astonishment. That was a famous book many criminologists had read.

"Yes, that's mine. Reggie wanted to include most of my senior thesis in his book so I agreed to a co-authorship." Robert smiled broadly, rightly proud of his academic achievement. I told him I was impressed and he grinned.

But by now, Jen was taking handfuls of cashews at a time and soon she was squirming in her seat. "Let's get dinner, Rachel. I could eat two horses and a unicorn." She abruptly stood up, which was my cue to follow her out.

"Goodbye, Martha and Robert, I enjoyed meeting you," I said as I was about to leave the table.

"I'd love to chat with you again when you have the time, Rachel." said Robert.

He handed me a business card and I took it, promising to call him. I doubted I'd follow through but wanted to leave open that possibility. As it turned out, I called him, all right. In fact, he saved my life, but that was much later, when everything was falling apart.

I do want to make one comment about my somewhat extreme reaction to Robert: Yes, I was impressed—bowled over, really—by Robert's accomplishments. More than that, I found him intelligent and attractive. So you're welcome to say my reaction to Robert was all in my mind, but so what! Love, romance, attraction—they're always "all in your mind."

16

Soon, Jen and I were seated in a booth at the Miller Tavern on Yonge Street. She had her Pentax camera next to her on the banquette, always ready to snap a picture that told a story. Through the open window, we heard a low buzz of car tires and conversations from the dimly lit patio below.

"Robert impressed me," I said. "He's fun to be around, also intelligent and accomplished."

"Don't forget hot," Jen said, laughing.

"Jen! You cradle-robber!" I joked.

"I saw you two looking at each other. I thought your face was going to explode."

"There was no looking," I lied, smiling. "And I heard him call you Aunt Jen. What's with the 'Aunt Jen' stuff?"

"That 'aunt' stuff is a term of respect. I helped him get his act together after he was expelled from Upper Canada College."

"Not for anything too serious though, I hope?" I asked.

Jen hesitated before answering. "It was pretty serious. Robert was in with a real bad crowd in those days. They caught him with a handgun at school. And one time he got into a squabble with another student who ended up dead. Not gun-related—the kid fell out a window—but Robert was a murder suspect for a while. He had to finish high school in Switzerland. After that, though, he was off to Harvard for his college education. By the time he graduated, he'd straightened out and there hasn't been any more trouble," she said, smiling.

Then she added in a more serious tone, "But lately, since Michael's murder, the police are showing an interest in Robert again."

"Really! Why? How could he be connected to Michael's death?"

"It must be suspicion by association. Robert told you he's an investment banker because that sounds respectable. But the truth is, most of the work he does is for a shady businessman named Yevgeny Tretnikoff. He's also a fixer for that guy, if you know what I mean,"

Then, Jen abruptly changed the topic. "Speaking of crime, the Coale family has suffered another calamity: this time, a break-in at Beth's house. Someone vandalized her home two nights ago. Unfortunately, her security cameras are still not working so she has no footage of who did it. Matt suspects it's the security camera installer himself—some hothead with a beef against Michael."

She leaned closer and I was afraid she was about to ask me about Dubash, but she went in another direction. "Do you know the cops have interviewed Matt about Michael's murder twice now—Matt, who'd never hurt a fly. I'm wondering if Trish McCormack led the police to suspect him. Trish and Matt were rivals at work, you know. She had lot of influence over Michael, and Matt thinks they were having an affair. If Trish's husband Preston knew about the affair and got jealous—well..." She left that sentence hanging.

"I talked to Trish McCormack the same day I met Matt at Westlake," I said. "But I didn't get the impression she has it in for Matt and wouldn't worry that she's trying to poison the police against him."

"Frankly, I won't stop worrying until they find Michael's killer."

"But Matt's alibi is solid, right? He was watching that big hockey game with you and Robert Delamont?"

"Right. And Beth's alibi will hold up too. She was in Jamaica with a friend the night of the murder. It's the other suspects who ought to worry. Like, where was Trish's husband Preston that night?"

"Maybe the police should be more interested in Tretnikoff and Guzman," I said, and filled her in on what I'd learned about those two. She shuddered when I said someone had called Guzman a Freddy Krueger type.

"Enough depressing stuff, Rachel," she said. "What else have you been doing lately, aside from looking into Michael's murder and trying to raise money?" She laughed as she completed that sentence, realizing how absurd it was. It was like asking someone, "So what else have you been doing this week, besides climbing Mt. Everest?"

"I've been working on a book about rage," I said. "I'm convinced that rage is a normal thing—not a psychiatric issue at all. Even ordinary people become enraged when they experience treatment that is humiliating and makes them feel worthless. Then, when they see other people get away with breaking the rules or mistreating others, they get angry, sometimes even enraged."

Jen nodded and said, "Yes, sometimes even to the point of violence. Your theory makes a lot of sense to me. Somehow, I'd always thought rage was a mental problem, not a social one.

But your theory helps me understand why so many people are so violent today, what with all the wealth and poverty around them."

We sat quietly for a few moments, sipping our drinks.

"On the other hand, some people manage to suppress their rage, despite humiliation," Jen said. "I have an intern working with me right now who should be enraged all the time, but isn't. She's about our age, in second year of the photography program at OCAD. I'm her adviser, and she worries me. She's so passive: awful things happen to her and she never says 'no' to anyone, not to me, not to her husband, not to her children. She always talks in a calm, rational voice, and I wonder if she ever fights back. I also worry she's going to crack one of these days. I reach out to her, but she just doesn't respond to anything I say. So I'm wondering how to help her."

"What makes you so sure she needs help? Maybe she's fine just the way she is," I said, gulping my tumbler of twenty-year-old scotch.

"She's drinking way more than she ought to. Her husband may be having an affair, and he has addiction problems too. Her daughter is in an abusive relationship. And honestly, my friend doesn't seem happy, deep down."

I thought this over for a moment. "All you can do is tell her what you've noticed and offer to talk about it if she ever wants to. And encourage her to hit back when people treat her badly."

"I agree with you, and I've been hinting at those things for a while. I haven't had any success but I'll keep on trying."

I felt a little presumptuous offering advice to Jen on people out of touch with their feelings. She's always had an eye for phonies and for people who can't see who or what they truly are. That's why her photography is so good. Jen is also the person who recommended Anita when I told her I wanted to get counselling.

Then, she said. "I wonder if you'd look at a book I've been working on and tell me what you think. I've never done anything like it."

"What's it about?" I asked, sipping an after-dinner scotch.

"Dead people. The people who published my other books asked if I'd contribute photos to a new edition of Edgar Lee Master's book of poems, *Spoon River Anthology*. They wanted to bring out a selection of these poems with photos facing each poem. It's taken me forever to do, but I've put everything in place now and it's going to the publisher next month. Would you look it over and tell me what you think?"

"I'd love to, Jen. I'd be honoured." She pulled a thick manila envelope out of a briefcase she'd brought into the restaurant. It contained photocopies of the poems and the adjacent photographs.

"Get it back to me by next week if you can, okay?" she asked, and I said I would.

"And since we're playing show and tell, here's my most recent publication," she said, pulling a glossy art book from the briefcase and passing it to me. "The Tate Gallery in London asked me to photograph people visiting an exhibition of pictures by an English painter I know. Her exhibition was called 'Greek Myths Revisited: New Paintings by Nadia Sutton.' I was fascinated by these pictures and the people viewing them."

The cover painting, titled "The Marriage Bed of Zeus and Hera," showed a sparse, dimly lit bedroom. In the background was a large figure in bed—presumably, Zeus—with his enormous back to us. In the foreground was a woman in a classic Greek tunic—his sister-wife Hera, I guessed. She was hunched over on the edge of the bed, staring at the viewer with her eyes bulging and her mouth open in horror. Her pose reminded me of Edvard Munch's painting, *The Scream.* The picture was shadowy—in black, gray, and white, except for Hera's face, which was electric blue with red eye sockets.

I started to panic, with my heart speeding up and my temperature rising about ten degrees. I felt like what was in the picture was happening to me—or had happened to me sometime in another life. I took big sips of ice water to bring down my temperature, and soon I felt normal again.

But as I glanced through the book, Jen looked around the room at other diners, sipping a brandy and maybe thinking of photos she'd like to take.

Finally, I put the book aside. "That's a frightening cover photo. I wonder what the artist was trying to say."

Jen just shrugged. "Bad marriage?" she quipped. I knew she could have said more, but Jen wasn't going to elaborate.

Eventually, feeling all talked out, we made our way to the parking lot. There, we hugged unsteadily, kissed goodbye, and got into the Uber cars we had ordered. At that moment, I loved Jen. I would have done anything for her, I thought in my alcohol-fueled haze.

I loved her even if I didn't fully know her. I hadn't realized what a caring person my friend could be. She had asked about me and listened to my answers. I had just learned that she'd once rescued a troubled teen from a life of crime. And she clearly cared about her intern too. I wished I could be so giving.

17

The night was dark and quiet when I got home. Our terrier Maisie greeted me with lots of tail wagging and, though I was tired, I took her around the block for an evening pee. Back home, I dreamed about inscrutable art and a hot investment banker with a tentacle draped over his shoulder. Oh yes, and my list of murder motives, which kept blurring in front of my eyes.

The next morning, I resolved to step up and help Jen. I'd get back to looking into her brother's murder and procuring the donation that would memorialize him. But both paths led back to Beth Coale and her family. By helping Jen help the Coale family, I'd keep my promise to Jen and be a good friend. Then my mind went into social science mode: organizing the data, grinding out a theory, devising a plan of action. I could practically hear the wheels of my brain spinning.

But the gears weren't meshing yet. I was still missing something important and couldn't bring a theory to consciousness. I was still missing important facts about some of the players.

The next day brought a postscript to my interest in Robert Delamont. I looked him up—or rather had Connie do it since she's so good at finding things. And I kept an eye out for Robert's name in Michael's diaries.

First, Connie found this old newspaper article from the time Robert was a teenage murder suspect. It came with pictures of two young men. One was a teenaged version of Robert, the other, a fellow student at Upper Canada College, William Brant. The article from many years earlier read as follows:

A tragic incident Tuesday night claimed the life of Upper Canada College student William Brant. The son of a Toronto lawyer and grandson of a senator, Brant fell from an open fourth-floor window of the freshman dormitory after a brief altercation with fellow student Robert Delamont. A lawyer speaking for Delamont said the two young men had been arguing over the possession of a tennis racquet when Brant lost his balance and tumbled out the window to his death on the flagstone pathway below. Police say Brant's death appears accidental. Had his head not struck a boulder on the pathway's border, he might have survived the fall. The college says it will carry out its own investigation and decide the future of Mr. Delamont's attendance there.

In the end, the college expelled young Robert.

And second, after skimming through multiple volumes, I eventually found this entry in Michael's diaries:

August 12, 2022
Had a "courtesy visit" from one of Gene Tretnikoff's helpers today—Robert Delamont. I'd heard his name before but never met him. One of the guys at the Club told me he does "wet work" for them occasionally, or at least used to. Funny, 'cuz he doesn't look like a tough guy. He's well dressed and pleasant, and I was impressed. My sister told me once that this guy is related to me somehow. So, I half expected him to try and tap me for some favour. But he never mentioned family ties and instead came bearing gifts. He brought me a case of Taittinger Brut Prestige champagne, a gift from Mr. Tretnikoff, because I'd mentioned in passing I liked that brand of bubbly-water. I invited Trish into the office and the three of us—me, Trish, and Robert—killed a bottle together.

I know Trish found Robert attractive—all the while he was there, her face was glowing and she kept squirming in her chair. So, he teed her up for me too, and that woman drives me crazy.

Did Robert's mother Martha know what doing "wet work" for a gangster entails? I had a vague idea but didn't know exactly and wasn't sure I wanted to find out. I liked Robert and wanted to keep on liking him.

With the mysterious Robert lurking in the back of my mind, I finally bit the bullet and phoned my friend Roxy. If I let any more time pass, she would get suspicious. And I didn't want to lose her friendship, which I really valued. Also, I wouldn't be able to pump her for information about Michael's murder investigation.

She picked up immediately.

"Roxy, I'm so sorry I couldn't get back to you before now but I've been up to my eyeballs in school business and fundraising. You left me an odd message and I wanted to answer any questions you might have."

She took a moment to remember what I was talking about. "Oh yeah, that. My god, it seems like weeks ago. I've been really busy too. It's nothing too important—kind of more theoretical than anything else, so I decided to come to the master theorist. Here's what I need to know, and please take your time with this, because it's complicated.

"Now, thinking about your rage theory, would someone who has committed rage violence in the past be likely to do it again? Or is that too broad a question? Does it all depend on what kind of rage violence they committed in the past? For example, would someone who has vandalized property or punched someone in the nose in a fit of rage be likely—more likely than average—to also kill someone in a fit of rage?"

"Gosh, that's a tough question, " I said. "Understand, it would be pure speculation on my part. I haven't done empirical research on that aspect of the topic, which would be necessary to answer the question convincingly."

"Okay, that makes sense. But here's the background, so just tell me what you think. We're looking at a possible suspect in the Michael Coale case—a guy named Dubash. He fitted Michael Coale's house with surveillance cameras and other security equipment, and he's a real hothead. He's been in one or two bar fights, and he was charged with dangerous driving in a case of road rage a few years ago. There have also been reports of sexual violence against at least one woman he was dating. So, we're wondering if he's a good fit for the Coale murder."

I quietly sighed with relief, glad to know I wasn't the object of police attention at this point, despite Dubash's seeming acquaintance with me.

"That's a good hunch, and it may point to Dubash for the murder, but it doesn't point directly at rage theory. You haven't told me why Dubash might have been enraged at Michael, except for failing to pay for the security work at his home. I'm not saying rage theory doesn't apply here, but normally, that theory addresses more extreme, longer term causes of rage and humiliation. Maybe I need to extend the theory to include people like Dubash, who are merely assholes with chips on their shoulders."

"I can't advise you on whether to expand your theory, but maybe you should. People who are angry at the world and think they are at the centre of the universe, people like Dubash, enjoy smashing things. They'd be just as happy smashing people's faces as smashing anything else. Anyway, thanks for hearing me out. I really appreciate it. Talk to you again soon."

I signed off and went to the bathroom to throw up. After splashing a gallon of cold water on my face, I felt a lot better: like I had dodged a bullet, and Roxy and I were back on speaking terms.

Recovered from the last conversation, I asked Clever Connie to find out what she could about Beth Coale. The next morning, my email contained a newspaper article from the October 3, 2014, issue of the *Hollywood Enquirer* that told me a lot about Beth Coale around the time she met Michael. The *Enquirer* was famous for scandalous and sometimes vicious articles about Hollywood personalities. The article read:

> Guess who we saw outside the Whole Foods Supermarket last week, wearing big sunglasses and enough makeup to cover multiple bruises (?) on her face and arms. Why, it was Beth Golding, wife of noted director Randy Golding. People in the know say this marriage is on the rocks. Randy's career may be on the skids too and he may be taking out his frustration on his glamorous wife. Rumour has it Randy has been drinking heavily. Busy Beth continues to host lavish swim parties at the Goldings' Hollywood mansion while raising a baby son and toddling daughter. But we hear she's found time for a lunch date or two with Silicon Valley mogul Michael Coale. Could he be probing her portfolio and supplying those happiness pills people say she's grown so fond of?

Under the story I saw two photos. One showed a young-looking Beth wearing large sunglasses and a baseball cap, pushing a two-seat stroller with an infant (Will Golding) in one seat and a toddler (Melissa Golding) in the other. The photo was captioned "Out for a little walk or meeting someone special?" The second photo showed a young-looking Michael Coale in a power suit arguing with three other men, also in power suits.

Poor Beth must have had a hard life. First, she'd been married to a violent narcissist in Hollywood, then to a non-violent narcissist in Toronto. At last, she was free of both husbands and charting her own course, with the help of friends-with-benefits like Susan Baccardi. With both husbands gone now, she had a chance to reinvent herself, as I had fifteen years ago.

I also looked through Michael's diaries for information about his relationship with Beth. His entries made it clear that, almost from the start, he and Beth had little or no sex life. She was just a trophy wife, for display purposes only. Michael continued to have brief sexual escapades with the women he met at work or elsewhere. Beth had occasional affairs with men, or more often, with women she met at social events or while traveling. One of Michael's diary entries that told me everything I needed to know about Beth's desires.

May 4, 2016
Beth finally agreed to leave California for Toronto. I have to get out of here. State investigators say they'll charge me with insider trading if I don't leave the country. Going back to Canada makes the most sense. I know people there and it will be easy to set up shop in Toronto. Beth is not keen on the move—Canada's too cold, she says—but she'll do it if I offer Susan Baccardi a job in the Toronto office. Beth and Susan are going at it hot and heavy these days and Beth wants to

see if this will turn into something long term. I told her Susan can come along if she wants to.

May 7, 2016
Susan told Beth she's okay with moving to Canada if I give her a job and a good income—at least six figures. I said that's fine, so we're all set now. I've told my people to set up an office for me in Toronto, big enough for thirty staff, and we'll take possession in September. If any of my California guys want to move there, I'll bring them along. Otherwise, we can hire a new staff before September.

This told me Beth had no interest in Michael's sexual activities and wouldn't have killed him for cheating on her. And even now, years later, Beth was still involved with Susan Baccardi. They were reportedly on vacation together in Jamaica the night Michael was killed. So I had to look somewhere else for a possible killer. I brought out my notebook and scribbled some notes to myself about Michael's marital relationship.

18

I called Beth and arranged to meet her for coffee at Future Bakery the next morning. Dean Grabol had suggested Beth could help me do an end run around Westlake if Matt was going to oppose my fundraising effort. So I had reluctantly agreed to feel her out on the topic.

I'd bumped into Beth a few times in the last fifteen years, always at Jen's house. We weren't friends but we were always cordial with each other. She'd done well for herself, a successful businesswoman in her own right, and I liked her. Unlike Michael, Beth was polite and charming.

During her first marriage to a TV director in California, Beth had started a cosmetics company, Astra Beauty Products. Now, fifteen years later, and thanks to financial help from Michael, her business was flourishing. Astra Beauty Products boasted the motto, "Be the star of your own life." With factories in Paris (Ontario), Greenville (South Carolina), and Guadalajara (Mexico), her company harvested growth hormones from baby rabbits. This, Astra claimed, is what gave product users "the skin of babies." Three million Instagram followers seemed to agree.

Michael, though he'd put money into it, had been less credulous about the enterprise. "You should call your company Bunnies R Us," he'd told Beth. "Your slogan should be 'Get your rabbit on!' and you should market your product with the slogan, 'Bringing your face all the mystery of Paris.'"

At least, that's what I'd heard from Jen. And those did sound like Michael-type jokes.

Beth showed up at the (very casual) restaurant dressed in an off-white designer suit and a tasteful gold necklace worth three or four months' of my salary.

After a few preliminaries, I said, "I know you've got a lot on your plate right now. So, I hate to bother you with anything else, but my boss—that's Dean Grabol—wants me to ask you something. Before Michael died, he told my boss that he was planning to donate twenty million dollars to a program on international crime at our university. Since I'm director of the criminology school, the dean asked me to follow up on that plan. I tried to reach Michael before he died but couldn't make contact. Since then, I've talked to Matt Carling who doesn't know anything about Michael's plan. So I'm wondering if *you* could tell me Michael's thoughts about this donation?"

I neglected to mention what Trish McCormack had said

about Michael's donation offer being bogus. Yeah, I know, this wasn't a nice thing to do, lying by omission and all. But I had to get Sandor Grabol off my back!

Not surprisingly, Beth looked puzzled. She stared up at the ceiling and around the room, squinting her eyes as she thought about this—looking everywhere but at my face. I almost wondered if she was actually choosing a pastry from the counter across the room.

"This is all news to me, Rachel. No, Michael never discussed this idea with me. He didn't leave directions about it in his papers, and when we read his will, there was nothing about a donation there either."

Continuing the Big Lie, I pressed on. "This is a big ask, but would you consider honouring Michael's memory by making this donation in his name? We could set it up as the Michael and Beth Coale Program in Global Crime Research."

"Hmm. That's a possibility and I'll give it further thought. And, here's a coincidence. I had a call from an odd man last week, a Mister Guzman at Jupiter Pharmaceuticals, asking if I'd carry forward Michael's interest in health research. I told him what just I told you—that I knew nothing about Michael's plans on that score, but I'd think about it. I also suggested he talk to Matt Carling about it, since Mister Guzman was proposing a business investment, not a donation. But there's only so much money to spend on these things, and it's either going to be an investment or a donation, but not both."

"You called him 'odd,'" I said. "I've actually met Mr. Guzman, so I understand the 'odd.' But do you mind my asking, how did he react to your words?"

"That's just it. He didn't react well at all. He started arguing with me—maybe I should say lecturing me—as if to guilt me into doing what he wanted. He said Michael had harmed his company and endangered the lives of little Mexican children by not honouring the deal. It was ridiculous. He was asking me for a truckload of money and being obnoxiously aggressive, at the same time."

"How did it end?"

"I cut him off and hung up. I wasn't going to put up with his rudeness."

"You may need to be careful how you speak to him," I told her.

Beth instantly bristled at this and said "Why would *I* need to be careful. He needs to be careful."

I explained what I had learned about Guzman's violent past and Beth's whole manner changed. In a much softer voice she whispered, "Freddy Krueger? That's awful. You know, Rachel, Freddy Krueger took his vengeance out on the children of adults he hated." Of course Beth (formerly of Hollywood) would have had this bit of movie lore at her fingertips.

"Yes," I whispered in agreement. I admit it: I was behaving shamelessly.

Still whispering, her voice gradually picked up volume. "When this Guzman guy started getting angry, in the middle of talking about how Michael had harmed the little Mexican kids, he brought up Melissa and Will. He asked me how I'd feel if someone hurt *them*. You don't think—Rachel, you don't think that whack job was threatening my kids, do you?"

"No, no, you shouldn't assume that." I felt bad now about scaring her and tried to backpedal on the warning I had delivered. It worked, and by the end of our conversation, Beth was calm again. As we were saying goodbye, she remarked, "Before you go, Jen tells me she passed on Michael's diaries to you. I was just wondering if you'd found anything interesting yet, anything the police might find useful."

"Not yet, but I still haven't read most of the entries. It's unlikely I'll find anything the police don't already know. Have they told you how their investigation is coming along?"

"They keep their cards pretty close to their vest, considering that the widow and the angry son are among their suspects. They're still whittling down the suspect list, checking out motives and alibis, and looking for links to the murder weapon. Poor Will. They keep trying to trip him up on his alibi because he was alone on the night it happened. So he's got no alibi."

"Who do *you* think might have done it?" I asked her.

"My guess is Michael screwed over the wrong person in some business deal. You know what he was like. For him, success meant sticking it to others."

That summed him up pretty well, I thought.

For weeks after that meeting, I'd often think about Beth's investment-versus-donation comment. My fundraising had made me J-C Guzman's competitor, and I'd later discover that competitors ended up in J-C's gunsights. My mind also kept returning to Beth's fear for the safety of her kids. It was hard *not* to remember this when terrible things started happening to Will and Melissa.

Saturday finally rolled around and Daniel and I slept in. Then, with Ellie at her apartment downtown and Josh at a friend's house, we went out for a late brunch. The sky was a cloudless clear blue and the air, warm and scented. Leaves on the big old maple trees were a gorgeous mixture of greens, yellows, oranges, and reds.

We drove to Café Landwer, a casual place nearby, and made ourselves comfortable. The cafe was quiet: past the breakfast rush and not yet filled up with a lunch crowd. I ordered a

Mediterranean mezze plate and Daniel chose pancakes and eggs. We also asked for mimosas and settled in for a chat.

I told Daniel about my recent visits to Beth and Matt, and my failure—so far—to nail down funding for the new criminology program.

In return, Daniel told me a story he thought I'd like, about an enraged Florida man who'd murdered his next door neighbour just last week. (He suggested I include it in my book about rage.) The neighbour had been letting his dog crap on the guy's lawn every day for six years, despite Florida Man's repeated complaints. Finally, Florida Man snapped, got his hunting rifle, stormed into the neighbour's kitchen, and shot him five times in the chest. Then, he scattered a garbage bag full of dog turds throughout the neighbour's house—kitchen, living room, dining room, and main bedroom. He even put turds in the neighbour's clothes closet. Seems he'd been saving up these turds for over a year, for just this purpose.

I pretended to find the story as amusing as Daniel did. Actually, it was pretty gruesome.

Then Daniel told me about his company's purchase of fifty-eight new trucks. Empire Trucking would go nationwide before the end of the year. For many decades, the Rosso family firm had served only the Greater Toronto Area. This time next year, it would own and rent out trucks in Ottawa, Vancouver, Calgary, Winnipeg, and the Maritimes as well. Daniel admitted it was a bit of a gamble to expand the business that much and that fast, but it was a calculated risk.

We drank to Daniel's business plan—also, to Florida Man— and fell silent for a few moments. Then, I realized the reference to gambling had given me the segue I needed.

"Speaking of gambling, you've been down to the Calypso in Picton a lot of times lately, and I'm a little worried about that.

Gambling hurts a lot of people, so I want to ask about your own gambling. How often do you gamble, and how much have you lost?"

"I've been going to the Calypso once or twice a week, and sometimes I lose more than other times. I netted $400 last Friday, as I told you before. Right now, I'm in the hole, compared with last spring when I started gambling, and I took a loan to cover the loss. But I expect to pay it off quickly by gambling smarter. Like Frank Sinatra put it, 'I'll do it my way.'"

"How much do you owe, Daniel?"

After hesitating he said, "Umm. About seventy-five or eighty thousand dollars."

I was shocked by those numbers. In a loud whisper, louder than I'd intended, I asked, "You've lost seventy-five or eighty thousand dollars gambling? That's crazy! Why didn't you reach into our bank account, pay off the loan, and stop gambling altogether?"

Surprised by my anger, Daniel whispered back, "I didn't want to do that. I had gambling debts last spring and they ate up a chunk of my savings. So, I took out a loan to carry the new debt for a while. I can probably pay it off this month. I've improved my poker game a lot in the past year."

Back to a slightly more normal voice but still freaked out, I shout-whispered, "That's pure fantasy, Daniel. That's the stuff gambling addicts say. Meanwhile, you're draining our bank account —*our* bank account—with losses and interest payments. Who loaned you that much money?"

Weirdly (I thought), Daniel smiled then. "Bobby Gupta. He's made it easy for customers at the Calypso to get short-term loans to cover their losses. I arranged all this through Bobby's associate, Robert. He provides loans to preferred customers." Now Daniel looked embarrassed. "Look, I know it sounds like a lot of money, but I'll win it back and then I won't gamble any more. It's just that gambling gives me something to do when I'm not working. And it's fun. I also make good friends down there. Josh likes it down there too."

That pushed me off the deep end. "You dragged Josh into this 'fun' so he could get hooked and go into debt too? What the hell were you thinking? It's not even legal for someone his age to gamble."

"Oh, sure, but underage gambling is illegal the same way underage drinking is. No one pays any attention to those rules. We let Josh have an occasional glass of wine at celebrations, don't we?"

"That's a ridiculous comparison. They're not at all the same and you know it."

"I just wanted to have a father-son experience with him."

"Then take him fishing or golfing! Go to a ball game or a movie like a normal dad."

"Movies are your thing and I hate golf and fishing. I like casinos."

"You're a fool, Daniel," I said, feeling my rage starting to bubble. "You're not gambling responsibly, or being a responsible parent, and I won't stand for it. Smarten up or you're going to find yourself without a wife—at least, without this wife."

All of a sudden, I was seeing Daniel Rosso at his worst. If my jaw muscles got any tighter, my head would explode. But as calmly as I could manage, I whispered, "Gambling is dangerous, and I don't want to live with someone who gambles his money away. Promise you'll quit gambling NOW! And stop recruiting Josh into that lifestyle."

Daniel agreed a little more quickly than I expected. "Alright, alright, I promise to fix this. I'll fix everything."

I shook my head in disapproval. In my normal voice again,

but through clenched teeth, I said, "This is the stupidest thing you've ever done, and you've done it behind my back. Stop gambling, right away."

Daniel shook his head. "One more week, honey, then I'm finished."

This wasn't the Daniel I thought I'd married, and for the first time ever, I didn't believe him. I knew I'd have to keep pushing him until I saw results. I decided then and there to move half the money in our joint checking account into a new account that only I could access. If Daniel was going down the drain with this gambling addiction of his, I wasn't going down with him.

19

I cut lunch short and left the restaurant, but I couldn't get Daniel's gambling debt out of my mind. That night, I'd sleep by myself in the guest room. I wanted Daniel to know I wasn't going to accept what he'd done—correction, what he was still doing.

I also phoned Anita to ask her for an emergency appointment. I really needed some support right now. But she was booked solid for the next two days and couldn't even talk on the phone. Her secretary suggested I head to Emergency at the Clarke Institute if I needed help right away, but all I wanted was to vent to someone. So, I phoned my sister Megan and told her what Daniel had just told me. She was as shocked as I had been.

"That's horrible, Rachel. Did you know he was gambling so much?"

"I knew he was going to Picton a lot, but had no idea about

the extent of losses. I guess it's good that things are finally coming out in the open."

And then my sister said, "Well, if that's really how you feel I should probably pass along some gossip one of my customers told me about Daniel's activities in Picton. I don't know if it's true but I heard Daniel regularly visits someone named Rusty, a hostess at the Calypso. My contact told me Daniel and Rusty are decorating a little farmhouse for themselves outside of town."

And just like that, my rage was back, stronger than ever. That night, I dreamed of standing beside a roulette wheel at a casino, losing every bet. I kept removing items of clothing and pawning them for betting chips until I was completely naked. The croupier, trying to keep a straight face, kept asking me for my next bet. In one dream, Daniel bet my wedding dress on a roll of the dice. Oddly, he looked like Fyodor Dostoevsky in that dream. Mr. Crime-and-Punishment had suffered from a gambling problem for about ten years, so I guess that put Daniel in good company. Haha!

I didn't need Anita's help to figure out what these dreams were about.

Maybe the thing that set me off was what Megan had told me about Daniel and Rusty. Or maybe it was what Trish McCormack had said about her open marriage and sex with Michael; or me remembering all those times Michael had cheated on me. Maybe it was the unusual sexual triangle involving Michael, Beth, and Susan Baccardi. Anyway, something reminded me of the conventional wisdom about murder investigations, the one after "follow the money." I'm talking about the need to "follow the sex." And again, I wondered if Michael's sex drive could have gotten him killed.

The provocation was a diary entry Michael had written about Susan Baccardi leaving Westlake following a sexual harassment incident and just before Trish joined the firm. Michael had written:

June 20, 2019

Thank God, Susan Baccardi is out of here. Prissy bitch. Beth can have Susan all she likes, I just don't want her stuck-up self around my office anymore. I hear she's lined up a job at Toronto-Dominion Bank, starting next week. In her place, I now have an incredibly sexy assistant named Trish McCormack who may be into playing sex games. I'll enjoy finding out more about that. She can't have missed my show of interest when I stood up to show her out of the office. A little embarrassing maybe, but she stared at the bulge in my pants and said, "Something tells me I've got the job." She laughed when I said, "You know you do." More later, dear diary.

That entry intrigued me, so I e-mailed Beth for Susan Baccardi's contact information. I told her Susan might shed light on some of Michael's diary entries. Then, after making sure that Susan was willing to talk to me, Beth gave me her number. Susan answered as soon as I dialed.

"Thanks for talking to me, Susan. I'm looking into some issues at Westlake Holdings, and thought you could help me. Can you spare fifteen minutes right now?"

"Sure," she said. "What do you need to know?"

"You've probably heard, I'm helping Beth Coale learn more about Michael's enemies. In particular, I'm wondering about enemies he may have made at work."

"Gosh, I haven't worked there for years now. I wouldn't know anything about Michael's recent dealings, much less anything about his current enemies."

"But he had enemies you knew about when you worked there?" I asked.

"Of course. Michael was always baking up a new batch of enemies. He was the opposite of a pleaser."

"I understand that you'd suffered sexual harassment at Westlake and received a settlement after signing a non-disclosure agreement. Is there anything—anything at all—you could tell me about working there?"

"Sure. I don't think anyone is going to sue me over the NDA now, even if I misspeak. Beth wouldn't allow it. Still, let's make it off the record; I can confirm I had problems with Michael's wandering hands—also, with his abusive language. Eventually, I couldn't stand working for him anymore. He had no boundaries. He wouldn't stop grabbing me even after I'd objected very strongly the first few times."

"And do you think he did that to others? Not just to you?"

"I assume he did. But that's the thing about NDAs. Victims who sign them are forbidden to talk to one another or share their stories."

"So, if Michael had abused the wrong employee, he might have gotten himself killed for it?"

"I don't want to speculate about that. As I said, Michael made as many enemies as Krispy Kreme makes doughnuts. A few people may have liked him, but I'm guessing there were many more on the other side of the ledger. People like me would have found it easier and safer to just get the hell away from him and take his hush money. Beth will tell you it was the same with family members."

"He gave hush money to family members?"

"Not exactly. Of course not. But often, when he went too

far at being a prick to Beth or the kids, he'd turn around and give them something—a gift, even something extraordinarily expensive, like a trip to Hawaii—to make amends. It was a bribe instead of a formal apology. For Michael, bribes and hush money meant never having to say, 'I'm sorry' and never having to stop being a prick."

"How did Beth react when she learned Michael had been harassing you?"

"I'm not going to talk about that," Susan said in a new, snappy tone of voice.

I'd touched a sore spot. So I thanked Susan for her time and hung up. I hadn't learned anything new about her relationship with Beth, or Beth's possible motives for killing Michael. But I made a mental note to check the diaries for other times Michael's behaviour at Westlake might have required NDAs with other employees. Susan couldn't have been his only victim.

In my head, I started to picture a Venn diagram, superimposing the Beth-Michael-Susan sex triangle on the Michael-Trish-Preston triangle. No doubt about it: Michael was in the middle of a lot of hanky-panky. So, the next morning I texted Connie to ask for any information she could find on Preston and Trish McCormack. Poor Connie, my demands were starting to drive her crazy. But she'd brought it on herself by being so good at her job. It was one of those no-good-deed-goes-unpunished cases.

Connie got back to me within the hour and announced this was the last thing she could do for me right now. She was falling behind in her grading and her doctoral research. Could I find someone else to help out on this project? I said I'd look for someone else and thanked her for all the work she'd done so far—and hoped I wouldn't have to ask her for even more work.

Her information was mostly from the US, where Preston

had grown up. As a high school football star, Preston had quarterbacked his high school team, the Waco Warthogs, to a state championship. That got him a chance to play quarterback at Texas A&M, but a bad tackle in training practice ripped Preston's Achilles tendon. Three surgeries couldn't fix the tendon, and Preston never regained his speed and agility.

After a frustrating year riding the bench, Preston retired from football. He completed his degree at Texas A&M, then took a coaching job with the Tiger-Cats football team in Hamilton. After two years there, he returned to school (at Penn State) to get an MBA. Since then, he'd held admin positions at four companies before landing at Jupiter Pharmaceuticals three years ago.

In business, Preston was always someone's helper, never a key decision maker. I guessed that, for Bradley Wong, Preston was also a Trojan horse: a channel through which Wong could gather information about Westlake Holdings and Michael Coale's thinking. So long as Trish worked at Westlake and Michael ran it, Bradley Wong had a use for Preston McCormack. So, Michael's death may have ended Preston's value to Bradley. That may have taken Preston off the list of suspects!

It was easier to find information about Trish than about Preston, because she had a thumbnail bio on the Westlake corporate website. Turns out, she'd grown up in Ontario, the daughter of a car salesman and an office manager. Trish went to elementary and secondary schools in North Bay, then got a scholarship to McGill University where she'd double-majored in English literature and classics. She took a master's degree in English at Cornell, then spent a year and a half working as the secretary in a London investment firm. As I was to learn later, while in London, Trish had studied accounting five nights a week, after regular work hours. It was there she'd also met Michael Coale, who persuaded her to work for him in Toronto as his personal assistant.

All this told me that Trish was punching well below her weight, both at Westlake and in her marriage. She was an extremely capable person hiding in plain sight as a seeming decoration. She had used her extraordinary beauty to get Michael to teach her a lot about business. In the process, she had also captured a high salary for her husband Preston; so Trish may have felt she was in charge.

That said, I still don't understand how Preston could have been okay with his wife screwing her boss, but that's me. I've never understood open marriages and could never be in one.

In all the pictures Connie sent, Preston looked like an Adonis. Maybe that made him not just sexually self-confident but even arrogant. He must have known he looked much more desirable to Trish than Michael did. And with that in mind, he may have discounted Trish's screwing Michael as a kind of business deal that didn't reflect badly on himself. Or maybe Preston evened the balance sheet by having his own affairs on the side.

I tried to picture Daniel and I turning our own marriage into an open one. If he was going to have an affair with Rusty, I should be able to screw Robert with a clear conscience. And that was an appealing thought. But as soon as I imagined it, I knew I could never handle the weirdness of such an arrangement. No matter how good Robert might be in bed, I would obsess about why Daniel and I were still together while he was sleeping with that bitch Rusty. Maybe I'll run that thought experiment past Anita in our next session.

In any event, it wasn't right to assume other people would be as jealous as I'd be—not if I wanted to figure out who might have murdered Michael, and why. Just because I was the jealous type didn't mean Preston or Beth would be jealous types. And just because I didn't like to think of sex as transactional, other people might think differently. Trish and Susan, not to mention Preston and Beth, may have taken that approach when they thought about Michael and his wandering hands.

20

I dealt with my own possible Rusty-Daniel-Rachel sex triangle the very next time I got a moment alone with Daniel. We were in the kitchen, washing and drying the dishes. I decided it was best to put the matter to him directly: "Megan heard you're spending time with a woman named Rusty down in Picton. Is that true?"

"I know Rusty, sure. She's a hostess at the Calypso. I see her delivering drinks and talking people up whenever I go there. We joke around sometimes too, but no more than anyone else," he declared.

"Megan heard you and Rusty are decorating a love nest together—an old farm house."

"No. That's crazy. I'm not having an affair with Rusty and we're not decorating a love nest. Megan's friend must be confusing me with another guy. Lots of men are interested in Rusty. She's attractive."

As my rage flared up at that, my whisper got even louder. "So if you and I drove down to Picton and talked to Rusty, she'd back up what you're saying, right?" I asked.

"One hundred percent right," Daniel said. "Or you could phone her now, if you want to. I don't want this hanging over my head."

Daniel looked upset but also aggrieved. Either he was falsely accused, or playing poker had honed his bluffing skills. I paused the dishwashing and stared into his eyes without blinking.

"I swear I'm not having an affair with Rusty," he repeated. He started to sob, which just made me angry. I wanted to punch him in the face, but I'm a Tile, so, of course I didn't. "If I find out you're lying to me, we'll make new living arrangements, Daniel. And I don't mean we'll buy a new house together. Meanwhile, you can sleep in the guest room."

Grabbing the bottle of scotch, I stomped upstairs to my home office and slammed the door. Daniel had made me look like an idiot, at least in my sister's eyes. And though I wasn't even sure he'd done anything wrong, I wanted to smash things, starting with Daniel's nose.

Do you know that song, "I saw the colours fade away from you"? It's about falling out of love. Well, I was coming to see a new side to Daniel and didn't like it. This was the day when I first started to notice the colours fade away from Daniel. And that conversation was only round one of our "Who's Rusty?" discussion. Round two came the next time Daniel returned home from Picton. And by then, there was a new wrinkle to his story.

The next day, Daniel got home around seven-thirty and announced triumphantly, "I won twenty-three hundred dollars today. The comeback begins!"

"That's fine, but weren't you down seventy-five thousand?" I said. "What you won today is a drop in the bucket."

"But I'm turning things around, Rachel. It's a whole new day! Another few visits and I'll get the demon debt off my back." He lifted me off the ground and swung me around. I enjoyed the giddiness of this moment but knew we had more to discuss. I poured myself a scotch on the rocks, then came back and confronted Daniel.

"Did you see Rusty today?" I asked him.

"Yes, she was there, as usual."

"Did you mention what people are saying about you and her?" I asked.

"I did, and she couldn't believe it. Not only are we not a thing, but she bunks with another guy—Robert Delamont—whenever the guy's in Picton. He comes and goes, she said. They're sort of an item."

"I've met Robert Delamont—I played tennis with him and his mother a week ago. The investment banker, right?" I asked Daniel.

Daniel looked surprised. "Umm … maybe. He works for Mr. Tretnikoff and takes care of loans whenever people need them. I've talked to him a half dozen times; seems nice enough."

"Why did you hesitate just now?" I asked, which made him pause again.

"It's just … no reason. I shouldn't have paused."

"Tell me."

"Rusty mentioned he has a gun. She finds that kind of fascinating and arousing. But do investment bankers usually carry guns?"

I nodded, recognizing the rhetorical question. "So, if I were to ask Robert Delamont, he would tell me he's with Rusty?"

"If he's honest," Daniel said.

"Okey dokey then," I said, still not convinced enough to let Daniel return to sleeping in the same bed as me.

"But just so we're clear—I'm still expecting you to erase that huge gambling debt of yours, Daniel. And soon."

"I know, I know. And I will, either through shrewder gambling or using our savings. If I can't turn this around in the next week or two, I'll quit gambling and never go back there again, so help me god," he said.

"I'm taking that as a promise," I said. "And 'shrewd gambling' is an oxymoron."

After he left the kitchen, I brooded, looked out the window, and sipped my scotch. I knew Daniel wasn't taking this debt as seriously as he needed to. And he didn't care how angry I was about his stupid behaviour. But I'd warned him. He'd be sorry if I found out he'd been sleeping with Rusty.

Then I found myself wondering if Robert was a good lover. Would I ever find out? And was he really sleeping with Rusty? I couldn't decide if Robert's alleged sexual connection with Rusty made me happy or sad. I resolved to check out this Robert-Rusty connection at the earliest possible opportunity, which, as it happened, came the next day.

The next day was cool and overcast, so I put on a sweater for the first time since last March. Then, dressed in my heaviest winter gear, I started walking down to Eglinton to check out the novels at Indigo.

As I passed Grazie, a casual Italian eatery on Yonge, I saw Robert and Gene Tretnikoff sitting at a table for four in the front window. I was just as surprised to see them as they were to see me. They waved for me to come in, so I did. As I approached the table, they both smiled and stood up. Each extended their hand for a handshake, then Robert hugged me and gave me a pretend air kiss on each cheek.

"Very French," I murmured. "I like that."

"What are you drinking?" asked Gene.

"I don't want to break up your lunch meeting," I said. "I just came in to say hi, and now I'm off to Indigo for new reading material."

"Please join us for lunch. You haven't eaten yet, have you?" Robert asked.

I admitted I hadn't, so they pulled out a chair for me and I sat down.

"I'll have a red wine, thanks," I said. Gene ordered us a bottle of excellent Italian wine—a 2012 Barolo, if I remember correctly. (Of course I remember correctly; it was one of the best red wines I had ever drunk!)

"What are you guys up to?" I asked.

"We meet for lunch every NOW AND THEN, just for fun," said Gene.

When the waiter had poured us each a glass of wine, Gene said that we must celebrate this unexpected meeting, each with our own toast. He then looked at me and nodded, as though ordering me to begin.

"I invite you both to toast knowledge. Nothing is more important than the eradication of ignorance and foolishness," I said. Then we all took a sip of wine.

Gene went next. "I invite you both to toast generosity. Nothing is more important than the elimination of selfishness and the people who live only to please themselves." Again, we took a sip of wine.

After that, Robert raised his glass. "I invite you both to toast justice. Nothing is more important than the punishment or elimination of people who please themselves by treating others unjustly." Again, we took a sip of wine, then Gene refilled the glasses. Having emptied the bottle, he ordered another bottle of Barolo. I was already feeling tipsy and we hadn't even started eating yet.

"Gene is an inexhaustible source of stories," Robert said, with a smile on his face. "He's seen every country on earth; isn't that right, Gene?"

"It is ALMOST true, Rachel. I have not yet visited Andorra, Belize, or Cambodia, just to name a FEW countries. Perhaps if I continued alphabetically, I could remember OTHERS. Now, Robert hasn't visited many countries at all. But in the FEW countries he HAS visited, he has made the close acquaintance of EVERY beautiful woman. Isn't that true, Robert?"

"You're right about that, Gene. And now that I have met Rachel Tile, my list is complete."

I tipped my wine glass to Robert, as a thank you for the compliment. "For my part, having spent most of my life in universities, I thought I had met the most extravagant storytellers in the universe. But this was not true at all, until I met you two gentlemen today," I chuckled.

"Touché," said Gene. "Robert is INDEED an extravagant storyteller. Why, just last week he declared he was probably the most COMPETENT bookkeeper in North America. To keep his HEAD from swelling, I had to name seventy-eight other SUPERIOR bookkeepers."

"Of course I had no way of verifying Gene's claim," said Robert. "But of the seventy-eight Gene named, seventy-two were dead and six were Russian, which is nearly the same."

"I swear I will NEVER understand what passes for HUMOUR in Canada. Half the time I do not know what Robert is saying, and the other half the time I am certain he is joking, though he is rarely FUNNY," said Gene.

"Boys, you are on the verge of insulting each other," I said. "In view of your troubled relationship, can you tell me why you continue to work together?"

"I CONTINUE to employ Robert because he works for nothing at all. In fact, he pays me every MONTH to keep him in his job, so he won't have to worry his mother with talk of UNEMPLOYMENT," exclaimed Gene.

"I keep working for Gene out of pity. No one else would work under the conditions I do, surrounded by week-old plates of blini, borscht, and kasha. The smell is soul-destroying," said Robert.

I had to laugh at Robert's pretend-Russian accent when he named the three Russian foods. At this point, even Gene cracked a smile.

"Well, ROBERT, this is your opportunity to eat non-Russian food—indeed, to eat ITALIAN food. I'm told the specialty here is pasta PUTANESCA. Did you know, Rachel, that they named this dish after Robert's longest-lasting girlfriend?"

"Oh, was her name Putin?" I asked him, smiling.

"No, that was her profession," he replied, smirking.

Taking on a school-mastery tone of voice with a fake Boston Brahman accent, Robert jumped in with an explanation. "In case you don't know, the name comes from the Italian word puttana, which means *whore*. Puttana in turn comes from the Latin word putida, which means stinking."

"Thank you," I said to Robert. "Your explanation is enlightening. I'll order that dish to find out exactly what you look for in a woman."

Gene couldn't hold back his laughter. He laughed so loud and long that other people in the restaurant stared at us.

Finally, catching his breath, Gene said, "You have ALREADY satisfied what Robert is looking for in a woman. But if you want to keep his interest forever, you might ADORN yourself in olives and anchovies. Their smell is EROTIC, don't you agree, Robert?"

Robert pretended to swoon with delight, fanning his face with his hand to revive himself.

Suddenly, I thought of mentioning Rusty in connection to Robert's taste in women, but I knew the only answer I'd get would be more jokes. This wasn't the time. I'd have to find another occasion—or maybe I wouldn't bother asking. There'd have to be other ways of finding out what I needed to know.

Finally the waiter came for our food order. We ordered pasta Putanesca and Caesar salad.

By the time the food arrived, I was starving, so I dug in and just listened. Throughout lunch, Gene and Robert continued to pretend-attack each other's looks, intelligence, reputation, and manliness. Their conversation was like a match between two tennis professionals, with neither willing to concede the point. Clearly, they knew and loved each other like brothers. They also enjoyed performing for me, trying to make me laugh at their outlandish statements. And I have to admit, I laughed a lot of times.

Gene recommended we finish with a glass of limoncello, to SETTLE the DIGESTION he said.

"All the way from the island of Capri," Robert noted, "which is famous for its lemons." As he said the word "lemons," he tilted his chin provocatively at Gene.

We laughed, ordered and drank our glasses of digestif, and asked for the bill. Gene demanded to pay the bill, because he was "without a DOUBT, the richest person AT THE TABLE." Neither Robert nor I could argue with that, nor wanted to.

I didn't feel like going to Indigo any more, or walking home either. In fact, I was woozy. But I walked home anyway, figuring the fresh air would clear my head as I reviewed our lunchtime silliness. When I finally got home, after what felt like hours of trudging, Maisie started barking at my heels. Resentfully, I bundled up again and took her to the park for a short walk; but I wasn't in the mood to play, even if she was.

That night, as usual, I had dreams but, surprisingly, not

nightmares. In one dream, Gene's face was superimposed on Zeus—ruler of all the gods and the father of Athena, Ulysses' protector. In the same dream, Robert's face was superimposed on Athena—well, not so surprising, since I had lunched with both of them that day. And in another dream, Jen's face was superimposed on Ulysses as she slashed through hordes of nasty suitors, using only her Swiss army knife (and Athena's help) to protect herself.

21

By mid-morning the next day, the afterglow from my pleasant lunch had begun to fade. Still, I was conscious of enjoying how different it was to spend time with sophisticated, worldly men like Gene and Robert, compared to dining with Daniel. Daniel was, like most long-term spouses, entirely predictable. I already knew all his interests and conversational gambits, and had memorized the favourite jokes he liked to recycle.

And although I felt a little guilty and disloyal to admit it, Daniel often struck me as goofy and "beige." He was all sports and headline news, never art or philosophy. He was a nice guy but no one would ever find him mysterious. Daniel was comfortable and safe without any hint of a dangerous dark side. That should have been a point in his favour, but it hadn't felt that way at lunch yesterday. I started to feel like I was talking myself into something risky.

For diversion, I started reading a book Jen had given me as a birthday gift. A book about Loki, the trickster god from Norse mythology. Among the gods, Loki was famous for his cunning and mischievous deeds. His tricks and schemes often created problems for the gods but sometimes helped them.

I couldn't imagine why Jen had chosen that book for me. Maybe she remembered that I'd written my honor's thesis about violence in Njal's saga. I'd titled my first lengthy piece of writing "Violence in medieval lore: The philosophy of justice in a Norse legend." I had to read the gift book, in case she asked me about it. So I dipped into it to sample what was there.

At first it was tough going, what with all the weird names. The plots of these stories were even more complicated than Njal's saga. Loki's most famous deed, it seems, involved the death of Baldr, the god of light. Loki, knowing that Baldr was invulnerable to everything except mistletoe, tricked Hodr, Baldr's blind brother, into throwing a dart made of mistletoe at Baldr. That caused Baldr's death. As punishment, the gods captured Loki and tied him up with the entrails of his own son, while a serpent dripped venom onto his face. Loki's wife, Sigyn, stayed by his side, catching the venom in a bowl. But whenever she had to leave to empty the bowl, the venom dripped onto Loki again, causing him excruciating pain.

What was I to take from this story, I wondered? Sure, Loki regularly does bad stuff and suffers horrendous punishments— that happens time after time in these stories. In fact, during a feast at Aegir's hall, Loki insults almost all the gods and goddesses with his sharp tongue, leading to his eventual capture and punishment. Yet Loki can also be helpful. That's why the other gods and goddesses put up with him, I guess. That's a trickster for you. You never know what to expect.

My favorite for the weirdest story? Loki sneakily cuts off the golden hair of Thor's wife, Sif. This really angers Thor, not to mention Sif. To make amends, Loki commissions a bunch of dwarfs to make new hair for Sif and, unexpectedly, creates several magical items for the gods to use. Another happy ending, and everyone likes happy endings. Me too!

Thank you, Jen. Now I'm ready in case you ask me about the book.

At the very least, lunching with Gene and Robert had been a welcome stress reliever and God knows I needed the relief. Besides everything else, my fundraising job had become downright obnoxious. And I'd mentioned this to Anita several times already. But I needn't have said anything; her eyes told her everything she needed to know. Anita was appalled by my weight loss. Because of my inability to keep food down, I had lost ten pounds in the last month alone. I was starting to look slightly skeletal.

Yes, I had grown to hate fundraising, because seeking donations from rich people felt wrong to me. I didn't mind raising money for my school, but hated having to celebrate the wonderfulness of awful people like Michael, who just happened to be rich. In this crazy world of ours, Michael Coale was a model of success. He'd amassed fortune and fame by treating everyone else like garbage, only to end up with fundraisers like me begging him for money in return for lionizing him.

Other shady characters like Gene Tretnikoff and Bradley Wong played supporting roles in this drama. But as a fundraiser, I couldn't afford to get too upset about the fact that awful people often donate money to worthy causes, to whitewash their reputation or impress one another. I bet if I said all this to Daniel, he would prescribe a nice rest. Or more likely, he'd just be puzzled.

True, I was getting some help with these emotions. Anita had taught me the value of unburdening myself. And her mood-calming pills weren't bad either. Then of course there was my pal Al—Mr. Al K. Hall himself—who had shown me how to forget stuff. But I'll tell you this—and it's no knock against Anita or Al: coping with stress via counselling, chemicals, and alcohol can only do so much. When the stress becomes truly monstrous—as in "Freddy Krueger monstrous"— more drastic solutions are needed. But once again, I'm getting ahead of my story.

I had made a date to meet Jen at the Faculty Club for a drink the next day. In theory, we were meeting just to catch up. But I also wanted to pump her for more information about Robert Delamont: who he was, and how he'd gotten that way. If Jen had an agenda—and she usually did—it may have been to receive my feedback on her *Spoon River Anthology*. I still hadn't looked at the manuscript and apologized when I sensed her impatience.

A few club members were already settled in at the bar drinking draft beers. As usual, the early birds were older academics who'd stopped doing serious writing or teaching decades ago. They came here several days a week for conversation with Fergus, the spirited and nearly incomprehensible Scottish bartender.

Jen was dressed in what she imagined was proper academic clothing, circa 1930. This included baggy black trousers, a gray and brown Harris tweed jacket with leather elbow patches, a white dress shirt, and a striped regimental tie. Oh yes, and heavy brown brogue shoes. Where did she find clothing like this in 2024, I wondered. She'd have looked just right at our university as late as, say, 1958. Instead, Jen just looked ironic, as she'd intended. She ordered a light beer and I ordered a scotch on the rocks.

"Okay, if you want the whole story about Robert, here it is,"

Jen began. "After finishing college, Martha Silver—his mom—took a junior position at Goldman Sachs in New York. Her manager was Joe Coale. Now, as you might guess from his last name, Joe and I are related. Joe's father and mother had divorced when Joe was young. Ten years later, his father married my mother, who'd been widowed. So, I became Joe's stepsister, though I've never met the guy.

"Anyway, back at Goldman Sachs, Joe harassed Martha until they slept together. Martha got pregnant and Joe pressured her to get an abortion. She refused and had the baby as a single woman. Later, Martha later married Warren Delamont, a guy she'd met at another financial firm. Warren adopted Robert, and that's why Robert is a Delamont and not a Coale.

"When things started to go wrong with Warren, Martha asked Joe for child support and he turned her down. Martha knew that Joe had a much younger stepsister in Toronto, so she wrote to me. I urged her to come to Toronto and when she did, I helped her settle in. Eventually, through a job at TD Bank, she met and married Harrison Crawford, the bank's President. She didn't need my help anymore, but we stayed close friends. I met my husband Matt through Martha and Harrison. At that time, Matt was Harrison's personal assistant."

"So, that makes you Robert's step-aunt, right?"

"Yes, I'm Robert's step-aunt—also, his 'spiritual godmother,'" she said, laughing.

"Did Michael ever meet Martha or learn that Robert was his step-nephew?" I asked.

"I tried to tell Michael about Robert but he stopped me after two sentences. 'I don't want to know anything about stray relatives,' he said. That ended that."

"And did Robert know he was related to Michael?"

"Yes, but he was never interested in discussing this relationship," Jen said. "I might just as well have told him he was tenth in line for the throne of Serbia."

We chatted a bit more, finished our drinks, and left. On my own again, I thought about all the joking around with Robert and Gene at Grazie. I knew that I wanted Robert, but what did I want him for? Not for a husband, despite my current rift with Daniel. And not for a friend. So, a fling? For something to be determined later? Robert was a mystery to me, and I loved looking into mysteries. I also liked happy endings, so what would be the happy ending in this case, I wondered. And what would smart Loki do in my situation.

Thinking back on that book of Norse legends, I remembered this story. Loki organizes the theft of Thor's hammer, Mjölnir, by the giant Thrym. Certainly, Thor holds Loki responsible for this theft of his beloved weapon and intends to punish him for it. But Loki helps to retrieve the hammer by disguising Thor as a bride. This disguise tricks Thrym into revealing the hammer's location, and Thor gets it back. The meaning of this story? Disguise is everything. Shape-shifting is the key to success. When in doubt, lie. If the lie doesn't work, disguise yourself. Present yourself in a different way—maybe, in multiple different ways until some disguise finally works.

So, in seeking to appeal to his beloved, Loki might present himself in an endless array of surprising, appealing disguises. Should I do that, I wondered? Could I pull it off, even if I tried? I'll have to think about this some more.

I came home with Robert still on my mind, still an unsolved mystery. Coincidentally, a text message from Robert—marked urgent—was waiting for me when I got back home from meeting Jen. It was short, even curt. It said, "You've got to keep Daniel out of the Calypso. He's getting deeper into debt every day. This could end badly. We can't ignore this, Rachel. I've given him three days to square his debt with us."

The tone had an edge to it, nothing like the breezy banter of our lunch meeting just a few days earlier. I suppose this was Robert being businesslike and serious. I hoped it wasn't Robert being tough and intimidating for his gangster boss. Anyway, I'd deal with Daniel as soon as I saw him again.

Then, I finally got a chance to look over Jen's new edition of the *Spoon River Anthology*. The anthology, first published in 1915, contained fictional free-verse epitaphs of people who'd lived in a fictional nineteenth-century American community named Spoon River. To this, Jen had added black and white photographs that captured the message or mood of each poem.

The original book contained 245 free verse epitaphs, from which Jen had chosen one hundred and matched them to one hundred photographs she'd taken. She had developed and framed some of the photos in ways that copied nineteenth-century photographic styles. Others were more modern and less adorned. The combination was great: Jen's photos made the poems come alive for a twenty-first century reader. They also reminded me that people don't change much from one century to another.

Unexpectedly, one poem, and the photograph beside it, brought me up short. The poem/epitaph read as follows:

Cassius Hueffer
They have chiseled on my stone the words:
"His life was gentle, and the elements so mixed in him
That nature might stand up and say to the world,
This was a man."
Those who knew me smile
As they read this empty rhetoric.

My epitaph should have been:
"Life was not gentle to him,
And the elements so mixed in him
That he made warfare on life,
In which he was slain."
While I lived I could not cope with slanderous tongues,
Now that I am dead I must submit to an epitaph
Graven by a fool!

On the righthand page facing the poem was Jen's photo of a male corpse, lying face up in a coffin. The image was blurry and I couldn't recognize the face, but I lingered over this epitaph and photo longer than over the others, puzzled by its meaning. I knew several people who'd "made warfare on life," among them Michael Coale. Is that who she meant?

I got myself another scotch and continued leafing through the book; then, another poem and photograph pairing caught my eye. This poem, titled "John M. Church," read as follows:

I was the attorney for the "Q"
And the Indemnity Company which insured
The owners of the mine.
I pulled the wires with the judge and jury,
And the upper courts, to beat the claims
Of the crippled, the widow, and the orphan,
And made a fortune there at.
The bar association sang my praises
In a high-flown resolution.
And the floral tributes were many—
But the rats devoured my heart
And a snake made a nest in my skull.

This poem was an indictment of lawyers and "fixers" every-where, and I half expected to see a picture of Jack Tile on the next page. Instead, I saw a picture of J-C Guzman wearing a tuxedo, with a flower in his buttonhole and a feral smile on his face. Jen obviously saw J-C the same way I saw him: as a wolf-like killer in sheep's clothing. A wolf in a tuxedo was still a wolf, even if he presented himself as a friend to widows and orphans.

Still, my biggest surprise came a few minutes later when I read the poem titled "Richard Bone" and saw the accompany-ing photograph. This poem, about a gravestone carver, read as follows:

When I first came to Spoon River
I did not know whether what they told me
Was true or false.
They would bring me the epitaph
And say, "He was so kind," "He was wonderful,"
"She was the sweetest woman," "He was a consistent
    Christian."
And I chiseled for them whatever they wished,
All in ignorance of its truth.
But later, as I lived among the people here,
I knew how near to life
Were the epitaphs that were ordered for them as they
    died.
But still I chiseled whatever they paid me to chisel
And made myself party to the false chronicles
Of the stones,
Even as the historian does who writes
Without knowing the truth,
Or because he is influenced to hide it.

On the page alongside it, I saw a photograph of myself at the Meet Market chatting contentedly with Gene Tretnikoff. I had a plate of caviar in one hand and a glass of white wine in the other. Was Jen saying I was the "historian who writes without knowing the truth, or because he is influenced to hide it?" And did she know something about Gene that I didn't? Something Robert had told her, perhaps? Or was this "truth" just the rumours about Gene's shady business dealings?

I put the collection aside and sent Jen an email message. "Sorry to take so long getting to your book manuscript. Congratulations on the masterful work, and thank you for showing it to me. Your photos are powerful. By the way, I hadn't realized you knew J-C Guzman, but obviously you do."

I'd discuss Jen's inclusion of my own photograph some other time. To see my own face in that book was weird and shocking. I wondered what, if anything, Jen's book was trying to tell me about Michael's recent death. Also, what it was telling me about myself. Remembering Loki, I realized that *Spoon River Anthology* was all about liars—people who present themselves in the best possible light to disguise their true motives. And many of these fictional characters—Cassius Hueffer, John Church, and Richard Bone—are tricksters like Loki. But are they helpful as well as harmful?

22

Was Jen suggesting that Michael was killed because he had "made warfare on life"? And that J-C Guzman had pulled wires to benefit his employer at the expense of widows and orphans? Did she think that I, as a fundraiser, had "made myself party to the false chronicles" to celebrate the lives of people I scarcely knew? Or worse, that I'd been "influenced" to hide the truth about them? That was the simplest explanation of what I'd seen in her book, and if so, the book was a shocking portrayal of me by a friend. So I felt betrayed.

I sipped a scotch and thought about these possible meanings. Collectively, they sounded like a judgment on all our lives, like that poem by Khalil Gibran that Jen had read at Michael's funeral. I still didn't know what Gibran's poem meant, so I Googled the poem to read it for myself. When I did, I discovered that what Jen had read was just an excerpt from a longer poem called "On crime and punishment." Now I understood: Jen hadn't been mourning Michael's death, she had been viewing it as a stroke of cosmic justice.

That night, I dreamed of the images in Jen's book—especially the image of myself drinking and laughing with Gene Tretnikoff. Then, abruptly I saw myself transposed into that picture of the corpse. I saw myself lying face up in a coffin, dead.

I sat up in bed, panting with fright. Daniel wasn't there, and it took me an hour to fall back to sleep. I kept remembering the images in Jen's book—especially, the blurry image of that unidentified person in a coffin. I'd have to talk about this with Anita.

Daniel's debts had finally gotten out of hand! I'd have to deal with Daniel firmly after that terse warning from Robert. And I was spoiling for a fight when Daniel came downstairs from the guest room. He was in his pajamas, his matted hair sticking out at crazy angles. His eyes were red, and he needed a shave. In short, he looked awful.

"You don't look so good, Daniel. How do you feel?" I asked.

"Not so good," he whispered.

"What happened yesterday?"

"I went to the Calypso and got home late."

"How did it go there?"

"Not so good."

"How much more did you lose?" I asked.

He hesitated and probably considered lying to me but finally admitted, "Another thirty-five thousand dollars," he said.

"So that puts you one hundred and ten thousand in the hole, right?"

"Roughly."

I slapped Daniel's face hard. It took him by surprise because I'd never done that before. In fact, it took me by surprise too. Not a Tile kind of thing to do. But my rage was too strong to suppress. "You have to pay that off! You HAVE to, Daniel. Get it? So, how do you plan to do it?" I asked him through clenched teeth, bouncing from one foot to another as I waited for his answer.

"I guess I'll have to empty my savings account and cash in some of our mutual funds."

"You know you borrowed the money from bad guys, right? You understand the situation you're in?"

"I know who I borrowed the money from. It was…"

"The loan man who carries a gun. And in case you didn't know, he works for a Russian gangster who scares the hell out of people because of his reputation for violence."

"Okay. I see your point."

"Do you, Daniel? Because you're not acting like you see it. I wonder if your bones would still be attached to each other if my dad wasn't working for Tretnikoff."

"I really don't think it's like that," Daniel half-whispered, without much conviction.

"Well, I don't know exactly what it's like and neither do you because these are not the type of people we normally deal with. But they are pissed at you and I've been warned this could end badly. You could get seriously hurt and I don't want to see that happen. Do you?"

"Of course not. I should never have let this get out of hand. I lost my head."

"I want you to pay back all that money today," I said.

"Sure, but that's a lot of money. I'll have to talk to our bank about releasing the funds. I'll go to the bank today and take a check to Picton as soon as it's possible."

"Make it today, Daniel. I don't want to talk about this again."

With nothing left to say, I took my coat and left the house, slamming the door behind me. I went for a walk in the cold to cool my temper and thought about the options. Should I have thrown him out of the house? Ended our marriage then and there? Maybe, but I also remembered the lecture I'd given my students just a week or two ago, asking them who's to blame for gambling addiction. Daniel might be weak and foolish but so is anyone who's addicted to anything. And that's millions of people.

Maybe Daniel would take this one last chance to redeem himself and fix this mess. I hoped he had enough strength to set it all straight. Then, I guess because I had gambling on my mind, I remembered Loki's bet with the dwarfs Sindri and Brokkr that they couldn't make items more beautiful than those of the sons of Ivaldi. To prove Loki wrong, the dwarfs crafted Mjölnir, Thor's famous hammer, thereby winning the bet. Loki, in an attempt to sabotage their work, then changes himself into a fly and bites Brokkr, but to no avail. Loki had bet his head on this and lost the bet. Still, in the end, Loki manages to keep his head by arguing that the dwarfs will damage his neck—not part of their bet—if they take his head. As always, Loki wins in the end.

I wondered if Daniel would prove as resourceful as Loki in dealing with his own gambling problem. Somehow, I doubted it.

When I got back home, I was happy to discover Daniel wasn't there. Maybe he had gone to the bank for a cashier's check, then driven out to Picton to pay off the debt. I went into the kitchen for a glass of scotch and found Ellie drinking coffee in the kitchen with the lights off.

When I bent over to kiss her on the cheek I saw her black eye. "Ellie, what's happened to you?" I asked. "How did you hurt your eye?"

"I don't want to talk about it, Mom. I got myself into a situation and need to get myself out."

A chill ran through me. I was pretty sure I knew who this "situation" involved and it had nothing to do with gambling or financial debts. But it also involved the Calypso, a place I was really, really beginning to hate.

"It's okay to need help with problems," I said to Ellie, staring at her black eye. "Who did this to you?"

"Bobby. He gets so mad sometimes that he can't help what he does. He'll get furious with something I do or say and fly off the handle. Last night, I asked him when we could move in together. He went nuts. He shouted he didn't want to talk about that right now. There was too much else going on in his life to think about it. Maybe we could discuss it next year. And I should wait for him to bring up the topic."

She paused before adding. "Well, I didn't like that. I reminded him that he said the same thing each time I asked him. It made me wonder if he was serious about me after all. He tried to calm me down, kissing me and stroking me, but I pulled away from him because this wasn't the time for kissing."

Now it all came rushing out.

"He said he wouldn't be pushed around, by me or anyone else. We'd talk about long term plans when he was ready and not a minute sooner. Then he tried to touch me again. I pushed him away. He slapped me and I slapped him back. Then he punched me in the stomach. I said he'd better not ever do that again if he wanted me to stay around. Yes, and I told him he was behaving like a jerk, and I wouldn't stand for it. That's when he punched me again, this time in the face. I punched him back, in his arm. He punched my face again and stomped out of the room."

Right then, I wanted to kick Bobby in the balls. But my reason told me to settle down and talk to Ellie calmly. I asked her, "When did this happen, Ellie?"

"Last night, at Bobby's place. Bobby grabbed his clothes, dressed in the living room, and stormed out the door. I haven't heard from him since then. So, I came here."

"Did you call the police?"

"No, and I'm partly to blame. I kept pushing him until he exploded. He couldn't help it. Bobby's so insecure about being respected. And he's emotional, so when he gets angry, he explodes. I shouldn't have challenged him like that."

I knew Bobby was one hundred percent in the wrong. In fact, I had gone through something similar with Michael when we were married: not so much physical abuse as emotional abuse, verbal abuse, gaslighting, controlling my movements—the whole shebang. Coercive control, criminologists call it. So I knew how much abuse by a partner can hurt someone. But I kept my calm and tried to get some background.

"Has this happened before?"

"Never this bad. But that's one reason I haven't visited here more often. Bobby didn't want you to see my bruises. Neither did I. Sometimes, I had to use a lot of makeup to cover them up."

"Ellie," I said calmly. "You need to bring the police into this. You're in danger," I said.

"Bobby would kill me if I went to the police," she replied. Her speech was soft and slurred, as if the seriousness of this was just sinking in.

"I know police officers who can help you discreetly. They'll protect you while the law deals with Bobby and makes sure he gets what he deserves."

"Bobby isn't afraid of the police. He's too smart and too well protected. He knows powerful people."

"We have to do this, Ellie. It'll get worse if we don't do anything." I was getting agitated again, and knew that wouldn't help her.

After taking a moment to calm down, I looked at Ellie's face again. "Do you know anything that would give the police a reason to lock up Bobby for a good long time?"

Ellie thought for a few moments, then nodded her head.

"Bobby's been making and selling drugs. I'm pretty sure that during our trips on the Queen Ellie, he's either delivered drugs or picked up drugs."

"Where have you traveled in the boat? And what makes you think Bobby was transporting illegal drugs?"

"We've been down to Picton dozens of times. Also, to Burlington, Rochester, Lewiston, the Thousand Islands, and Brockville. Wherever we stopped for a meal or drinks, people boarded the boat. Sometimes they carried boxes on to the boat; other times, they carried boxes off it. There were always a lot of boxes. The storage area could hold dozens of boxes—maybe hundreds."

"What day of the week did you usually take these boat trips?" I asked, thinking about ways to trap Bobby.

"Different days, but we usually dropped off stuff at Picton on Mondays."

"That's tomorrow," I said. "I'll see if I can get the police to seize Bobby's boat and search the hold for illegal drugs."

Ellie panicked. "If Bobby finds out I'm behind this, he'll kill me."

I'd never seen Ellie so frightened. She was almost screaming with fear and it broke my heart to see her that way.

"I won't let that happen, Ellie. Give me a few minutes to set this up, then we'll go downtown and pick up some clothes so you can stay here for a while."

23

I called Roxy Duncan, told her about the drugs on the boat, and asked whether she could get a search warrant.

"It's possible," she said, "but we'd have to move quickly and I'd need to talk directly to the tipster. Second-hand info isn't good enough."

Eventually I told her Ellie was the source and the drug seller was Ellie's abusive boyfriend. But what sealed the deal was when I said, "The boat owner is Bobby Gupta."

"Oh, we know all about Bobby Gupta and his pals Gene Tretnikoff and Robert Delamont," Roxy answered. "If I tell the judge we have a bead on those guys, I can probably get a search and seizure warrant by the end of the day."

Roxy got me to put Ellie on the phone so she could take down the boat's details. She wanted to know its name, size, appearance, scheduled departure time and exactly where in the Scarborough Bluffs marina it was moored. Roxy also promised to keep Ellie's name out of any interactions she might have with Bobby, but warned that Bobby might still figure out who had tipped off the police. Roxy also offered to take a statement from Ellie about the alleged abuse if Ellie wanted to press those charges against Bobby too. But Ellie declined to take that risk, saying, "Is it okay if we see what comes of the drugs thing first?"

Roxy said she understood; they could always revisit the abuse charges later. And she offered to keep us posted on what came of the request for a search warrant.

As soon as Roxy hung up, Ellie and I started to worry about how this would all turn out. We worried together until Ellie, completely exhausted, finally bedded down in her old room.

When Daniel got home and learned what his daughter had gone through, he was enraged. He wanted to wring the neck of that bastard Bobby. But we also started to feel guilty—to beat ourselves up for failing our kind, beautiful daughter. Somehow, we had let her think she needed to take such abuse from a piece of shit like Bobby.

Eventually Daniel called it a night too, and I was left alone with my sole remaining friend. The esteemed Mr. Al K. Hall, tonight in the costume of Captain Morgan, stayed with me until the wee hours, when blessed unconsciousness took me away from my so-called life.

The next morning, I awoke on the couch feeling unaccountably better: in fact, as giddy as a kid at Christmas. That glorious day—Gupta Goes to Jail Day—had arrived! And though it seemed like an eternity, we really didn't have to wait long before our gift was delivered, via telephone.

"Professor Tile?" asked an unfamiliar voice on the telephone. "This is Inspector Mahler from the Toronto Police Department. Constable Roxy Duncan asked me to call you about a tip your family gave us," he said.

"Thank you for calling, Inspector. Were you able to search Bobby Gupta's boat?"

"Everything went as planned. We seized the boat and found illegal drugs and drug-making supplies. And we arrested Mr. Gupta."

"My daughter will feel safer knowing you have Bobby in custody, Inspector. Is there any chance he'll be released from jail awaiting a trial?"

"I'll do everything I can to prevent that," said Mahler. "Bobby's a known felon. It would help if we could tell the judge we're charging him with domestic assault too. Would Ellie testify to that?"

"She's considering it," I confided.

"That's all for now, then. Please thank Ellie for her help. We couldn't have done this without her."

Relieved to hear Bobby was under arrest, Ellie said she'd testify against him if it would keep him in jail for a good long time. Plainly, that final punch in the head had cleared up any confusion Ellie might have had about her relationship with Bobby.

An hour later, I was down at Criminology, trying to work but not succeeding. My mind was filled up with thoughts about Bobby Gupta and Gene Tretnikoff, Brad Wong and J-C Guzman, and a million other people and things. But I kept trying to concentrate and, finally, somehow the day passed.

Back home around dinner time, I was with Josh when a text came in from Robert Delamont. "Call me. This is important." I wasn't feeling kindly disposed toward Robert after hearing more about what went on at the Calypso, but I knew I had to follow up on this. So I grabbed a scotch on the rocks and went upstairs to my home office.

"What do you want to talk about?" I asked Robert when I had him on the line.

"The police have arrested Bobby Gupta on drug charges. They're offering him a deal and pressing him for information about me and Gene Tretnikoff. Bobby may cave under pressure, and he's more likely to implicate me than blow the whistle on Gene. But if Bobby puts the police on to me, I won't be able to protect you. Bad things will happen to your family. So I need you to convince your daughter that she mustn't help Inspector Mahler put the squeeze on Bobby."

My temperature was rising—my voice too! This was the second time in a short while that Robert had threatened my family with "bad things" happening to us. In a whisper-shout, I said "I won't lift a finger to protect you from Bobby."

Robert stayed as calm as always. "You're making a big mistake, Rachel. This won't go the way you think if you cross us. I'm trying to protect you."

I was shaken by this conversation. Robert had threatened me even while claiming to protect me. And it felt like he was helping the man who had beaten Ellie. I had liked Robert, even wanted him, yet now he was turning on me. Who was this person I thought I knew?

I didn't have to wait long to find out what he meant about things going differently than I thought they would.

In less than two hours, I heard from Inspector Mahler again. "Professor Tile, new information has come into my hands that I'll need you to verify. I can come there or, if you'd prefer, we can discuss it at the police station tomorrow morning."

"Okay. But what's this about, Inspector?"

"Please meet me at 53 Division on Eglinton Avenue at ten tomorrow morning. We'll discuss it then. You may want to bring legal counsel with you."

After the phone call, I rushed downstairs and found Daniel

in the kitchen. "That was Inspector Mahler on the phone. He's going to interview me tomorrow and suggested I bring a lawyer. But I've already told him everything I know about Ellie's boyfriend. If there's anything I don't know that you know—anything at all—now's the time to tell me." I waited for an answer.

"Honey, there's nothing. I only found out that Gupta is a piece of shit when you did. Ellie never confided in me."

"Well, Mahler is suspicious about something and I swear to God, Daniel, if Gupta has something on you that you're not telling me, I won't forgive you. I'm sick of being blindsided—of being the last to know what you're up to. So if this is your doing, we're finished. I mean I'm divorcing you." As they rushed out of my mouth, those words surprised even me.

I left Daniel gawking at my threat and went back upstairs to phone a criminal lawyer with whom I'd collaborated a few years earlier. He heard my story and agreed to meet me at the police station before the interview. Then I phoned Anita in hopes of talking to her right away, but instead I got a recorded message. It said if this was an emergency, I should go immediately to the Emergency Service at Clarke Institute. I decided against doing that.

Instead, I went into the washroom and threw up my dinner—possibly, several days' worth of dinners. I cleaned myself off, then tried to figure out what to do next. I wondered if Gene Tretnikoff knew about Robert's threat, or his loan-sharking activities, or Bobby's abuse of Ellie. So, when I recovered from puking, I phoned Gene and we talked for a few minutes.

As usual, Gene was blunt and seemingly honest. He admitted he'd given Bobby and Robert permission to offer Calypso's customers short-term loans, so long as the practice was aboveboard and complied with the law. He claimed ignorance of any drug dealing activity, saying this was something Bobby had done without consulting him. And he said he was shocked to hear about Bobby's abuse of Ellie. In fact, he said he would've sacked Bobby if he'd known about that. He also seemed surprised to hear that Robert had threatened me. He asked me whether I could have mistaken Robert's tone. I said that was impossible.

Still, this conversation made me feel a bit better and gave me the courage to ask him something that had been on my mind for weeks. "Gene, you've always been nice to me. Why is that? I can't give you anything in return."

There was silence on the line, then Gene answered very carefully. "The first time I saw you, I was struck by your resemblance to my sister Irina. Your red hair and freckles and modesty, and many other qualities, reminded me of her. Irina died at the age of sixteen, after being sexually assaulted and beaten by three boys in our neighborhood. I took my revenge on them, of course; but I've missed Irina. Not a day goes by that I don't think of her. And when someone reminds me of her, as you do, I try to help them. That's the whole story."

"I'm sorry to hear about your sister, and want to thank you for your kindness," I said softly.

"And I know that I can always count on you to do the right thing, Rachel, just as I could always count on my sister Irina. Am I mistaken in this belief?"

"No, Gene, I will always do what I know to be the right thing. And I hope we will always agree on what that might be."

"Then good night, Rachel. I send you my very best wishes."

I was certain Gene had been telling me the truth and now I felt somewhat better. But my likeness to Irina might not keep me safe if I caused Gene trouble—or at least that's what I took from our conversation. Exhausted from the conversation, I fell off to sleep and dreamed about a sexual attack by neighbour-hood boys. I couldn't see Irina's face—didn't know it—and instead saw Ellie's face. And a saw a younger version of Gene beating the attackers to death with an iron rod. One at a time, slowly, methodically, coolly.

24

The next day, I met my lawyer before the police interview and answered all his questions about recent events. Then Inspector Mahler and an associate interviewed me in the lawyer's presence.

Mahler proved to be a short, chunky man of about fifty-five in a gray suit, gray tie, and heavy black shoes. His light brown hair was cut short, almost to his skull. And he was wearing an aggressive cologne or aftershave I found hard to handle. Worse still, Mahler's manner was not just businesslike but almost hostile. Maybe this was how he intimidated criminals into cooperating.

Still, I answered all his questions. Some of them were not what I had anticipated. For example, his first question was why I had "failed to disclose" the full extent of my family's financial entanglement with Bobby Gupta and the Calypso. He was referring, it turned out, to more than just Daniel's (and Josh's) gambling debts.

For instance, he asked why I hadn't told him Ellie was a part owner of the *Queen Ellie* (which was news to me and, I was certain, would be news to Ellie too). He implied that Ellie had a business as well as a romantic relationship with Bobby. There was also a suggestion Ellie was helping Bobby to smuggle the drugs, either for profit or to help her father, Daniel, repay his gambling debts.

Another of Mahler's questions was premised on the possibility that Daniel had blamed Bobby and Robert (and the Calypso) for letting him get so deeply in debt. Mahler even raised the possibility that my father might be dissatisfied with his contract to represent Gene—dissatisfied enough to want to hurt Gene's business. He even asked whether my failure to raise donations for Criminology had hurt my career.

Then he asked me how I knew Joe Dubash, who had greeted me when he came to Michael's office demanding payment for the security cameras he had installed. And what did I know about the security arrangements at Michael Coale's house? I said I knew nothing about any of this. I told him, truthfully, that, while I had seen Mr. Dubash when I visited Westlake Holdings, that was the only time I recalled meeting him.

"So, you're saying you never met Mr. Dubash at Michael Coale's house the night Mr. Coale was murdered?"

"As I said, I don't remember ever seeing him before that one time at Westlake Holdings."

"Well, he says he remembers you. How do you explain that?"

"I can't."

"Have you ever been to the Coale home?"

"I don't recall ever being there."

"Ms. Tile, it's a yes or no question, isn't it?"

"Yes, it is," I admitted. "No, I was never at his home."

Then Mahler asked me a by-the-way question about how harshly my marriage to Michael had ended. Had Michael had been a good father to Josh and given me a fair divorce settlement? he asked aggressively.

Finally, he queried my whereabouts on the night Michael was killed. He said, "I understand you told one of our detectives you were at a faculty-student colloquium that ran until ten-thirty that night. But we haven't been able to confirm that.

No one seems to remember seeing you there. Can you tell me who you talked to on that occasion?"

I was too embarrassed to admit I couldn't remember any of it, because of a blackout I'd had that evening. My social calendar told me I was supposed to be at that faculty-student symposium, so I had probably gone. Shaken, I blurted out something that sounded suspicious even to me. "I go to a lot of functions like that and they all kind of run together in my mind. And the small talk is rarely memorable. Who did I talk to that night? —I'm afraid I'll have to think about that and get back to you."

"It wasn't very long ago, Ms. Tile."

"No. I agree. It wasn't."

Mahler waited for me to add something but I shut up. After thirty minutes of questioning, I was rattled. My heart was pounding and I knew the inspector could see me starting to sweat. He sent someone to get me a glass of water and waited until it arrived. But this effectively ended the interview. Mahler thanked me for coming in and even offered to have one of his officers drive me home. I declined, wanting to be on my own as quickly as possible.

Back home, I ransacked my memory for clues about what might have happened on the night of Michael's murder. Maybe I *had* gone over to Michael's house while Beth was out of the country. And maybe Dubash had seen me there. But then what? Could Michael have done something that enraged me so much that I killed him? But no, I said to myself, that's a crazy speculation. I can't have killed Michael; I don't have a gun. Unless … shit, unless Michael had a gun that I used to kill him. But why didn't the police find the gun? Because I took it away … because of fingerprints. But if I was the killer and took the gun, where might I have hidden it?

This was getting me nowhere, so I reverted to the "character defense." I'm an unlikely suspect because I have no history of violence. It's much more likely the killer was someone like Guzman or Dubash. Dubash may have seen someone who only *looked* like me. And he was trying to divert the cops' attention from himself. That's more likely, right?

I worked hard to discredit the possibility that I might be a killer—to clear myself in my own mind. But then I undid all that good work by getting drunk again. Then, by sheer luck, someone else died that day—someone I hated—and I was definitely not involved. Bobby Gupta, who had been released on bail that afternoon, was murdered on his front doorstep that night.

The police had no suspects in the Gupta murder, but they ruled out robbery as a motive. I began to wonder if I might have killed him while I was in the middle of a "fugue state." This was something I had read about but didn't really understand, so I asked Anita about it the next day.

"Fugue states? Yes. I'm familiar with them. But what's your interest in them, Rachel?" Anita asked me at our scheduled session.

"I'm just asking if they are a real thing or more of a made up, urban legend kind of a thing. Like something that almost never happens except in Hollywood movies?"

"Fugue states are real enough. They're rare but they do happen. A severely traumatic event can trigger a form of amnesia. If a person does something, or experiences something, terrible and horrific, the mind may protect itself by suppressing all memory of the event. The person goes into shock and loses time, returning to consciousness after the traumatic event has passed."

"A traumatic event like a murder, you mean?"

"Yes, that, or a violent accident or injury. But, why do you ask, Rachel?"

"Recently, I learned that a man had violently abused my daughter. I immediately hated his guts and wanted him dead, and a few days later he turned up dead—murdered. I wonder if I might have killed him but can't remember doing it."

"It sounds like you had reason to hate him. But you know, thoughts don't kill. So what's the big deal."

"Anita, the man was murdered. The murderer hasn't been caught and I can't remember where I was on the night it happened."

Anita was clearly having trouble grasping my thought process. "Sounds like a coincidence to me, Rachel. Just a coincidence. Do you really think you could have killed someone in a fugue state? No one has accused you of anything have they?"

"No."

"You have no history of violence, right?"

"Right."

"And there's no evidence linking you to this crime, is there? Like someone seeing you in the vicinity? Or that you woke up with unexplained blood on your clothes?"

"No. There's nothing like that," I admitted.

"And do you feel you would be capable of murder?"

"Well … no. I don't think so."

"Still, the memory loss is a little strange, I admit. The pills I've prescribed shouldn't do that to you. Have you had any other unusual physical symptoms? Did you, maybe, hit your head?"

"No, but—"

"Rachel?"

"Okay. I've been having blackouts whenever I drink too much alcohol."

"You have? Then the mystery is solved. Forget fugue states. You've been drinking too much. Seriously Rachel, we've talked about your alcohol consumption a few times now. You have to stop drinking."

I was almost happy to hear Anita's anti-alcohol lecture yet another time. Just as I had hoped, she was reassuring me that I hadn't killed anyone. But even though I liked Anita and trusted her, I decided not to push my luck. I didn't feel a need to tell her that there were actually *two* men who had enraged me who, then, had been mysteriously murdered while I was blacked out. Michael and Bobby, both mysteriously dead. I had wanted them dead and didn't know if I had killed them!

Sure, doctor-patient confidentiality says that everything we talk about is kept secret. But there may be an exception that says doctors can rat out patients who are a danger to others. Why take chances, I thought. So I didn't mention my concern that I may have also murdered Michael.

And if I was turning into an avenging murderer, I might—just possibly, might—do away with J-C Guzman too. He was driving me crazy and posing a threat to all of us. Still, I couldn't see myself killing the man.

Even Michael, who had made room for every kind of bad behaviour, had seen this potential in J-C, and he viewed the horribleness as something in J-C's favour. A diary entry revealed that he had even considered hiring Guzman as his personal monster. Here's what Michael had written about J-C shortly before his death:

October 3, 2022
I've changed my mind about J-C Guzman. I interviewed him today and might hire him to do personal security work for me. He's nuts but nuts in a good way. Good for me, any-

how. I taped the interview and I'm glad I did!

He said that working for Brad Wong is the best job he's ever had because he gets to "help people." And I'm pretty sure Wong knows exactly what Guzman's "helping" is all about—he just doesn't want to have to hear about it. Guzman is Wong's muscle, his persuader, his fixer.

J-C told me that in past jobs, there was always unpleasantness: conflict with competitors and sometimes with his bosses and co-workers. I tried to get him to confirm what Trish says Guzman told her husband Preston—about Guzman getting fired unfairly "by Jews" or because of gossip, and being passed over for promotions because of racism or personal reasons. According to Preston (via Trish), in his previous jobs, Guzman always felt isolated, frustrated, and angry. Sometimes he "got back" at the people who had made him unhappy. But Guzman did not repeat any of that to me. So maybe Preston is full of shit and was badmouthing Guzman because the Mexican intimidates him.

J-C isn't living with anyone right now, but he told me a bit about his ex-wife. He stopped communicating with her years ago. He says she cheated on him with his best friend, tried to poison him, and finally left him. According to Preston, Guzman views all women as vipers who can't be trusted and said he wants to pay back his ex-wife for her treachery. But Guzman didn't say that to me. And to be fair, if the bitch tried to poison him, no wonder he's ticked at her.

Women aside, Guzman is also a loner, without friends or family. He told me his parents had abused him in childhood, always badgering and criticizing him. His mother had even tried to poison him and his father had beat him with a belt almost every day. He claims the nosey neighbors were no better. They kept making up false stories about him stealing, vandalizing property, partying every night, and drinking underage. They kept ratting him out to teachers, cops, and his parents. Then, finally he figured out that threatening them with weapons got them to back off, shut up, and mind their own business. To escape all this, he left home at the age of fourteen and joined a gang, sleeping on the street or in deserted buildings. Pretty soon, he was strong and tough, and knew a lot of ways to hurt people.

J-C was vague about work he'd done for the Mexican police in the 1990's—maybe, he didn't want to boast. Or maybe he's in legal jeopardy. All he would say is that soldiers understand that cruelty is sometimes necessary. J-C's one crazy dude but, if I could control him, he'd be an excellent human pit bull. And everyone could use a good pit bull now and then, right? Maybe I should offer him more money and responsibility than he has at Jupiter. I'm going to sleep on that.

This was all more than I really wanted to know about Michael and J-C, but there it was, nonetheless.

My interview with Inspector Mahler had left me deeply worried but unimpressed with the police. How would Loki have investigated this murder, I wondered. And could I use any of these methods myself to find out who had killed Michael Coale?

Undoubtedly, Loki would use his cunning intellect, his shape-shifting abilities, and his love of mischief to solve a murder mystery. His process is unconventional, of course, but that's part of the fun. First, he would use his shape-shifting ability to take on different forms. This would allow him to eavesdrop on conversations and gather clues without arousing suspicion. To gain insider information, he could literally become a fly on the wall or assume the identity of someone close to the investigation. I could do some of these things, though not others (e.g., transforming myself into a literal fly on the wall.)

For sure, Loki would take every chance to manipulate suspects and witnesses, using his silver tongue to its best advantage. By doing so, he would get them to reveal more than they intended. He would also use a mix of intimidation, persuasion, and deception to uncover people's hidden motives and secrets. Loki might even set up elaborate traps or tests to provoke people's reactions. Designed to reveal the truth, these tricks might range from magical illusions to psychological games. Done right, they might even get the guilty party to confess. Now, that's something I could try, I thought to myself.

By analyzing people's motives, jealousies, and past conflicts, Loki could pinpoint potential suspects and motives that other investigators might overlook. Sure, I've been doing that all along, I thought to myself. That's my go-to strategy.

And how about Loki's tendency to keep shifting his allegiances? Loki was always collaborating with other gods and mortals to solve his problems, then betraying or abandoning his allies when they'd served their purpose. I wouldn't feel good about doing this, I thought. Besides, this tactic could also backfire, leading to unexpected complications. And I don't have the kind of access to magical artifacts that would keep me safe from revenge, as Loki does. What's more, I can't cast any spells or bring back the dead to give testimony. Too bad, I thought.

No matter how he did the job, Loki would end his investigation with a dramatic reveal, complete with twists that no one saw coming. For example, he might unmask the murderer in a public, humiliating way, mainly to satisfy his own ego and sense of drama. In short, Loki's methods would be unconventional—maybe even immoral by my standards—but dramatic and undeniably effective. He would solve a murder mystery not just to serve justice, but also to amuse himself and settle personal scores.

Damn, I thought. Go, Loki! I would model my own investigation on Loki's methods, I decided as I sipped a second scotch. Or was it a third scotch? The methods Loki used weren't completely out of keeping with what I'd read in the literature on police education.

25

I heard the front door close and went downstairs to see who it was. It turned out to be Ellie, who had come in and was sitting by herself in the living room, getting ready to do some homework. When I told her about Bobby Gupta's murder, she broke into tears. "I loved him, even though he was so awful to me" she told me. "I hated him for hurting me, but I loved him too. What's wrong with me?"

"There's nothing wrong with you." I said. "We can't control who we fall in love with. Love isn't rational. But at least the violence is over now. You're safe and that's the important thing. But if you're grieving, you can stay with us as long as you want."

Ellie thought for a moment. "I'll just stay one more night, Mom. You guys have been great, but I want to be back at my own place again. I need to get back into my routine."

It was lucky my daughter was so resilient and self-reliant. Soon, I would have my hands full trying to cope with a wave of terror unleashed by J-C Guzman.

It all started with an act of petty vandalism at Beth Coale's mansion. Then it escalated into physical harm to both of Beth's children. Then, Jen's home was invaded, my home was broken into, and one of my family members ended up in hospital. These weren't coincidences, I knew that for certain.

And all the threats and violence pointed to Guzman. He was trying to strong-arm Michael's wife into investing in Jupiter Pharmaceuticals, as Michael had once been about to do. My family got caught in the middle of this, because of my fundraising. As another competitor for Coale funds, I had become J-C's enemy and a threat to Jupiter's survival. That's because, if I landed a donation from the Coale family money, Jupiter would get nothing.

And J-C wasn't going to let that happen.

At first, Beth and I didn't even recognize these acts of terror for what they were. Sure, someone had broken into the Coale mansion and trashed it. Expensive items were smashed and slashed—furniture, paintings, pottery, and so on. Paint was splattered willy-nilly. It looked like nothing more than senseless vandalism, the kind of thing teenage punks might do in a tantrum or after an out-of-control drunken party. Some cops thought Will Coale might have even orchestrated this himself. Even the note the vandals left behind sounded like something teenagers might have written. The note read, "It's a sin to care more for material possessions than for children in need."

But Will insisted that he'd had nothing to do with this. He was indignant and acted hurt at being suspected; and his mother and sister believed him. Besides, there was no physical evidence linking him to the crime. Nor did the handwriting in the note match Will's writing. Maybe the most convincing evidence had to do with the content of the note itself. It sounded moralistic and appeared to condemn materialism, but Will was neither opposed to materialism nor even vaguely moralistic.

On the other hand, Guzman, in his own warped way, was both of those things.

I heard about the next calamity from Jen, who phoned me to say "Will is dead. I just heard it from Beth, who heard it from the police. He died of a drug overdose last night and his body was found in a park, where he had stopped on his way home from a party. He had a needle sticking out of his arm and they say he'd been shooting heroin. There'll be an autopsy, but the police are pretty sure a drug overdose killed him."

"That's terrible, Jen. I was afraid of something like that when I saw Will at the funeral. He seemed completely unhinged. Do the police suspect suicide?"

"Beth didn't say. But she's freaking out, so could you give her a call? She needs all the support she can get."

When I called, I told Beth, "I just heard the awful news about Will. I'm so sorry."

Beth's voice was hoarse. "Yes, it's terrible news. There's been one awful thing after another these days, first Michael and now Will. What's next, I wonder? I'm being punished for something, I guess, but don't know why. I just can't imagine why."

"Was Will injecting drugs very often?"

"I know he'd been using drugs, off and on, for years: cannabis for sure, and pills now and then. I never imagined him shooting heroin. But losing his dad and then being treated like a suspect really ramped up the pressure on him. The poor kid. He tried to act tough but he's always been sensitive and vulnerable. He must have gotten a bad batch of drugs, with something in it he hadn't expected."

"Can I do anything for you, Beth? Anything at all? The next few days will be especially hard," I said.

"Thank you, but no one can do anything for me now. I'll

just have to deal with it, and Melissa's here to help out. We'll announce the funeral arrangements today or tomorrow, and I hope you'll come."

I went to Will's funeral three days later and it had to be one of the saddest funerals I've ever attended. We all assumed it was suicide. But right after the funeral, Beth received an ugly note in the mail that sounded like Guzman. It said, "Now you know how the mothers of other dead children feel." It was a horrible thing to write to a grieving mom, something only a sicko would send. But it also suggested an even more sinister possibility. We didn't really know who had plunged the needle full of poison into Will.

Sure, it could have been bad luck on Will's part. But it also could have been murder. And Guzman might have been the murderer.

Melissa suffered the third and fourth calamities and there was no mistaking the malice behind them. Beth called me, just days after Will's funeral, with the news that "Melissa's in Sunnybrook Hospital with cracked ribs, a broken arm, and a possible concussion. Yesterday, her brakes failed while she was driving on the 401. Her car was totaled, and she was lucky an emergency vehicle was nearby. She could have died in that crash."

"Oh my god Beth, that's terrible!" I said. "The brakes failed?"

"Someone must have tampered with them, because Melissa had just had her car serviced last month. According to the mechanic, the brakes were one hundred percent fine at that time."

Fifteen minutes later, I called my friend Terry, who does the repair work on my car. She said it was easy to tamper with the brakes on any car. With a certain kind of tampering, the brakes would fail as soon as the engine temperature reached highway driving conditions.

"Could anyone rig the brakes that way, or would you have to be an expert?" I asked her.

"Videos on YouTube show anyone how to do this. You just have to get into the engine and attach a transistorized capacitor to the brake controller. The video shows you where to find the brake controller on different car models. It also tells people where they can order the capacitor for twenty-nine ninety-five."

"So, anyone who got into my car engine could murder me with a cheap piece of electronics?"

"That's right," Terry said. I could imagine her smiling grimly and nodding her head in agreement.

My first thought was, Melissa has to leave town as soon as possible. Someone's trying to kill her, and she should put as much distance between herself and Toronto as possible. Maybe my cousin Nikki in Calgary could help out. I hadn't seen Nikki for years but knew she'd help me if I asked. I phoned her, and when I explained the situation, she said Melissa should book a flight to Calgary as soon as possible. If I texted Nikki the details, she'd meet Melissa at Calgary Airport and Melissa could stay in her guest room as long as she wanted. I thanked Nikki, then showered and dressed.

If Melissa felt any hesitation about going, it disappeared when she received flowers at her hospital room. They came with an unsigned get-well card containing a corny joke about "putting the brakes" on illness. We didn't need a signature to know this was Guzman again. With my prompting, Beth told Melissa to leave town as soon as the hospital released her. And around noon the next day, I got a text message from Melissa saying, "I'm out of the hospital and heading to the airport. Thanks for your help. I'll see you again soon, I hope."

I texted back, "Remember, don't tell *anyone* where you are, and let me know if you need anything."

That evening, I texted my cousin Nikki in Calgary. "Did Melissa get there okay?"

Her answer was immediate. "She wasn't on the plane, and I haven't heard from her. She must have changed her mind and stayed in Toronto."

I called the hospital immediately. They told me a nurse had rolled Melissa down to the front door in a wheelchair, where they saw her enter a waiting taxi. Then I called the taxi company and talked to the dispatcher. He told me the driver who'd picked up Melissa at the hospital said Melissa asked him to drive her home. She planned to grab another cab to the airport when she was ready. I guess she went home to fetch something she needed to take to Calgary. But, according to the dispatcher, Melissa never called for another cab.

Melissa had either stayed at home or asked someone else for a lift, and I didn't like either alternative. This news sent me to the washroom where I threw up, kneeling over the toilet. After cleaning myself up, Daniel and I drove to Melissa's apartment, where no one answered our repeated rings. Her roommates must have been out so we rang for the caretaker but got no answer. Finally, we called 911 and explained our concerns. Then we called Beth and told her to meet us there.

Within minutes, a cruiser arrived. Two police officers, one tall and thin, the other short and stout, approached us and I told them what was going on. "What's the woman's name, Ms. Tile?" asked the taller officer. The officer kept pressing buttons until someone buzzed open the front door. At the door of Melissa's apartment, the police knocked and called out "Melissa" five times, each time more loudly than the time before. Still no answer.

The burly officer returned to their cruiser and got a battering ram out of the trunk. After three tries, he smashed open

Melissa's apartment door. We saw a body lying in the hallway and you can imagine what I thought at that moment.

But Melissa was just unconscious and still breathing, though covered in blood. Someone had hit her on the back of her head with a heavy object. The police called for an ambulance; also, a scene-of-crime team to search for fingerprints and other evidence. They advised Daniel and me to go home, promising to contact us when they knew something. I couldn't stop shivering as Daniel drove us back home.

I was terrified by what had just happened, and what seemed to be happening almost every day now. This was beginning to feel like a *Friday the Thirteenth* horror flick. Were the police doing anything to protect us against Freddy Krueger, I wondered? I'd get an answer soon enough.

The next morning, I got a call from Roxy, who'd heard about the attack on Melissa.

"We don't know who attacked her. But a witness saw someone tampering with Melissa's car on the day before her auto accident, in a parking garage downtown. It wasn't a very helpful description—just an average looking guy between the ages of twenty-five and forty. But that's enough to rule out Guzman. He could never pass for forty. And by the way Rachel—you didn't hear this from me—but you can also cross off Bradley Wong and J-C Guzman as suspects in the murder of Michael Coale. We confirmed yesterday that they were both in Mexico City on the night of the murder, just as they had claimed."

"Really? Shit." I said. I was disappointed that Guzman's alibi checked out. So I added, "But there's still the possibility of thugs working for Guzman, right?"

"Sure. There's always that possibility."

I was glad that Roxy was still telling me things about Michael's murder. She'd been irritated with me for a while over whether I'd misled her about being at a criminology event when Michael got murdered. She even came close to accusing me of giving the police a false alibi. But, in the end, she let me smooth it over by characterizing it all as a "miscommunication."

Roxy had previously told me that Michael's murder scene looked like an execution style murder with a twist. The two neatly placed bullet holes—one in his heart, one in his head—suggested it was a professional hit. But an autopsy revealed the killer also stomped on Michael's genitals. That was something an amateur or psycho killer might have done, but not a professional. Roxy said the police still weren't giving out this information to the public yet so I couldn't repeat it to anyone.

That stomping had immediately turned my mind towards Guzman. As a member of the secret police, he had specialized in both killing and torture. But if Guzman was in Mexico at the time of the killing, who else might have stomped Michael's genitals? An ex-lover, perhaps? Someone he had cuckolded? Or just someone who hated him enough to give him a little extra pain before he died? Still, Guzman appeared to have the best motive for hurting Michael and his family.

Certainly, Guzman had to be behind the post-murder attacks on Beth's family. No one else made any sense. And no one else made any sense for the Michael Coale murder either.

In my new persona as Loki, I started to wonder who might be my worthiest and most dangerous adversary, so I (once again) consulted the book Jen had given me. After considering various options, I concluded that if we had to identify one particular figure as a principal adversary, it might be someone like Heimdall, the watchman of the gods. Heimdall is the guardian of Bifrost, the rainbow bridge that connects the world of the gods (i.e., Asgard) to the world of humans (i.e., Midgard).

Known for his keen eyesight and hearing, Heimdall can see for hundreds of kilometers and hear grass growing out of the ground.

During the events of Ragnarok, Heimdall and Loki are prophesied to fight and kill each other. But what does Heimdall have going for him? First, as mentioned, he possesses extraordinarily acute vision and hearing, which are said to be better than any other god's. And as the ever-vigilant guardian of Bifrost, Heimdall makes sure that only those creatures who are meant to cross into Asgard can do so.

As a god, Heimdall also possesses stamina and durability that make him capable of enduring long periods of vigilance without rest and surviving in battle against formidable foes. Despite their differences, Loki and Heimdall share certain similarities, such as their intelligence and strategic thinking. But unlike Loki, Heimdall possesses the Gjallarhorn, a powerful horn that, when blown, can be heard in all worlds. Heimdall will blow it to signal the beginning of Ragnarok. In short, Heimdall is a formidable warrior, equipped with armor and a sword. He is expected to be one of the last standing in the battle of Ragnarok, where he will face Loki in their final battle.

As I read this, I thought that Heimdall doesn't sound all that tough as a foe, except for his extremely keen senses—his ability to see and hear everything. Who do I know who's like that, I wondered? Maybe J-C. He seems to be everywhere at all times, knowing what everyone is doing. Is J-C to be my final foe at the battle of Ragnarok, I wonder? And if so, will I prevail?

26

When I called Beth two days after the second attack on Melissa, she was drained of emotion. Her voice was a flat whisper. She sounded like a robot as she told me Melissa had been discharged from the hospital again and they were leaving town in a few hours. This time they were going to try a place Jen had recommended, but they were keeping its location secret from everyone. I told Beth how sorry I was about the latest calamity and again asked, "Is there anything I can do?"

"No, thank you, Rachel. Melissa and I will stay away until we feel safe again. Right now, here, we're sitting ducks. And there's no one who can protect us. We have to protect ourselves." With that, she hung up.

Jen and I had hoped the wave of terror would end once Beth and Melissa left town—that Guzman would be out of victims to frighten. But we were wrong. Now, he just turned his attention to us.

First, someone invaded my house when no one was home. The invader (or invaders?) didn't do much damage beyond smashing a back window to get in. Once inside, all they did was toss Maisie's dog crate down the basement stairs and leave behind a blurry polaroid snapshot of somebody's massive, gloved hands wrapped around Maisie's neck. Our little dog looked terrified in the photo. Those big hands could have easily snapped her neck with one twist.

On top of the dog crate we found an unsigned message in an ordinary envelope, printed on ordinary paper by an ordinary printer. "Stop asking the Coale family for money that would be better spent elsewhere. I am watching your selfishness every day and you will suffer if it continues."

This frightened the crap out of me for a couple of days; Daniel and I thought about fleeing the city too. For a moment, we even considered reporting this to the police. But they'd been monumentally useless up to now—sorry, Roxy, no offence intended—so there wasn't any point bringing them in. And while we dithered, news arrived that Jen and Matt's place had been hit too.

I needed Anita's help more than ever during this wave of terror. My health was going downhill fast and I didn't know what else to do. I had developed an infection in my esophagus from throwing up so often. The lining of my stomach was shot from all the alcohol I'd been drinking on an empty stomach, and it was hurting all the time. And there was a serious chance I might pass out while driving the car, or while lecturing a class. That wouldn't be good for my professional reputation.

My nightmares were getting more violent each week, keeping me from ever getting a good night's sleep. So I walked around in a daze most of the time now. I'd had to cancel speaking engagements in the US, Singapore, and Taiwan.

After two sessions of discussing this, Anita told me, "You're pushing yourself far too hard, Rachel, and I'm afraid of what might happen to you. I'm upping your prescription, so you'll feel a little calmer. But please, I beg you, lay off the booze. You can really hurt yourself if you take these pills and keep on drinking. And don't make any more travel plans just now."

She scribbled a brief note on her prescription pad, ripped off the page and handed it to me. It was written in that illegible script doctors seem to use everywhere. "Get this filled at the pharmacy downstairs, right away. And take your first two tablets as soon as you get home. Then stretch out on your bed and read a magazine or nap—whatever you prefer. The main thing is, get off your feet for the rest of the day."

Anita meant well. She was trying to help, I know that. But how could I be calm and rest on my bed during a wave of terror? Seriously? That was easier said than done, and I knew I couldn't do it. Probably, Anita knew that too, though she was professionally bound to advise it. My mind was rolling from one thing to another now and I started to think about Loki again.

Did I mention that Loki's firmest ally and supporter is his wife, Sigyn? Just the way Anita is loyal to me, Sigyn is loyal and devoted to Loki, as she showed through her actions during Loki's punishment. Do you remember Sigyn's willingness to endure hardship for Loki's sake, continually catching the venom and only leaving Loki's side briefly to empty the poison-bowl? Sigyn was a figure of immense loyalty and compassion. What's more, her actions contrasted sharply with Loki's deceit. Sigyn proved herself a steadfast supporter in a world where Loki had few if any other true friends.

Anita's like that too, I thought. My truest friend and supporter. She's helped me deal with many problems this year—for example, my drinking problem—I would have had trouble navigating on my own. And in her own way, Jen's like that too. My best friend forever.

Meanwhile, Gene Tretnikoff and Robert Delamont were, each in his own way, dealing with the aftermath of Bobby Gupta's murder. Roxy told me that when the police interviewed Robert about his connections to Bobby, Robert made it sound like he barely knew the guy and had rarely even spoken to him. Apparently, Robert did a masterful job of disconnecting whatever dots Mahler had been trying to connect.

Gene took a different approach to the police's newfound interest in him, as I found out when I returned a missed phone call he had made to me. He was leaving town, and so was Robert.

"Thanks for calling BACK, Rachel," he said. "I was just phoning to say GOODBYE. I've enjoyed the time we spent together. But REGRETTABLY I must leave and may not see you for a WHILE. I look forward to the NEXT opportunity, WHENEVER that may be."

"Where are you going?" I asked.

"I'm going back to London to spend time with my beautiful wife. My daughter Irina will remain here; she has settled in well and does not need me any longer. The housekeeper will keep an eye on Irina and make sure she eats properly."

"I'll miss talking to you, Gene. What are you doing about your businesses here? Is Robert staying behind to run things?"

"No, Robert is leaving too. I've asked him to manage my antiquities business from the Middle East. Within the next few days, he'll set up a new office in either Tel Aviv or Cairo."

"Well, goodbye then, Gene. Have a safe and healthy trip home."

"Thank you. Before parting, let me give you my personal phone number in London. Don't hesitate to call if you ever need my help. The number is +44 20 7887 8000 --- did you write that down? Meanwhile, GOODBYE and GOOD wishes."

I felt certain I'd see Gene and Robert again, though I didn't know when. And it turns out my intuition was correct. They'd be crucial to completing my murder investigation.

Even Dean Grabol, of all people, tried, in his own way, to help me during the wave of terror. But the "help" he offered was suspiciously self-serving, and based on more dubious logic than the kind of help Anita offered. When I hinted at my suspicions about Guzman's role in all this, Grabol argued that Guzman was only terrorizing people in the hope of procuring Coale money for Jupiter Pharmaceuticals. Therefore, the way to end the terror was to end the uncertainty. Beth would have to get off the fence and decide how she wanted to spend her money. And I would have to help her get down off the fence.

After all, Beth had admitted she was going to make *either* an investment *or* a donation, but not both. So if she gave some of her family's money to our university, Guzman would realize the contest was over and his side—Jupiter Pharma—had lost. At that point, Guzman would accept defeat, give up, and leave us alone. Anyway, that was the logic of Grabol's argument.

Unfortunately, Dean Grabol did not factor in the possibility that defeat might enrage Guzman and cause him to go completely berserk. The dean was prepared to have Beth's family, my family—also, Jen and Matt—take that risk. Perhaps Dean G. would have felt differently if J-C's warnings had been arriving at his own home instead of mine. If so, Mrs. Grabol might have knocked some sense into his head, assuming there was a Mrs. Grabol. Actually, I couldn't picture a Mrs. Grabol; what did that mean?

In any event, Dean Grabol told me to write a new proposal for Beth. The last time we had talked, Beth and Melissa had both shown an interest in a program on domestic violence, so I wrote a new proposal for that. But I also knew from Jen that Beth was in no state of mind to entertain pitches at this time. So, whether Dean Grabol liked it or not, my new proposal was destined to sit on the shelf until Beth got through this current crisis.

All I had to stabilize me were the theories I had first considered the night Michael's murder was reported. I came back to them now and considered how well J-C might fit into any of these categories. In my den, I had made a list of the reasons someone might murder someone else. Having come up with fifteen well-known criminological theories, plus a theory of my own, I wrote them all down. Then I put them into seven rough groups:

1. People kill to gain something if they don't think the risks are too high. They're motivated to kill and an opportunity has presented itself. They've never been punished for past crimes and see no risk or downside to committing the murder.

2. People kill if something (for example, drugs or alcohol or brain injury) has twisted their emotions. They've never learned to control their violent impulses, especially when depressed or angry.

3. People kill if they think murder is exciting or fun, or unimportant. They attach no value to other human beings and make excuses to erase any feelings of guilt or responsibility.

4. People kill if they know other people who also commit murders. They're used to seeing murder in their community and don't feel attached to law-abiding people or customary ways of behaving.

5. People kill if they don't have a legal way of getting the things they've learned to want desperately: especially, wealth, respect, and power.

6. People kill if other people see them as "bad people who do bad things" and they've come to see themselves the same way. So, they're just doing what people expect them to do.

Then, there was my own theory, a seventh theory. I called it "rage theory" and it ran like this: People kill when they've suffered extreme, prolonged, unjust, and humiliating treatment by the person they (eventually) murder.

I couldn't help thinking J-C satisfied all seven of these theoretical groupings. But I wasn't sure and certainly didn't have any evidence he was connected with Michael's murder.

Meanwhile, the university expected me to keep teaching and I did so. I like to teach; what's more, I'm good at it and enjoy it. So I gave a lecture on rage theory while Guzman was terrorizing us, and that amusing coincidence got me smiling for the first time in many days.

I got to class early on the day of this lecture and watched my students arrive. The eager faces of students hoping for an *A* sat at the front of the lecture hall, while indifferent or actively hostile students sat at the back. The largest group, sociable students with a casual interest in criminology, sat in knots of two and three in the middle of the room chatting about social media posts (I guess). When the last of my students had straggled in, I began to lecture.

I told them ordinary people—people just like them—become enraged when they experience treatment they consider unfair and humiliating. And since rage is a result of humiliation, it is connected to social inequality. That's why crimes of rage are common in societies where social inequality is the most extreme. Crimes of rage are especially common in Latin America, where the recorded homicide rate is the highest in the Western Hemisphere and still rising. That is a lingering result of Spanish colonization, the vastly unequal plantation system of agriculture, and a sharp social divide between fair-skinned and dark-skinned citizens.

Throughout the world, young men, especially, are drawn to murderous gang activity in the suburbs and shantytowns of large, low-income cities. As they grow up, they learn to kill one another, kill the police, and kill the law-abiding citizens.

Some eventually change sides and join the police or military, letting the government use them in violent actions against slum dwellers and anti-government protesters. Many of these killings, on both sides of the law, are concerned with protecting one's honour and reputation.

As in previous lectures, I talked for an hour, then invited debate. After answering questions, I gave the students a brief writing assignment. As I left the hall, I saw people pulling out fresh sheets of paper and starting to write. Most of them looked like they were already deep in thought. I loved to see that!

As much as anything, I enjoyed delivering my lecture about rage because it reminded me of the good old days. Those were the days, a few weeks ago, when murderers and criminals were imaginary figures I could safely study, analyze and discuss in a purely academic setting.

But nothing—not a stimulating lecture, nor Anita's counsel, nor even alcohol—was going to rein in Guzman. I needed a plan, and Jen and I finally hatched one. That's when we started to fight back.

Back home that evening, at first, I didn't even hear the doorbell. When I finally got to the door, Jen was standing there looking irritated. "Where were you? I must have buzzed fifteen times."

"I was deep in thought, Jen, deep in thought," I said flippantly, smiling. "What's up?"

Without waiting for an invitation, Jen strode into the house and whipped off her coat. She was wearing black corduroy pants and a New York Yankees sweatshirt. Her long blond hair—a mess, comparatively speaking—framed a beautiful pale face. She looked like a crazed but gorgeous demon.

"The psycho's hit our place now too," Jen said. "Someone

came into our house during the night and turned on the gas stove. We could have died in our sleep. By sheer luck, I got up for a drink of water and noticed the smell of gas. If I hadn't turned off the gas right away, we wouldn't have survived the night."

"What did the police say?"

"Those keystone klutzes? I didn't even call because there was nothing to show them once I turned the gas off. There was no sign of forced entry. Whoever did it must have picked the lock."

"Did anyone leave a note?"

"Not this time. But I know what it's about. It's a spillover from earlier in the day when Guzman was harassing Matt at the office, then me at home. He called Matt for an appointment to re-start the discussion of an investment in Jupiter Pharmaceuticals. And he called me at home this morning to ask how he could get in touch with Beth. He wants to talk to her again about Jupiter's medical research program."

"What did Matt tell him?"

"Matt passed J-C over to Trish, who told him he's only hurting Jupiter's case with his pushy antics. Apparently, she said something like 'this isn't Mexico and we don't do business that way here.'"

"Really!" I said. "How did he like that?"

"He started calling her a bitch and making a lot of misogynistic remarks, among other things. Trish said she was glad they were speaking on the phone and not in person. It gave her the opportunity to hang up on him."

"And what about when J-C called you?" I asked.

"I told him Beth is still recovering from the deaths in her family and isn't available right now. But he insisted I tell Beth that Jupiter's work was a matter of life and death, and time is of the essence. Rachel, he's not going to stop bugging us, and this is driving me absolutely bonkers. We have to stop it."

27

Easier said than done, I thought to myself. But that's Jen for you—always able to see the big picture but not always the smaller parts that make it up. That's my job, I guess.

"I agree with you," I said. "And I see five possible courses of action. One is to give J-C what he wants. Two is keep thwarting him and live with the negative consequences. Three, which is related to two, is hire a bodyguard to keep you and Matt safe. Beth and Melissa would need a bodyguard too—maybe my own family as well. Four, we ask the police to protect us. Or, five, we ask Bradley Wong to bring Guzman under control."

"Wow," Jen exclaimed. She started looking around the room in wonder, as though something on the ceiling or hallway might give her the answer. "So, where does that leave us?"

"I'm not keen about relying on the police," I told her. "I hear from Roxy that Guzman's alibi for the night of Michael's murder checks out. He and Bradley Wong really were in Mexico City that night. And although a witness saw someone who might have tampered with Melissa's car, the man was apparently too young to be Guzman. Roxy also says the evidence that Guzman is terrorizing us is circumstantial. It's not solid enough to justify police action."

Jen briefly pondered our options and then said, "I don't like solutions one or two. Even if Westlake and Jupiter finally work out a deal, I can't see anyone being comfortable with Guzman around now. Solution three, involving bodyguards, is hit and miss. What do we know about choosing bodyguards? Solution four, involving the police, is probably out too, for the reasons you just said. Which leaves solution number five. Do you think Wong would help us bring J-C under control?"

"There's no harm in asking him, I guess. But something I saw in Michael's diary makes me think Wong won't provide the solution."

"What did you see there?" Jen asked, looking puzzled.

"Michael thought that Guzman probably does Wong's dirty work without telling his boss how he does it. That gives Bradley deniability. Michael was pretty certain Wong knows what Guzman does even if he pretends otherwise. If we tell Wong about J-C, he'll just act surprised and do nothing. I'm inclined to believe Michael on this, but I'll call Wong if you want me to."

"No, I agree; Michael probably had a good sense of how other creeps operate. And that means all our choices are bad, right?"

"I have a sixth idea but it's an absolute last resort. Perhaps your nephew Robert could convince J-C to behave better," I suggested.

Jen smiled and nodded. "Robert would probably do that for me," she said. "And I'm sure he could handle J-C. But he's living in Tel Aviv now and trying to avoid the Toronto police. Coming back here might be risky for him. Plus, Gene Tretnikoff might get angry if Robert acted on his own. He wasn't happy to find out that Bobby Gupta—that creep Ellie was dating—had his own side gigs. And you never want to get Tretnikoff angry, at least that's what I hear from Robert. Mr. T. holds a grudge for a very long time, if you get on his bad side."

"Then let's consider option seven, which in a way is Josh's idea. I could talk ask Tretnikoff to do something about J-C. Gene promised me a favour and I could ask him to let Robert off work to deal with J-C."

"Terrific! But how is this Josh's idea?"

"He came up with it when I told him about Guzman's Freddy Krueger reputation. Josh had already heard me talk about Tretnikoff's shady past, so my son suggested a monster-versus-monster solution. He said the movies do that all the time: pit one monster against another. Apparently there's a movie featuring Freddy Krueger versus Jason from the *Friday the Thirteenth* flick. Also, a King Kong versus Godzilla movie and an Aliens versus Predators movie."

"Hmm. Smart kid. Will you do it then?" Jen asked, smiling sweetly. "Will you ask Tretnikoff to unleash a monster for us?"

"Let me think about it. I don't want to be in debt to Gene if I can avoid it. Meanwhile, we'll take every possible precaution. As long as J-C's in the picture, he's a danger to all of us."

I don't think all of my message registered on Jen, because she responded, "Okay, wonderful! We've got a plan then! You'll consider asking Tretnikoff for a favour!" Then, shrugging her coat back on, she burst out of the house as speedily as she'd entered.

I didn't see an easy way to get out of this new "promise," short of telling Jen to do it herself. But she probably didn't know Gene as well as I did, I thought. And she may not have reminded Gene of his dead sister Irina. Although who knows, maybe Gene had other dead sisters (or brothers) he hadn't mentioned—including some who looked like Jen.

That night, I had my first nightmare in nearly a week and naturally it was about J-C Guzman. In the dream, Freddy Krueger and a giant octopus circled each other in a cage match, while I sat in the stands watching, sandwiched uneasily between Godzilla and King Kong.

It didn't take long for Guzman to force my hand. A few days

later, Jen phoned to tell me Beth had heard from J-C again. Somehow, he had tracked her down her hiding place in upstate New York. A large package had been delivered to her hotel room and it was creepy in the usual Guzman way. It contained a large red clay flowerpot and photos of the garden outside the Coale mansion. Other photos showed the interior of the home, including one of Beth's bedroom. A note that came with it read, "Enjoy your vacation. I'll see you when you get back."

"The bastard must have broken into her home. He's letting her know she can run but she can't hide. But what's with that flowerpot? Is he planning to dig up her flowers?"

I thought for a moment and suddenly realized Guzman was making a cute reference to something that had been filling the Toronto newspaper in recent weeks. The police had been finding bodies crammed into large flowerpots in various Toronto gardens. Perhaps Guzman was suggesting the same fate awaited Beth if she failed to do what he wanted.

"How's Beth dealing with this?"

"How do you think? She's a mess; completely frazzled. Rachel, we've got to do something. This can't continue. Beth asked me if I'd given him her location, and of course I hadn't. But he seems to know our every move. Have you decided about calling Tretnikoff yet?"

Reluctantly, I agreed. "Okay, I'll do it." I saw no other choice. The flower-pot imagery was just a step too far.

Gene must have recognized my number, because he picked up the phone immediately in London. "Yevgeny Tretnikoff here. Is that you, Rachel?"

"Yes. Hi, Gene. I'm afraid I may have to call in that favour you promised me."

"Of course, but first let's obey the niceties of polite conversation. HOW are you?"

We made small talk for a while until he decided it was enough and we could finally get down to business. "Now, how can I help you Rachel?"

"Bradley Wong's personal assistant J-C Guzman is making a real pest of himself. He's been threatening people and, frankly, he's pretty scary. I wonder if you can do anything about that."

"There's ALWAYS something a person can do. How does this problem affect YOU, if I may ask?"

"Guzman is affecting Beth Coale and Jen Carling more than he's affecting me. But he appears to have me in his sights too. I received an anonymous note warning me to stop asking the Coale family for a donation. He may have put Beth Coale's daughter in the hospital with serious injuries and threatened even more harm if Beth didn't invest Westlake money in Jupiter Pharmaceuticals. And Jen's husband Matt—Michael's second-in-command—has also been pressured to revive Westlake's deal with Jupiter."

"Let me get this straight. This man is trying to force people to revive the Westlake-Jupiter deal, and he's using violence and threats of violence to achieve that goal. Is that correct?"

"Yes, that's about it."

"What a disgrace that man is. Completely out of CONTROL. But I'd GUESS he's just doing what his boss Bradley Wong expects him to do, and that's too bad for both of them. Now, I can get J-C off your back, but it may take a week or two. Can you WAIT that long? A faster way would involve Robert, but it's more dangerous. So, tell Beth and Jen to stay indoors as much as possible and I'll make this problem GO AWAY. Will you please tell them that?"

"I will, Gene. Thank you for this. I'm indebted to you. And good wishes to you and your family."

"You TOO, Rachel." Gene hung up the phone and my line went dead.

I told Jen what Gene had said and she promised to pass the message along to Beth right away. Then I went back to work but couldn't stop thinking about ways to keep my own family safe until J-C was out of the picture. If J-C somehow learned that I'd asked Gene Tretnikoff for help, he might get even nastier.

In any case, I had to tell my family about the danger we were facing. I wanted them to stay home as much as possible until the danger had lifted. So I texted Ellie, Josh, and Daniel, asking them to be home by seven tonight for an important family meeting.

At the meeting I told everyone "We have a problem, and for the next two weeks, we need to take special precautions. You kids still have school and Dad and I still have work to do. But when we finish school or work, we all need to come right back here. We can't visit friends or go shopping or hang around outside." I explained that we might be in danger from someone who'd been threatening the Coale family. Though we were secondary concerns to J-C, we were still in his gunsights, so we had to spend the next two weeks keeping each other safe.

Then I had a well-known security firm send over someone to stay with us for a while. The fee was a hefty two thousand dollars a day, and I intended to try this for a week or two. It was a huge cost, but I couldn't avoid it.

An hour later, a woman of about thirty-five arrived. Dressed in a business suit, she introduced herself as Nancy Branch, an employee of Terrazzo Security. She agreed to stay around the house from nine to five every day, pick up the children from school, and do other jobs we might give her. She could stay in the house or watch the house from her car, if we preferred; and she could extend her hours, if we wanted. We'd adjust the arrangements as necessary.

Daniel was restless, though. He missed the Calypso and his friends there. Maybe he missed seeing Rusty. Or maybe he just missed losing money. For whatever reason, he was edgy and short-tempered. So, after fussing for an hour, he left the house, claiming he had important things to do that he couldn't do from home. He promised to be back before five.

But that never happened.

I got a panicky call from Daniel around eleven-thirty that morning. "I played hooky from the office and headed down to Picton for the day. But I lost control of the car around Cobourg. I guess I was tailgating. I couldn't brake quickly enough and smashed into another car, then went into a ditch. My car was totaled and now I'm in Cobourg hospital waiting for surgery on my right leg. Can you come down here?"

"Was the guy in the other car hurt too?" I asked.

"I hear he's okay. His car rolled over, but he's fine except for a few bruises."

"I'll be there as soon as I can," I muttered, relieved to know that Daniel's injuries were not serious. But now I knew I was at the end of the line with Daniel. We were done. We'd split up the household as soon he recovered from this accident.

I told Nancy that I had to go out and might not be back before tomorrow, though I didn't say why. After packing a change of clothes for Daniel, I drove down to Cobourg in a rental car. (I wanted to be sure I wasn't driving a car J-C had tampered with.) When I got there, Daniel was still in the emergency department of Cobourg Hospital, waiting for a room.

A doctor and nurse came into our little waiting area and introduced themselves. Doctor Li, a man of about thirty-five in a white coat and stethoscope, said Daniel was lucky to get away with minor injuries, all things considered. "We'll do the surgery on Daniel's leg in a few hours. Your husband will stay with us overnight, and if everything looks okay, we'll send him back to Toronto in an ambulance. He'll have to stay in a hospital there for at least four days, to make sure the leg is mending properly. Then he can come back home. But he'll be off his feet for a few weeks, at least."

Nurse Rafferty said she would start checking the Toronto hospitals for a vacancy, ideally one near our home.

It was then I started to learn something about my husband's checkered history.

28

After Dr. Li and Nurse Rafferty left, two police officers came in. "Mr. Russo, can you talk to us about your car accident?" the older of them asked.

Daniel gave them a brief account like the one he'd given me earlier. Then the officer declared, "We see you have a record of dangerous driving, Mr. Russo. You had a serious car accident in 1994, causing death and property damage. Do I have the right information?"

"Yes. But I was just a kid then. This accident wasn't anything like that."

"We'll look into today's incident and get back to you if we have more questions, Mr. Russo."

"What's this about?" I asked Daniel after they'd left. I'd never heard about previous trouble with the law.

"When I was nineteen, my parents bought me a Maserati for a birthday present. I was reckless in those days and sometimes I drove when I'd drunk too much. Anyway, I was driving up Yonge Street about eighty klicks over the speed limit when an elderly couple started to cross the road. I swerved to avoid them and plowed into three parked cars, killing the passenger in one car. The police wanted to charge me with manslaughter but my lawyer pled the charge down to impaired driving and I spent two years minus a day in a provincial jail."

I was stunned. I couldn't believe this was the same guy I'd lived with for fifteen years. "That's not what happened today, is it Daniel?" I asked.

"No," he murmured. "I never drink and drive any more, and I never drive over the speed limit. I learned my lesson when I was a kid—learned it the hard way."

I couldn't shake the suspicion J-C might be sending us another message through another case of brake tampering and said as much to Daniel. I even began recounting all the different ways Guzman had been terrorizing the Coale family, Jen's family, and our family. But the look on Daniel's face caught me up short. He wasn't taking me as seriously as he should have, which made me angry.

"What are you smirking at?" I demanded. "Do *you* think it's funny that a psycho is threatening us, stalking us, and hurting us? Or that you could have been killed?"

"Honey, no. I'm sorry. I wasn't smirking. Or at least not on purpose and not at you. I didn't mean anything. I'm just worried that maybe this Guzman nut has you spooked. Your imagination may be running wild."

I couldn't believe he'd said that. "My imagination! What the hell, Daniel. I'm not *imagining* anything. Michael was actually murdered. Will is actually dead. Melissa actually got attacked and now you are actually in a hospital. Guzman has a terrible criminal past and he's sending us threatening letters. You need to take this all seriously."

"Yes. Of course. And I *am* taking this seriously. But Rachel, I'm not sure you know how you sound sometimes when you talk about those two thugs, Guzman and Tretnikoff. It's like you are in awe of them. Freddy Krueger and the Russian's tentacles? It's like they're supervillains—like no one can be safe from them anywhere. But they're just people like you and me."

"They are *way* more dangerous and powerful than you and me, and that's just the truth."

"Okay. Fine. Thugs can be violent and dangerous and powerful. Granted. But you don't have to give them more credit than they deserve."

"What on earth do you mean?"

"I just mean that, in our trucking business, Pete and I have had a few run-ins with criminals and thugs. Trucking is attractive to smugglers, and we are susceptible to extortion demands. Vandalizing our trucks could put us out of business."

"And?"

"And in our experience, most criminals and thugs are pretty uncomplicated. They're bullies. When they want to scare someone, they threaten to beat him up or kill him, but usually, that's just a bluff to intimidate or extort. If you stand up to them, most of the time they look for someone easier to victimize. Of course, if it's not a bluff, you'll know that soon enough too. They'll smash your face in or shoot you, or kill your dog instead of just threatening it. You won't find yourself having to wonder how angry they are or what they're capable of doing. They'll show you."

"So what are you saying about Guzman then?"

"I'm just saying, try not to spook yourself about my accident. I'm pretty sure it's my own fault I'm in this hospital with a broken leg. I drove unsafely. Recklessly. That's my fault. And Will may have killed himself with an accidental overdose. As for Melissa—if some psycho had wanted her dead, don't you think she'd be dead by now?"

"You've got an innocent explanation for everything, huh Daniel? Why do you think the Mexicans call J-C Guzman a killer—a Freddy Krueger—if he's so harmless? Harmless people don't get compared to Freddy Krueger."

"You're right, Rachel. I can't explain that away."

I didn't tell him so, but Daniel had made some good points. Still, that flowerpot message Guzman had sent Beth was gruesome. Normal people didn't do that, I thought.

I checked into a Cobourg motel so I could be near the hospital when Daniel had his surgery the next day. And since I was still trying to get a clear fix on Daniel and his somewhat shocking past, I called Daniel's brother Peter from my room there. After confirming his take on criminals was similar to Daniel's, Peter filled me in on Daniel's driving history, criminal record, and gambling addiction. I learned more about Daniel in that twenty-minute conversation than I had learned in the last fifteen years of marriage.

Peter told me, "Daniel was a wild kid when he was young, Rachel. You wouldn't have recognized him then. Probably wouldn't have liked him either. He got into all kinds of trouble at school, and he was always arguing with our parents. Then he started drinking and there were many times—more times than I can count—that I had to drive him home or cover for him with our parents."

"When did he turn this around?" I asked him.

"He took that jail sentence seriously. After getting out, he cut back on his drinking. He always stayed within the speed limit, or close to it. And as far as I know, he never again drove while he was drunk. He had a terrible fear of going to jail again. He hated that place. The people he met there scared the crap out of him."

"Did you know that Daniel's developed a gambling problem? He's lost more than a hundred thousand dollars gambling in Picton."

"I'm disappointed to hear that, but not surprised. Our dad had a gambling problem when we were kids. Our mom had a drinking problem for a while and Dad's gambling made it much worse. I'm not excusing it, just saying that Daniel comes by his addiction problem honestly. He'll have to work hard to overcome it. Our dad never did beat his gambling addiction altogether. That's why Mom finally left him."

I paused to let this sink in. "Daniel was so embarrassed about his gambling debt that he took out high-interest loans to pay it off. Then he went asking people for help in paying off the loans. Did he ask you for help too?"

"I guess he did, in a roundabout way. A few months ago, he said he was looking at investment possibilities but was short of cash. He wondered if I could lend him fifty thousand dollars for a month or two. I said we couldn't manage it right then; we were tight for cash ourselves. All our cash was tied up in buying new trucks. Maybe he had planned to use that loan to cover his gambling debt."

"He even asked Michael Coale for a loan to cover the debt, but Michael told him to forget it. That had to feel humiliating, coming from Michael—who Daniel hated with a passion."

"I'm sure Daniel didn't like it," Peter agreed.

"Peter, I feel like an idiot for not having known—or even suspected—anything about this side of Daniel. Why didn't you or other members of the family ever tell me about Daniel's prison sentence or your parents' addictions?"

"Daniel probably didn't tell you because he was embarrassed and didn't want to scare you away. And Mary and I never felt we had the right to tell you anything Daniel was keeping secret. And no one else who knew about these past problems is still alive."

Finding out that my husband had kept me in the dark about all this was very disconcerting. I cracked open a mini-bottle of vodka and downed it in one gulp. To be fair, though, any day ending in "y" was enough to drive me to drink these days. So, after talking to Peter, I made my way to a local watering hole to drown my worries. Then, at the bar, serendipity intervened. I overheard a fellow bar patron ordering a Rusty Nail which got me thinking, Who is really nailing Rusty—my husband, Robert, or both?

Picton is only a short drive from Cobourg. So, I cut short my plan to drink all evening and set out on a road trip to visit Rusty, Daniel's new friend in Picton. It was the best decision I could have made. I was about to learn something important about the state of my marriage; also, to gather a vital clue in the mystery of who had murdered Michael.

29

I saw no need for guile when I got to the Calypso. I had only come to talk to Rusty, so when someone pointed her out to me I went right up to her and said hello. She gave me a warm smile in return and said "Hello. Is there anything I can help you with?"

I guessed she was somewhere in her mid-thirties, which made her a few years younger than me. She was also very attractive, if you happen to like fit, trim, red-headed healthy types with a nice build, big blue eyes, perfect teeth and skin, and basically perfect everything. On top of that she was friendly and lively and ready to be helpful. Of course, I tried to spot a flaw, but Rusty wasn't giving me much to work with.

"I just wanted to introduce myself. We may have a mutual acquaintance. Do you happen to know a Daniel Russo who gambles here sometimes?"

"Oh, everyone here knows Danny. He's always the life of the party, when he's here. He's got a hilarious sense of humour and endless interesting stories. You mean that Daniel?"

I was tempted to say no, there must be two Daniel Russo's, but that seemed unlikely.

"The one I'm thinking of has a son, Josh, he brought here…"

"Sure, I know Josh, too. Sweet boy. And you are…?"

"My name is Rachel Tile. I'm—"

"Danny's wife. Josh's mom. And, if I remember correctly, a professor who is no fan of casinos."

"So Daniel and Josh talk about me," I said.

"Yup. But don't worry. It's always positive. They're obviously proud of you."

"Can I ask how you and Daniel met?"

"We're both talkers. We first started to gab at a meeting of 'The Tribe.'" She made those funny quotation-mark signs with her fingers as she said this.

"The Tribe? Sorry, I don't understand."

"Leaf Nation. There's a lot of Toronto Maple Leaf fans here and we often watch the big games together. Sometimes at my house. And at one of the games Danny and I discovered we both have the same favourite Leaf."

I nodded approvingly. Actually, I couldn't tell you Daniel's favourite hockey player if my life depended on it.

"And then the more we talked, the more we discovered those little coincidences that make you think 'What a small world it is.' You know? Like I'm from Truro and look a little like Denise. And my parents used to play that Stompin' Tom Connors song 'Little Wawa' in our house a lot too."

I must have looked completely baffled, so Rusty started giving me helpful prompts to jog my memory. "Truro, Nova Scotia … that's where Denise was from? And Stompin' Tom sang that song about the goose from Wawa, Ontario?" Rusty did some kind of body movement that I couldn't interpret, but I suppose it had something to do with a mysterious goose from Wawa.

Once again, I nodded knowingly without the slightest idea what she was talking about.

"Sorry," I said. "Can you just remind me, jog my memory? Who is Denise?"

Rusty was taken aback. A look that flashed across her face told me she thought I was either mentally defective or an imposter. Regaining her composure, she answered slowly in a polite and neutral voice, as though talking to someone whose native language was Serbian, "Denise MacLean of Truro, Nova Scotia. Your husband's first wife. As a girl, her parents used to play the 'Little Wawa' song in their house. And my parents did the same."

I was suddenly and deeply embarrassed by how much more this casino hostess knew about Daniel's first wife, and Ellie's mom, than I did. She had only known Daniel a few months, yet in fifteen years Daniel had never talked about Denise to me. Never ever. I only knew her name from Ellie's birth records—Ellen Denise MacLean. I never even knew she went by her middle name, let alone that she came from Nova Scotia.

I hurried to change the subject and Rusty was kind enough to let me do it. "We may also have another mutual acquaintance. Do you know a guy who works here named Robert Delamont?" I asked her.

"Sure. The loan arranger. Hah, that sounds funny, like The Lone Ranger. That guy from Harvard." She pronounced it contemptuously, as 'Hahvahd.'

"'Hahvahd'? Why did you say that?" I asked.

"He's a graduate of Harvard University, you know. In Boston?"

"I'm aware of that," I told her.

"I'll bet you are. Robert dropped 'Harvard' into the conversation about four times in the first four minutes after I met him. I guess he was trying to impress me."

"Do you think he's conceited? Or a bit of a snob?"

"Sorry. If he's a close friend of yours, I don't mean to be rude."

I told her, "No, no, not that. It's okay. Actually, I heard somewhere that you and Robert were close. Maybe even a couple."

"Me and Mr. Hahvahd? God no. Never. We are *not* compatible. And he is definitely *not* my type."

"A lot of women find him attractive."

Rusty nodded. "Yes. He is good looking. Smart. Rich. Interesting. But he's not particularly nice to people. A lot of people find him hard to relate to. Hard to understand. Don't get me wrong. I've flirted with him. I might even have a one-night stand with someone like that, if I was feeling lonely. But he's not serious partner material."

"What do you mean, he doesn't relate to people?"

"I mean he doesn't hide his snobbery well when thinks something they like is inferior."

"For instance?"

"For instance, God forbid you might offer him a baloney sandwich or some of your KFC. Or here's another one. The hockey fans here are a pretty friendly bunch. We like to include and welcome new people. So, when we had a party at my place to watch this big hockey game a while back, somebody—it may have been your Danny—invited Robert to join us. I didn't think he'd come, because he always says he doesn't like team sports. But he showed up."

"And?"

"There's not much to tell. The whole time he's there—which wasn't very long—he fidgets and looks bored. He makes it clear he only came as a favour to us, because he hates hockey. He deep down really hates the sport. I don't think he made it halfway through the first period before he leaves and misses the biggest game of the season." The look of astonishment on Rusty's face was hilarious—as though she had just seen a creature with eight limbs and four heads from outer space. I couldn't help laughing, then I got serious real fast, as I remembered Robert's alibi.

"I thought the Nick Dempster pre-retirement would have been the biggest game."

"That's the one I'm talking about."

"Robert was here in Picton for that?"

"The first half of the first period he was. Then he left, maybe for Toronto. I don't really know where he went. And I don't care."

Wow, I thought. This is big. If Robert was on the highway during that game, then three alibis are shot. Robert told the police he had watched the big hockey game with Jen and Matt the night Michael got shot. I'd try not to leap to any conclusions, since I had also (accidentally) given the police a wrong impression about my own whereabouts the night of the murder. But I would have to investigate this further.

I cancelled my motel room in Cobourg and headed back to Toronto.

On the way back, I had time to ruminate about this murder case and all its weird bits. For example, I finally remembered something important about Dubash. A month ago, I had been chatting with my admin assistant Kathy about what we had spent on equipment in the past year. We got to talking about our expensive new video technology in the main seminar room. Because the faculty's IT staff was already overstretched, we'd had to contract the job out and bring in representatives from three different companies to bid on the job.

She reminded me that one of the three companies to bid on the job was BASH-TEK. You guessed it, the company representative—also, the company owner and technician—was Joe Dubash. Joe came in, made a ridiculous pitch, behaved in a rude, obnoxious manner, and offered to do the job for ten thousand dollars more than our next highest bidder. So naturally we turned him down. Of course, we were polite and said, "Thank you for coming in, Joe." Anyway, that's where I'd met Joe Dubash before—not at Michael's house. Cross that off the list!

Relieved of that niggling (but life-threatening) issue, I also had time to reflect on my most recent appointment with Anita. I had come prepared to talk about Daniel and his gambling. But she didn't want to talk about Daniel, she wanted to talk about me.

So we talked about me: Why did I marry Daniel? Did I want to stay married to Daniel? How did I feel about his gambling? How did I feel about Gene and Robert? How did I feel about my father being involved with Gene's gambling business? How did I feel about my mother's support for my father's involvement in Gene's gambling business? How did my mother feel about my career choices? How did my mother feel about my fundraising? How did *I* feel about fundraising?

I answered all of Anita's questions as honestly as I could, curious to see where she was going. And I quickly realized several things. First, a lot of those questions touched off mini-panic attacks and Anita had to calm me down before we could continue. Second, I was angry about every single thing she mentioned, though I had rarely expressed my anger about any of them before. Third, and most revealing, I admitted hating fundraising—hating it with a passion.

When Anita pushed me to tell her why I hated fundraising so much, I told her it was because it allowed horrible people like Michael Coale to parade around like saints and saviours. It made my university, which I had viewed as something like a temple of knowledge, pander to the likes of Michael Coale for money. And it made me behave like a fool and a supplicant trying to get Michael's money. I went on and on about that last point until I ran out of steam. God, my voice got hoarse from talking so much. All the while, Anita listened and took the occasional note.

Finally, she said "I'm afraid our time's up for today, Rachel. We made a good start, so let's continue with this next week. Meanwhile, take your pills and stay away from alcohol."

I started to panic again. "Wait, I still don't know what to do. I can't keep feeling this way. I need you to tell me what to do."

Anita smiled at me. "I'll see you next week, Rachel. Try to relax. This was a good session today and we made real progress."

30

When I got home after our session, my body was shaking. It took me a half hour to calm down. I guess that's because I had trouble sharing Anita's confidence in the value of mere talk. So I called Gene, a man of action, to see whether he was having any success with our Guzman problem. He tried to reassure me, saying, "I've already put my plan in motion to get J-C out of the way. Meanwhile, I'll ask Robert to return to Canada and get J-C's associates out of the way. I'll phone you after I've spoken to him."

Gene called back fifteen minutes later. "Robert will be in Toronto tomorrow night, and he'll phone you when he gets in. Then he'll get rid of J-C's helpers. I have a separate plan for handling J-C, and I'll try to speed it up."

I latched on to that word "speed" and, since my adrenaline was at record levels, I tried to convince myself I had a need for speed. Speed is good, I thought to myself. Speed will power me through these stressful times to better times and better days. But, you know, it's also hard to control things at high speeds. And I doubted *my* foot on the gas was driving things forward. So I needed to stay calm. As I reflected on the possibility of a crash, I started to panic—gasping for air, feeling faint, and heating up like a nuclear reactor.

On top of everything else, a very disturbing idea about who might have killed Michael started to form in my head. It made me panic even worse than all the rest of the experiences I'd been having. Now I had a new suspect to match against my seven murder theories.

Maybe I should have told Roxy Duncan what I'd learned about the false alibis—especially, Robert's false alibi. But since Robert was going to risk his life to protect us from J-C, I didn't want to rat him out to the police. I'd give him a chance to explain himself before calling Roxy about it. And I made a mental note to confirm with Daniel that Robert had been at Rusty's when the hockey game started on the night of the murder, but that he had left early.

Meanwhile, Robert was headed back to Toronto to deal with J-C, and I learned later that he'd already set his own plan in motion. After hearing from Gene, Robert had phoned Kosta Spiros, an associate in Toronto to ask if John Friendly and Billy Burtch were still doing odd jobs for J-C. When Kosta said they were, Robert asked Kosta to arrange a meeting with John and Billy for the next night at Kosta's home. He also asked Kosta to tell them that he—Robert—needed their help. "Make up any story you like; just make sure they're at the meeting," he told Kosta.

Robert got back to Toronto at five in the afternoon after a flight from Tel Aviv. He'd slept on the plane so he didn't feel too tired. Back at his Toronto home, he showered, relaxed, and cleaned two of his revolvers, then drove out to Kosta's house just before nine. He told Kosta that J-C and his boys were interfering with Mr. Tretnikoff's business. He'd come back from Israel to sort this out. Robert specifically asked Kosta to keep a gun handy, in case he needed backup.

When John and Billy arrived around ten, they all sat down around the dining room table, and Robert told them he knew they'd been doing jobs for J-C. He needed them to do a job for him instead. Robert said he'd make it worth their while.

They didn't warm to the idea right away. After hearing what had happened to Bobby Gupta, they were more than a little nervous about dealing with Robert and Gene. But Robert offered them ten thousand dollars each to *stop doing* J-C's jobs and stay hidden for the coming week. John hesitated, then said he'd agree to do what Robert wanted for $15,000. Billy needed persuading but finally agreed to the same deal.

"Come on down to the basement then, and I'll get your money out of the safe," Kosta said. In the basement, Kosta pulled a gun on them and ordered them into a room with two cots, a toilet, a sink, and a TV set—oh yes, and with barred windows. They protested loudly when he locked them inside.

"You'll get your money as soon as we've dealt with J-C. It shouldn't take us more than a day or two. Meanwhile, relax, watch TV, and Kosta will make sure you get enough to eat," Robert said. "Kosta, be sure to give them some of that special moussaka you do so well."

Robert also told Kosta to tell J-C that Robert had killed his men for interfering with Mr. Tretnikoff's business. The same would happen to J-C if he didn't catch the next plane out of town. Later, when Kosta told J-C that Robert had killed his men, J-C thanked Kosta for letting him know who was responsible, and said he was going to try to verify the information.

With this part of the plan completed, Robert shook Kosta's hand and left the house in Scarborough.

An hour later Robert was at my own door. "I may have solved your problem tonight," he said, smiling. "I predict J-C will leave the country within the next twenty-four hours. He and his associates won't bother you anymore."

"And if J-C doesn't leave?"

"Gene and I will tidy up the loose ends. Gene has prepared a creative ending to J-C's story, so one way or another, he's finished."

"Does this mean I don't need a bodyguard at our home any-more?" I asked.

"Keep the bodyguard in place for now, if that gives you peace of mind. I'll stay in town for another day, in case of any more unpleasantness."

Robert and I looked at each other for a long minute, then unexpectedly, we kissed. It was a long, tender, loving kiss. We stood in the doorway, pressed close to each other with Robert's hand in the small of my back. We rocked back and forth, still kissing. I wanted him and he wanted me, I knew that much. I shivered with delight and then he shivered. It only lasted a moment but felt longer—like years, maybe. Then we pulled apart—reluctantly on my part—and Robert left. I felt a crazy mix of surprise, desire, and shame. And maybe a little rage at not controlling my own emotions.

To calm myself down, I got a scotch on the rocks and sipped it. But after a few minutes I left most of it on the kitchen counter and went up to bed. I had sweet, frenzied dreams that night. I dreamed of love and sex, and Robert was my partner in my dreams.

But what will the endgame look like? I wondered when I finally awoke. Translating this into fable-talk, what's supposed to happen when the world of Loki and Heimdall finally ends? During Ragnarok, gods, giants, and other mythical beings fight to the death, destroying the current world and opening the door to a new world. After unleashing a series of natural disasters, Ragnarok finally submerges the world in water. After that, the world resurfaces, new and fertile. The surviving gods return, and two human survivors start to repopulate the earth. A happy ending, I guess.

But which humans will survive, I wondered? According to legend, Loki, who has been bound by the gods as punishment for his role in the death of the god Baldr, is freed at Ragnarok.

He leads the forces of chaos—I'd call them the forces of change—against the gods of Asgard and forces of stability. Heimdall, the watchman of the gods, stands in defense of the gods and the existing order.

So, the final battle between Loki and Heimdall is a culmination of the long, seemingly endless conflict between order (represented by Heimdall) and chaos or change (represented by Loki). And the deaths of Loki and Heimdall at each other's hands wipe away the old order, making way for a new beginning: for a renewal of the cosmos.

So where does all this leave me? If I'm Loki, am I to be destroyed while trying to solve the Coale murder mystery? And will I be destroyed by the forces of order and the old gods? Or will I prevail, through cunning and shape-shifting and the help of my true allies. Only one thing seems certain now: the end of my story will be cataclysmic and at least one more death will result. But who will die? I fell asleep in my home office, head down on the desk, with this thought still on my mind.

The next morning, I woke up to the first snowfall of the season. The snow looked clean and pure on the pavement, though after an hour it had melted. I told Nancy the security guard and the kids we were probably safe now, but we'd need another day or two to be sure. They were all relieved to hear this.

Then I called Jen and gave her a brief version of Robert's story, leaving out the kiss and so on. "Has there been more trouble since yesterday?" I asked her.

"Nope, it's been quiet," said Jen. "I'll be careful for the next few days, just to make sure."

"Please phone Beth and fill her in. She and Melissa can probably come home now."

"I doubt she'll want to come back just yet. But I'll pass along the information, and she'll decide for herself. Talk to you later."

This had all gone a little too smoothly and I was afraid J-C would make at least one more appearance before leaving the country. As if to confirm that fear, I received another envelope by bicycle courier later that morning. The note inside read, "Your thug can't protect you and he doesn't frighten me. You'll pay for this, or Josh will!"

I freaked out when I read that and called Robert, who told me, "I'll see if Gene can make things move along faster, then get back to you."

Twenty minutes later, Robert called back. "It'll take another two days to close the trap on J-C, using Gene's method. Meanwhile, I'll watch over your family and friends. I could kill J-C now but that's not what Gene wants." I didn't know why it was taking Gene so long to close the trap on J-C when it had been so easy to sic the police on Bobby Gupta. But as I'd learn later, several different police forces (and governments) would be involved.

That morning, while Jen and I fussed about J-C, Daniel completed his treatment in Cobourg. I had planned to visit him in Cobourg but, after the threats against our family, I didn't feel right leaving the kids just with Nancy. So I stayed home with Josh and checked in with Daniel over the phone instead. The good news was, his operation had gone just fine though he expected to be out of commission for several weeks. And here's the silver lining: being out of commission meant Daniel would also be out of the Calypso for a while. By noon, an ambulance had brought Daniel to Humber River Hospital in Toronto, which had an empty bed he could fill.

Daniel's car accident had accomplished what my anger and his will power couldn't. It put Daniel's gambling on hold. And, so far as I knew, it also kept Rusty at a distance.

At this point there was nothing to do but wait for word from Robert. I felt like we were under siege, waiting for the calvary to rescue us. But eventually the longed-for call from Robert came. "I've captured J-C." Robert said. "He won't hurt you anymore."

"Thank God!"

"So now I'm following Mr. Tretnikoff's plan. Watch the news today and you'll understand what he's been arranging. Meanwhile, let Jen and Beth know they'll be safe now too."

I thanked Robert and got Jen back on the line to relay this information.

That evening, about ten minutes in, the newscaster interrupted a story about trends in early Christmas shopping with this item:

The RCMP has just arrested a man who'll be returned Mexico to face trial. Manuel Mendoza has been living in Canada for the last five years under an assumed name, J-C Guzman. When Mexican police received a tip the wanted man was in Toronto, they asked the RCMP to arrest him. Police found Mendoza tied up in an empty apartment in the St. James Town housing complex.

As a member of the Mexican military police in the 1990s, Mendoza is alleged to have ordered the torture and murder of Mexican civilians under the guise of a crackdown on crime. Since the year 2000, the Mexican government has brought several hundred such killers to justice, returning them from the UK, the US, Germany, Singapore, Chile, and now Canada. In recent years, though, Mexico has stopped searching for alleged killers like Mendoza and has even granted amnesty to several.

Though Mendoza could face a sentence of life imprisonment, no one has been tried in Mexico for crimes like these since 2014. It remains to be seen how the Mexican government will deal with him now that he's been caught.

This had been Gene's plan all along and it had worked faster than he'd expected. He'd guessed that Mexico's government would have little interest in capturing criminals from long ago—people like J-C who'd actually killed for the government. Arresting and trying such people would stir up too many bad memories and create political unrest. However, once the RCMP, the Canadian government, and the international media were involved, the Mexican government had to take J-C into custody. Surface appearances counted for everything, yet again.

At his trial, J-C would probably claim he was a better person today than he had been three decades ago. Just look at the evidence, his lawyer would say: he's been promoting a cure for infectious diseases that have killed thousands of Latin Americans every year.

At least, that's what they would probably argue, and it might even work. They wouldn't acknowledge J-C's more heinous activities in Canada. Nor, it seemed, would the Canadian government.

31

After the news of J-C's capture, I felt better than I had in weeks. But I still needed help with my anxiety, my drinking, and my blackouts. So I took Anita's advice and went to the

Clarke Institute to enquire about their addiction programs. While waiting to talk to someone, I saw a framed photograph on the wall. Immediately I identified it as one of Jen's early pieces, even though it was unsigned. At the bottom I saw the words, "Thanks for all your help" in what appeared to be Jen's handwriting. It was dated April 2001, a long time ago. This made me wonder what kind of help they gave her. And help for what?

The earliest of Michael's diaries had some answers for me. I hadn't paid much attention to the earliest volumes, since they didn't seem relevant to Michael's murder. But when I skimmed through them, I found this entry:

March 14, 2001

Heard from Mother today that Jen's in the Clarke again for observation—could be there for ninety days. Her stunt of jumping on to the subway tracks so some guy would play hero and pull her up has everyone convinced the little drama queen was really trying to off herself. As if suicide is hard to do when you're serious about doing it! She's such a coward, Jumpin' Jennie.

But she got what she wanted. Mother went back to hinting that somehow I'm to blame for Jen's mental problem, but I wasn't having that. I told her she and Dad were to blame, if anyone. They never paid her much attention—never paid either of us much attention. They were always too busy drinking and fighting, and going off on "rest cures," leaving us on our own. Mind you, I liked the extra freedom when they weren't around. Basically, it never mattered much to me if they were there or not. Anyway, Mother said I should phone little Ms. Over-sensitive or send her flowers, and I said I would. But I won't.

Back in the Clarke again? Suicide? And look at Michael's stone cold reaction to his sister's state of mind. That man was a monster.

Later that day, I heard from Roxy that the police had questioned J-C until the Mexican officers arrived. They were trying to find out about his possible involvement in recent Toronto crimes. Beth, Matt, Jen, and I had already told the police everything we knew and suspected about J-C's activities. But J-C denied everything and the police had no proof of any local crimes. The police also interviewed Bradley Wong about J-C. Predictably, Bradley said he was amazed to learn that J-C was wanted in Mexico for crimes he'd committed in the 1990s. I found his claim of ignorance hard to believe. Correction: impossible to believe.

But J-C was in custody now and, I hoped, out of my life forever. I was getting used to the idea that my life was safe and normal again and I liked that feeling. Unfortunately, this new feeling of comfort turned out to be a little premature.

I called Gene Tretnikoff to thank him for what he'd done and he was modest about his services, as usual. "You're welcome, Rachel. I'd heard years ago that Mr. Guzman was wanted in Mexico but never had a good REASON to turn him in. You gave me a good REASON, so thank you. Everyone will be better off without him around."

I said, "J-C couldn't have been responsible for Michael Coale's death since he was out of the country that night. Do you think he might have hired someone else to kill Michael?" I asked.

"You should ask Robert about that. He knows Toronto far better than I do and knows the local criminals, if Guzman hired someone to do the job. Anyway, I'm not the right person to discuss this."

Gene's answer puzzled me. "Are you suggesting Robert knows who killed Michael Coale?"

"I'm only saying that Robert could make a better guess than I. But here's something I *can* tell you about Robert and Michael Coale. A few months ago, Michael and I were discussing a business deal and Robert was present. Later, Michael praised the role Robert had played in laying the groundwork for our discussion. He asked me how I'd feel if he, Michael, offered Robert Matt Carling's job. Matt, I take it, was not much good as a right hand man. Michael said all of this jokingly but also half seriously, and it made a big impression on Robert when he heard about it."

"How so?" I asked.

"Robert said he thought Michael was a huge asshole for talking like that. Robert knows and likes Matt Carling, so the casual job offer did not amuse him. In fact, I've never seen our Robert so angry."

No one had told me Matt's job had been on the line. It was one more thing I'd have to check out when I asked Robert about the false alibi he'd given the police.

Later in the same conversation, I mentioned to Gene that my boss, Dean Grabol, was still hounding me to deliver a donation from the Coale family and he expected a progress report on Monday. "Your commanding officer—the dean—is INSENSITIVE, isn't he," Gene noted. "Does he know about the DANGERS you and the Coale family have faced in the last few weeks?"

"I've told him, but he's preoccupied with raising money. He wants me to get my hands on that twenty million Michael dangled in his face."

"Don't do it, Rachel. Tell your boss it WASN'T POSSIBLE. Or tell him you'll try again in six months. Just don't let him PUSH you around."

"If I don't bring in this money, Criminology may not get the funding it needs this year. My people are depending on this. So I can't just say no to my boss."

"You know BEST, Rachel. Just don't worry yourself to death about it. But I must go, so goodbye for now. I hope we meet again under happier circumstances. Meanwhile, I know you'll be VICTORIOUS." With that flourish, Gene hung up the phone.

Gene's advice was wise, so I followed it. When I called Beth to celebrate the arrest of Guzman, I deliberately avoided discussing a donation. I'd get to that a little later.

"Welcome home, Beth. I've finished reading all those diaries you gave to Jen and looked over the photos of your house that J-C sent you in New York State. Should I return them all directly to you or leave them with Jen?"

"Either way is fine, Rachel. Whichever way is more convenient for you. But I'm curious. Did you learn anything interesting about Michael and his life from those diaries?"

"I did. I'm not saying they helped me crack the murder mystery. But I realized I'd never known Michael as well as I thought. And lately I've been finding that's true of a lot of people I thought I knew."

"Well, I'm giving you an *A* for effort. I wouldn't have had the patience to wade through seventeen volumes of his irritating opinions. I got enough of the 'world according to Michael' from hearing him spout off at home every day."

"Michael did have strong opinions on a lot of things and a lot of people, that's for sure. But did you say seventeen volumes?"

"Yes."

"You're sure there were seventeen diaries?"

"I'm a hundred percent certain. Why?"

"No reason," I told her. "I must have miscounted."

But that wasn't true. I'd counted accurately.

Robert called later to gloat over the capture of Guzman. "I just hope the Mexican police can handle him. He's a slippery character and he's broken out of jail several times over the years. That's how he happened to be in Canada. He escaped from custody in Spain five years ago and needed a brand-new country to infest. He might have stayed here in Canada forever, hiding in clear sight, if he hadn't made a pest of himself with you and the Coale family."

I didn't want to ruin the mood by challenging Robert's alibi right after he'd saved us from Guzman, so I kept that question for later and said goodbye. Jen had been Robert's mentor and was implicated in his alibi, so I wanted to clarify some points with her before having it out with Robert. And I had some questions for Jen about her own past, based on what I'd seen at the Clarke. So I called her up and offered to pop over whenever she was available. That turned out to be the next day.

But in preparation for that visit, I needed to do a little more research. And for once, I didn't think of Clever Connie. This time, Robert's mother Martha Crawford would be the best source of information.

32

Jen had given me an email address for Martha, so I emailed her and asked if we could chat. Martha got right back to me with her phone number and said she was free to talk now. So when I got to my office, I phoned her.

"To what do I owe the pleasure of this call?" she asked me pleasantly.

"I'm still looking into Michael Coale's death—something Jen asked me to do. I've talked to Matt Carling about it but didn't learn much. I'm wondering if you can tell me anything about Matt and his relationship with Michael. You've known Matt for a long time, I hear."

"Yes, I've known Matt for ages. He worked for my husband Harrison before taking his present job with Michael. And because of my link with Jen, Harrison and I often socialized with Matt, both before and after he left TD Bank."

"Matt didn't say much about his relationship with Michael. Does this surprise you at all?"

"Not really. Matt is a very private guy, most of the time. He's tight-lipped, and that may be one of the things that drew Matt and Jen together. They don't like to talk about their feelings, or sometimes, even about what they're thinking."

"So you don't think I should read anything into Matt's reluctance to talk to me about Michael? That it was just Matt being Matt? Or the loyal right hand man protecting the boss's privacy?"

"Goodness, I'd be surprised if loyalty had much to do with it."

Martha was an impressive lady. She'd thought a lot, knew what she thought, and didn't mind telling people about it. She had a bit of rich-person's manner as well: a little *noblesse oblige*. I don't know if she'd always been like that or this was a result of having married Harrison Crawford, one of the richest men in Canada.

By way of explaining her last remark, Martha added, "I understand from Jen that Michael often treated Matt in a disrespectful way. They weren't friends, or even friendly with each other."

"Michael treated a lot of people that way, and yet Matt stayed on at Westlake. Why did he put up with Michael's rudeness, do you think?"

"I really can't say. You'd have to ask him."

"But if you had to guess?" I pushed.

"Luckily I don't have to guess" she answered, but then she caught herself, thinking she may have been rude to me. She added, "I can tell you my husband Harrison's guess, if you promise to keep it just between us. I wouldn't want this getting back to Jen."

"Sure. Just between the two of us then, I promise."

"Harrison thought that Matt was lucky to have that job at Westlake. He thought Matt was overpaid there and wouldn't be able to command that high a salary or that much responsibility anywhere else. This view was based on what Harrison saw when Matt worked for him. Matt was … I'm not sure how to say this diplomatically … a very nice young man but … low energy and, well, not the sharpest knife in the drawer, if you know what I mean. It always amazed Harrison that Matt had risen so high at Westlake."

I knew what she was saying but wasn't sure what to make of it. Was Michael being generous to his brother-in-law but also bullying him? That didn't make a lot of sense and I'd have to think it over for a while.

"And now it looks like Matt will take over as the head of Westlake Holdings," I said.

Martha's only response was, "Yes, I've heard."

It was time to wrap this up but I didn't want to let Martha go without asking if she knew why her son had to carry a gun. How could I ask this delicate question in a polite way, I wondered. So I circled around the question.

"By the way Martha, I ran into Robert recently. And once again, I was struck by what a fine and accomplished young man he is."

"Thanks for saying that, Rachel. Jen deserves a lot of credit for how he's turned out."

I played dumb about what I'd heard from Jen about Robert's teenage troubles. "How so?"

"Jen was an angel. For a while, as a teenager, Robert was going down a very dark path: drugs, violence, hoodlum friends, a bad attitude, and failing at school. He even stole Harrison's gun and took it to school on one occasion. And there was an unfortunate incident with another boy that got the law involved. I shudder to think how it might have ended if Jen hadn't stepped in. God knows, I was at my wit's end."

"What did Jen do?"

"She gave him a new life. She swooped in, took all the bad stuff away and replaced it with more wholesome alternatives. She took away his drugs and drug paraphernalia and stripped away the stupid, depressing posters he had hung on his bedroom wall. More important, she confiscated the weapons he had started to collect, helped me find him a new school, and deleted the contact information for friends who were a bad influence.

"Robert was livid at first, of course. Mad as hell. But then Jen gave him things she knew he would like. She bought him books, took him to plays and art shows, introduced him to kids with a future, and broadened his mind. She showed him he could be so much more than he had been. And once she'd showed him a better way, he took it."

Martha was glowing with maternal pride—I could sense that even over the telephone—and I didn't have the heart to tell her that guns were back in Robert's life. So, I let her keep her maternal pride intact. I'd find somebody else to tell me why Robert needed a gun to work for Gene Tretnikoff. I wrapped up our conversation with pleasantries and we said goodbye. I was getting close to the truth now, and that meant I needed another chat with Jen to tie up loose ends.

I looked forward to tonight's meeting with her, but with a touch of trepidation.

I got to Jen's around eight and she met me at the door dressed smartly, as always, this time in a plum-colored velvet miniskirt and grey silk blouse.

"Is Matt at home?" I asked.

"Nope, just us. It's hockey night in Canada. Matt's at the Leafs game, in his happy place."

"Yeah, Daniel's a big fan too. You wouldn't believe how angry he got about Nick Dempster's last game. I gather some useless bench-warmer punched the superstar in the face. In the third period, of all things. To Daniel, that was like a peasant assaulting the king."

"Yes, well, hockey superstars *are* Canadian royalty," Jen said.

Jen brought out a bottle of wine and two glasses. "You're okay with a glass of red, I assume?"

"Yes. That's fine."

Looking around the artfully furnished living room, I remembered many previous visits. "I was just thinking about all the times I've been here, Jen," I said. "I even remember seeing Beth here a few times, but never Michael."

"No? Well that's probably for the best, right?" said Jen. "After the divorce, he wasn't exactly your favourite person."

"No, he wasn't. But still, I would have thought maybe once…"

Jen shrugged but said nothing more on the topic. She had already started looking all around the room, for reasons I never understood. So I tried a different conversational gambit. I asked, "Jen, do you remember that day when the first female astronaut walked on the moon and we got stoned out of our heads with that big orange bong of yours?"

"Sure do. It was fun. But that was centuries ago. What made you think of that?"

"I was just wondering if you still had that thing?"

"It's around here somewhere, but I don't have any weed in the house. We'd have to get some."

"Oh god no. I just mean, that may have been the last time I got high. Where did you ever get that crazy thing?"

"Oh?" Then, hesitatingly, "Sorry, I can't remember."

"Because when I spoke to Martha, she mentioned you'd confiscated Robert's bong when he was a teenager."

I could see Jen's guard go up. "I guess that's right; it *was* Robert's bong. I'm the hypocrite who stole the kid's bong and used it herself. Do as I say, not as I do! That's my motto." She laughed and started looking around the room again, then picking lint off her miniskirt.

"Martha mentioned you also confiscated Robert's gun back then: the one he'd stolen from his parents' house. I understand Martha told the police it was a Glock 19."

"Was it? So what?"

"So, did you know that was the same kind of gun that killed Michael?"

"How would I know that, Rachel? I took that gun and

tossed it out because Martha wouldn't have in her house anymore. I barely even looked at it. And that happened centuries ago. Where are you going with this?"

"I'm going to ask you for Michael's last diary."

"I gave you all his diaries."

"Beth says she gave you seventeen diaries, but you only gave me sixteen."

"So she miscounted."

"She insisted there were seventeen. Besides, the earliest one you gave me is marked Volume Two. Where's Volume One?"

"How should I know?"

I excused myself and went to the bathroom. My body was shaking all over, so I breathed deeply, washed my face in cold water, and waited for the shaking to pass. I may have taken a few minutes to recover; I can't recall it clearly. But I looked through the medicine cabinet and looked at the reading material beside the toilet. *GQ*, for Matt I suppose. *The Literary Review of Canada* for Jen?

Back in the living room, I pressed on. "What does the missing diary say, Jen? Does it describe something that happened that made you want to kill yourself? Maybe, something Michael did to you when you were young?"

"Shut up. That's none of your business. And you should be on my side, Rachel, not grilling me like a police detective."

"I would be on your side, if you hadn't lied to me about the hockey game."

"What do you mean?"

"You agreed when I said that Nick Dempster was treated like royalty after his face was smashed."

She looked bewildered now.

"No one punched Nick Dempster's face in that game, Jen.

You would have known that if you'd watched the game, like you told the police."

"So I'm guilty of not paying attention. Big deal! Matt's the hockey fan, not me. I only sat next to him while he watched. I was probably reading a magazine anyway."

"You, Matt, and Robert watched together?"

"That's right," Jen insisted.

"Bullshit! You've got to stop lying to me, Jen. Robert wasn't there, he was in Picton or on the road back to Toronto. Daniel and several others were in Picton with him at the start of the game. Robert couldn't have driven to your place before the game was over."

I'd finally cornered Jen. For the first time, she looked scared and her eyes teared up.

"Why are you trying to trick me, Rachel? I can't believe it's for Michael's sake. Michael was a much bigger pig than you'll ever know."

"I'm beginning to realize that. So let's talk honestly about Michael, and especially about the years before I met him. Because I think you hated his guts."

"Okay," Jen said. "I'll admit it, I hated Michael's guts."

"And I think I know why, but I'd like you to tell me, from the beginning."

"Ah, the beginning! I started hating Michael from the moment I was born, which was the moment he started treating me like a piece of shit. He mocked everything I said and did. He ridiculed the way I looked and dressed, and all the people I knew. He upset all my plans and destroyed all the stuff I valued—even pictures I had painted and photos I had taken."

A look of anguish came over her face. "But worst of all, he wouldn't keep his hands off me once I hit puberty. He raped me almost every day. I objected. I cried. I threatened to tell our parents. But he laughed at me and said they wouldn't believe me.

"And he was right. When I told my mother what Michael was doing, she said I was exaggerating and that I had too much imagination. She also said I was just trying to get Michael into trouble. Only once did she ask him about what I'd said, and he denied it all. And our parents were hardly ever around anyway, so I never raised the matter again. But I had to protect myself. I started kicking and biting and scratching him whenever he approached me at night. I even started taking my Swiss army knife to bed with me. Finally, I had the best idea, and it worked."

I was dying to hear what she'd come up with now. This was a side of Jen I'd never seen before.

33

"What was your great idea?" I asked her.

"I introduced Michael to you. He liked you; and wonder of wonders, you liked him too. Once the two of you got together, he never bothered me again. Never, not once. I was safe from his disgusting urges and demands. You wanted him, and as far as I was concerned, you could have him."

Jen held out her hands to me then, like she was giving me a gift. A donation, even.

Some gift! "You mean you set me up with your rapist? You must have hated me too," I said, feeling shocked and angry.

"I didn't hate you, I liked you. I still do. But I needed to save my life, and you did it for me. You took my disgusting brother out of my bed forever. And it wasn't rape for you. For a while, you were happy with him, weren't you?"

"Yes, you're right. For a while I was happy with him."

"So, in the end, everyone got what they wanted. Michael got you, you got Michael—you even got Josh—and I was free of his dirty hands forever. But I never stopped feeling damaged. He left me feeling like garbage. So I vowed to be a better person than Michael. That's why I helped Martha and her son Robert, when I got the chance."

What she said made a lot of sense. I couldn't deny it, and it squared with all my theories, especially with rage theory.

"Why didn't you tell me about this, Jen? I was your closest friend."

"I never told anyone what had happened to me—not even Matt or Robert—until a few weeks ago. I was too ashamed and too frightened about what they might do. Before that, I had only ever told two people about this—my mother and our cleaning lady. And only the cleaning lady believed me."

"Yet you continued seeing Michael socially. Matt even worked for him."

"I wanted to exact something from Michael, so I made him hire Matt. That drove Michael crazy—he could never stand Matt—but he did it anyway. And the bastard acted like hiring Matt and paying him a lot of money squared his debt to me, which it didn't. In the end, he treated Matt like shit, so I did my best to avoid Michael, whenever possible. I continued to hate him and hated the way he treated Matt. For that matter, Matt hated him too. But at least I didn't have to see my horrible brother very often. I almost never set foot in Michael's office or home."

"You're running a big risk, Jen. If the police ever home in on you, you'd better hope some bit of forensic evidence doesn't trip you up. I'm thinking of your cell phone records, your car GPS, some traffic camera—or Matt, for instance."

She looked me in the eye and said, "Right now, Rachel, I'm just hoping my best friend isn't planning to betray me to the police. And if you've been listening carefully, you'll know I haven't said I've murdered anyone."

Jen was right. She'd chosen her words carefully and hadn't admitted killing Michael.

"Besides," she said, "you were there with me that evening, Rachel. Or at least, you were supposed to be there with me. That was the evening Michael had invited you to drop in, wasn't it?"

So Jen had known about Michael's invitation: about the note I had found in my pocket only recently. Jen hadn't set up this situation but she was sure willing to capitalize on it. Worst of all, I still couldn't remember anything that had happened during or after the faculty-student colloquium. Maybe I *had* gone to Michael's house and helped Jen kill him. I couldn't be sure I hadn't done just that. But I wasn't going to fall for another of Jen's tricks either.

"Tell me, Jen, after all this time, why did you kill him now, after so many years?"

"Don't play dumb with me, Rachel. I'm sure you know Michael was planning to sack Matt. Robert heard him say so. Michael was tired of even pretending to repay his debt to me, and that was the last straw."

"Was it?" I asked, knowing she wouldn't answer. The question hung in the air. Jen was looking around the room again, then stared directly at me.

"What made you think I'd killed Michael anyway, Rachel? I wasn't that obvious, was I?"

"It was a collection of little things, actually. Your fake alibi. Robert's old handgun being the same as the murder weapon. And your easy access to Michael's home; he would have let you in even if the security system had been working. More than that, it was your art: your preoccupation with death, and your anger at people who considered themselves high and mighty. That rage is in all of your pictures. And maybe you thought you could hide your anger in plain sight because the rest of us aren't smart enough to catch on.

"Another big clue was the wound to Michael's genitals. Stomping his balls was a bad mistake, Jen. The police don't know what to make of Michael's wounds, but I know—and maybe they know—they're marks of personal rage. The rage of an abused woman. The research on abused women confirms that much. And then, there was another thing."

"What?"

"Guzman. You never doubted the whole Freddy Krueger thing. In fact, you egged me on to see J-C as this horrible boogeyman. But now I'm wondering how much of that was real. Did anyone actually break into your house and turn on the gas? There was no forced entry, no creepy note left behind. You're the only witness and, though your life was supposedly in danger, you never reported this to the police. You could have made it all up. And how did Guzman find Beth in upstate New York? Only you knew where she was hiding. Plus, the photographs taken inside her house: they were high quality pictures, much more like your work than the shitty little Polaroids someone left behind after breaking into my house. You used our fear of Guzman to confuse us—to keep us off balance.

"But now that I think about it, your signature act—the thing that made me absolutely sure you were involved—was that flowerpot you sent Beth with the photos. That was a primo Jen Coale piece of humour—the kind of thing only you would think of doing. As I'm sure you know, J-C doesn't have a humorous bone in his body. No, that flowerpot photo was all you."

Jen went silent and fixed me with the coldest stare I'd ever seen. Then she said icily, "We're done, Rachel. You need to go."

I was out of there in seconds, barely reaching my car before I threw up in the gutter. When I got home I fixed myself a scotch on the rocks and downed it in three gulps. Then reality took over again. I started feeling terrible pains in my stomach and thought I might be getting an ulcer from all the drinking. Or all the thinking.

Like the Norse legend predicted, my world had collapsed tonight. But I hadn't been Loki after all; the trickster was all Jen. Did that make me Heimdall, with his preference for order and tradition? But if so, where was my supposed legendary ability to see and hear everything? I sure missed a lot of information in solving this case, it seems. About thirty years' worth of vital information, at a modest estimate.

I took several swigs of Pepto Bismol to steady my stomach, then pulled up Roxy's phone number in my list of contacts. I intended to tell her about Jen and what I suspected about Michael's murder. But something stopped me and I put my phone away. I wasn't ready to put Jen in prison for the rest of her life for what she'd done to Michael.

But I'd have to do something about Jen. No wonder I slept fitfully that night. I had colourful, noisy dreams, full of slamming prison doors, though when I woke up I couldn't remember what I'd dreamed. Still, I was exhausted, as though I'd run a marathon. Finding out who had killed Michael was supposed to be my finish line, but somehow I couldn't stop running.

This feeling of unfinished business—unfinished business that just wouldn't end—was surreal and nightmarish. For a fleeting moment, I wished I was dead, so at least the anxiety would be over. "To sleep, perchance to dream," as another stressed-out person is rumoured to have said. But then what? I couldn't come up with an answer.

After that confrontation with Jen last night, I needed to hear a voice of reason so I phoned my sister Megan. I caught her just as she was on her way out to work.

"I'm in a terrible situation, Sis. I won't go into all the details, but I'm having trouble figuring out how to make things simpler. My home life is a mess, my work is a huge burden, and it turns out my best friend, Jen, has been lying to me about really important things." I started crying and couldn't stop.

After about ten seconds, Megan said, "Why don't I come over and we'll sort this out together?" I blew my nose and said okay. Fifteen minutes later, we were sitting in the living room with cups of coffee. I told her all about Michael's murder and Daniel's gambling and J-C Guzman's threats and Dean Grabol's demands. She listened and didn't say a word until I'd finished.

Then she asked me a really simple question. If I wanted all this to stop, why didn't I just stop it? Wasn't that within my control?

I realized then that it *was* within my control. It wasn't my job to solve Michael's murder or bring his murderer to justice. And if I couldn't make Daniel stop gambling, I could at least stop having him in my life. And if Dean Grabol was a pain in the ass, I could stop fundraising. I just had to make those changes. I didn't tell Megan what I had learned about Jen, but on that topic I assumed Megan's advice would be similar. Make up your mind if you want her behind bars for killing her horrible brother, then act accordingly. I hugged Megan and thanked her for all the good advice. I cried some more about Daniel and Ellie and Jen and how my marriages had turned out, then Megan went off to work. I felt better than I had in weeks. In fact, I thought all my problems were solved.

But I was about to face the biggest problem yet.

After Megan left, I drove downtown and trudged to the dean's office. This is how the Bataan Death March must have felt, I thought. The dean's cheery assistant told me that Sandor had been in Saudi Arabia visiting university alumni and recruiting new undergraduate students. While there, he'd also secured commitments of thirty million dollars towards setting up an Islamic Chair in Women's Studies. Donors expected the chair to promote a favorable understanding of the Saudi approach to gender relations.

Or as the dean's assistant put it, "They want to correct our Western misunderstandings about Saudi Arabia, and especially about the role of women there."

"Do they?" I asked, with raised eyebrows, wanting to make sure I got this right.

"Yes, pretty much. Mainly, the dean was impressed by the wealth in that country."

"You're right," I said. "I've heard there's a lot of money in Saudi Arabia." Then I started laughing and couldn't stop. The dean's assistant started laughing too, and when we had both run out of breath, we stood there silently, facing each other. Neither of us knew what to say, so I sat down and zoned out while I waited for the dean to invite me into his office.

Suddenly, the dean's fundraising mission to Saudi Arabia gave me an idea that would suit the dean just fine. Entering his office, I saw the dean seated in his usual easy chair. After exchanging niceties—"How are you?" "I'm fine," and so on—I got to the point. "Dean, I just heard about your fundraising trip to Saudi Arabia. Congratulations on raising all that money for a new chair in Women's Studies. That's excellent news."

"Thank you. Yes, the trip was a huge success. Now I just have to find a way to sell the goal of our donors to our colleagues in the Women's Studies Program. They hold a more critical view of Saudi culture than our donors do. But down to business: how are you coming with the Coale donation?"

To make a long story short, I outlined an ambitious new plan. First, I proposed we stop pursuing the Coale donation. Second, I proposed that, instead, I raise money from rich alumni in the Global South, as the dean had done. According to this new plan, I'd focus on the criminal victimization of rich people in low-income countries and the harm it did to economic development. Many of those benighted rich people get kidnapped for ransom, I told the dean. Some are even murdered. We could capitalize on this problem by offering solid research.

Once he was satisfied I wasn't being sarcastic or "snippy" as he used to say, Dean Grabol was delighted. He saw the fund-raising potential of this approach as well as I did. He proposed only one amendment to my idea: why not raise money from rich people in the Global South AND from Beth Coale at the same time? I said I'd consider this two-pronged attack if I could find the time. So, for the moment, I had calmed the dean and given myself a chance to think about how to proceed.

I felt great when I left the dean's office, but my good humour disappeared when I started to work on the details. That night, I had a nightmare about Dean Grabol dragging huge burlap sacks of money to the Canadian Bank of Knowledge. Sweating under the heavy load, he had to stop three times to catch his breath. Then, when he had completed his deposit, he kneeled before an enormous University Provost, who knighted Dean Grabol with the flat edge of a sword.

For some reason, this ceremony took place at a desert oasis. Lightly dressed young women appeared suddenly and began to dance for the middle-aged men seated in a circle on the ground. Some of the men were dressed in traditional Arab clothing—flowing white robes, that sort of thing—while others were dressed in Western business suits. Dean Grabol loved the dancing girls and chatted easily with the man next to him.

34

The next day, I visited Daniel at Humber River Hospital. Despite his high spirits, I felt more than ever that my marriage was in intensive care and not long for this world. I wouldn't end the marriage while Daniel was convalescing. That would be too much like kicking someone while he was down. But though I felt sorry for Daniel, my feelings for him were unromantic: more like the affection one feels for a friend or a brother. How different this was from the passionate infatuation I felt for Robert! And I couldn't help wondering if Daniel would have preferred a visit from Rusty, not me.

Back home from the hospital, I turned on the TV to hear disturbing news. J-C had escaped from custody. On a stopover in New York where he was to board a plane for Mexico City, J-C had overwhelmed one police officer and used his gun to shoot the other. He'd then escaped in a cab to Manhattan. The cabby reported leaving him at the Port Authority, where he could catch a train, bus, or car to almost anywhere.

No one knew where J-C was headed. The CBC reported that border guards from British Columbia to the Maritimes had received photos of J-C and been told to watch out for him. He'd be smart to head south, I thought—to Miami, for example, or Houston. There, he'd find a friendly climate and a large Spanish-speaking population to hide in. He might even continue further south, into Latin America. The FBI said they'd keep an eye out for him in the southern United States. Megan phoned with the news and urged me to relax. J-C's escape wouldn't affect my life, she said; but I couldn't relax. As I watched the news story, all I could think was: Freddy's loose! After the news of Guzman's escape I felt emotionally and physically drained. So, I let myself drift off to sleep on the couch, but then I woke up to something very, very bad.

When I managed to wake up, my phone was ringing and Jen was on the line. I looked at the clock and it said 11:15 p.m. "Can you come over to my place?" I heard her asking me.

"I'm sleeping right now, Jen. Can we put this off until to-morrow?"

"No. You have to come now."

After how our last meeting had gone, I didn't feel comfort-able being alone with Jen. But I couldn't come up with a good excuse for turning her down and after a few lame attempts to weasel out, I relented.

"Okay," I said. "I'll be there as soon as I can."

I told Nancy, asleep upstairs, that I had to go out and would be back soon. I didn't know if this was true, but I didn't want to frighten her. Then I thought of Robert and called him. There was no answer and I left him a message to meet me at Jen's place. I wanted him there because I didn't want to be alone with Jen. But, as it turned out, it wasn't Jen I needed to worry about.

When I got to Jen's home, only one dim light was shining and the rest of the house was in darkness. Trying the front door, I found it unlocked so I came in. Once inside, I heard a familiar voice I identified as J-C's. He told me to lock the door and though I couldn't see him, I sensed he was near. I could smell the sandalwood perfume I associated with Jen, so I knew she was near too.

"Sit down on the couch," J-C said. I did, and as my eyes adjusted to the dim light, I could make out Jen on the couch, her mouth gagged and her hands and ankles tied up.

"Where are you, J-C, and what do you want from us?" I asked him.

"I don't want anything from you two. You're just bait to lure Robert. I expect Robert to arrive soon, and it's him I want to see. And kill. And if you think that Robert, that little prick who's on his way here, is some chivalrous knight, you are badly mistaken. That bastard tried to have me locked away for life. He escalated this conflict, not me."

"What makes you think Robert will come here?" I asked him quietly, hoping to calm the situation.

"I figured you'd probably call him. But to make sure of his company, I called him myself. Robert knows I'm holding you both prisoner, and he'll have to come by to free you."

For close to an hour, we sat without speaking. In the darkness, unable to see more than a few inches in front of my face, my other senses took over. I could still smell Jen's sandalwood, also J-C's body odor and my own smell—a smell of fear. I could hear the electrical appliances humming and the sound of traffic on Eglinton Avenue half a mile away. I touched my face and it was greasy; I badly needed a wash. Then, Jen started writhing around, moaning words I couldn't understand. J-C removed her gag and asked her what she wanted.

"I have to use the toilet," she whispered.

"I'll untie your ropes, so you can do that. But if you try to escape, I'll kill Rachel and come after you. Do you understand?"

"I understand," she mumbled. He untied her ropes and Jen stumbled into the washroom, unable to walk straight. By the time she came back, the circulation had returned to her legs and she was walking better.

"I'm cold, J-C."

"No tricks. Sit down on the couch," J-C growled, and Jen sat down beside me. I put my arms around her to stop her shivering. She rested her head on my shoulder and we waited for what felt like hours but was probably only forty-five minutes.

Suddenly we heard a car horn honking repeatedly in front of the house. After five honks, J-C went to the front window and looked out. The car was still honking, with its lights flashing, but no one was inside. Someone had pushed the emergency button on their key fob. I could imagine people all along the street coming to their doorways and windows to look for the source of this noise. Surely, someone would phone the police if the noise didn't stop soon. Meanwhile, the horn kept honking, over and over.

J-C sank back into the shadows and waited for something else to happen. Soon enough, we heard quiet footsteps at the back of the house. "Hello, Robert," J-C said. "Come in and join us. But don't do anything foolish or I'll shoot your ladies."

The horn outside continued honking and, I can tell you, it was starting to drive me a little crazy. I thought of Anita and wondered what she would have told me to do, if she were here. Then I realized she wouldn't have told me to do anything. She would have asked me to think about the best course of action. I was just starting to review my alternatives when I heard a noise nearby.

All of a sudden Robert appeared in the door of the living room with a gun in his hand, aimed directly at J-C's head.

"Let's not end this in bloodshed, J-C," Robert said. "Let's

make a deal instead. If you agree to leave right now, I'll give you one hundred thousand in US currency and an American passport, then have a man drive you across the border. You can spend the rest of your life in freedom and comfort anywhere in the world."

Robert's calm reasoning was interrupted by noises from outside. Someone pounded on the front door, shouting. "Is that your car honking? Turn off the horn, you moron, we're trying to sleep." Meanwhile, they kept pounding the door. I wondered if Robert was going to say anything more, but he didn't. He stood quietly and waited, his gun still aimed at J-C's head.

"That's an attractive offer, Robert. But I must repay you for turning me in to the police. So my plan is to kill you, then kill Jen and Rachel, and only then to leave the country."

We heard even more pounding on the door, and then the doorbell starting ringing too. But J-C and Robert continued to ignore these noises. Suddenly, Robert rushed at J-C and knocked him to the ground. The gun flew out of J-C's hand and the two men struggled for it. Seeing a chance to help, I jumped on J-C and tried to pin his arms, but he pushed me away. I jumped on him again, putting all my weight against his legs and torso. Meanwhile, Robert kept punching J-C in the chest and head.

"Get away, Rachel, you'll get hurt," Robert shouted at me.

Until now, Jen had watched the fight in horror, too frightened to do anything. Then unexpectedly, she jumped off the couch and smacked J-C on the forehead head with a table lamp. Together, we tried to pin down J-C's arms while Robert looked for the lost gun in the darkened room. But J-C was too much for us. He had incredible strength for a man of his age and, more than that, a demonic dedication. He kept thrashing around, trying to bite me and then Jen while we held him down.

Abruptly, calling on all his strength, he pushed us off him. I went flying into the wall and Jen landed back on the couch. Freed of our interference, J-C crawled around the room on his hands and knees, finding his gun just seconds before Robert did. Standing back a few steps, Robert raised his own gun and fired it a split second before Guzman's gun went off. Then I heard a terrible scream I'd never forget.

I can't tell you how many times since that night I've re-played those gunshots and that scream in my memory. I wish I could forget them but I can't.

In the dim light, Robert had missed J-C's head and hit his left shoulder instead. J-C screamed in pain and then, having recovered his own gun, stood and fired at Robert. Robert fell to the floor, his blood streaming on to the carpet. Without thinking, I rushed at J-C and kneed him in the groin. As J-C buckled to the ground in pain, I grabbed the gun out of his hands and smashed his face with the gun butt. He looked stunned and I hit him a second time, this time breaking his nose. Then, passing the gun to Jen, I rushed over to Robert and held his head in my lap while I stroked his face.

"You'll be okay, Robert. You'll be fine." And to Jen I barked, "Call 911! Right now." We didn't realize it then but Guzman's bullet had pierced Robert's heart. He was dying. Robert looked at me and smiled weakly, and I kissed him lightly on his forehead. When the kiss ended, Robert closed his eyes and died. And as I continued to stroke Robert's head, Jen took her eyes off J-C to stare at Robert too.

While we both stared incredulously at Robert's lifeless body, J-C leapt up and hobbled out the back door of the house.

About fifteen seconds later, we heard a car start half way down the block. J-C had escaped and we'd probably never see him again; but outside our front door, the other car had continued to honk. Finally, Jen found the key fob in Robert's pocket and pressed the right button. Almost as unexpectedly as it had started, the honking stopped.

I heard someone screaming, and Jen put her arms around me and hugged me close to her. After a few minutes I stopped screaming—my throat now too hoarse to make a sound—but I couldn't stop crying. For endless minutes Jen held me, then leaned over to kiss Robert on the forehead too. When the police finally arrived, I let the officers in and found enough voice to tell them what had happened. A paramedic checked us for shock and drove me home.

When we got to my home, the paramedic called Megan, who promised to come over right away. I wanted to sleep for a week and wake up to find that none of this had ever happened. But I was covered in blood—Robert's blood—so I stripped off all my clothes and took a hot shower. After scalding myself with hot water for what felt like hours, I slipped into bed and fell asleep. In my first of several dreams, Robert's blood seeped endlessly on to the pale carpet. The world had ended, and I couldn't imagine what would follow.

Megan stayed beside me all night, her arms wrapped around me as I slept. She murmured words of comfort into my ears whenever I woke from a bad dream. Tonight had been Ragnarok after all. J-C had killed the trickster Robert and Robert had neutralized, if not killed, J-C—the historic defender of wealth and power. Was this finally the end of days and the end of the story, I wondered?

No, it wasn't.

35

When I finally woke the next day, snow had fallen and the ground was covered in a white blanket. Megan was still next to me, giving me occasional hugs. From the kitchen, I called Gene Tretnikoff, and he picked up right away.

"Robert died last night, Gene," I told him in a raw, hoarse voice. "He was defending me and Jen against J-C Guzman. Robert wounded Guzman but Robert's dead. I thought you'd want to know."

"Thank you for phoning me, Rachel. You're RIGHT, I do want to know. Robert was like my younger brother. I'll miss him very much. For years, he was my comrade in arms and my trusted FRIEND. But I'm glad he saved your life. You meant a lot to him, so I'm not surprised."

"How do you know what I meant to Robert if I didn't even know myself?" I asked him.

"I watched him and listened to him more carefully than you did, Rachel. I could see and hear his FEELINGS, though you couldn't. You must learn to pay better attention to people's feelings."

"You're right, Gene. If it hadn't been for you and Robert, I'd be dead now too. How can I repay you?"

"Just come to the funeral ceremony and help me bury our friend."

I told him I'd be there. As always, Gene had behaved with kindness and generosity. Now I knew how deeply he'd cared about Robert, and he knew how I felt too. That gave us a new bond. We might differ from each other in a thousand ways, but Gene and I shared something important.

Then I emailed Martha and asked her to phone right away. She got back to me in less than twenty minutes. She knew that

Robert had been shot but little else. "Martha, I was there. He protected me and Jen from a violent attacker," I croaked.

"Yes. Jen called this morning and told me. Thank you for calling me too."

"Robert was brave. He protected us to the best of his abilities, I know that."

"I'm sure that's true, Rachel. Robert was brave and always put other people's wellbeing before his own." I wondered then if Martha knew as much about Robert's dark side as I did. If not, I wouldn't be the one to tell her.

"Would it be okay if I came to Robert's funeral?" I asked.

"Yes, certainly" she answered. "I'll email you the details as soon as they're settled."

I'd made an appointment to see Dean Grabol the next afternoon to update him on my fundraising. The dean may have muttered something about how work might distract me from my grief. But, honestly, I don't remember much of what he said. To me it sounded like: blah, blah blah. I just couldn't concentrate. Or care.

I had discontinued Nancy's protection service and both my kids were back at school. At home alone, I started to feel awful again. I didn't know what to do with all these terrible feelings: feelings of guilt and rage, but mostly feelings of loss. I'd made my living by thinking, but now I was starting to suspect I'd spent too much time thinking.

And I had a theory about that: I think to keep myself from feeling too much. I don't want to feel guilt or rage, so I think about them, then write about them. As though I could banish those feelings by putting them down on a page! But now I couldn't do that anymore. I didn't want to feel I'd lost someone important to me, but I had. Oh, Robert had done terrible things, even I knew that. But though I tried to stop feeling this way, I felt awful.

When the police had searched Robert's clothing, they'd found a note that he had written to me just before coming over to confront J-C. It read "Rachel, if you're reading this note, I'm already dead. I'm sorry I'll miss the rest of your life. We could have been perfect together. Keep being yourself. I hope you don't forget me. Your Robert."

As I read that, I started to gasp for air and felt my legs give out under me. I sat down quickly and tried to slow my breathing, the way Anita had taught me. Then, when the strength had returned to my legs, I got an ice pack and held it to my face. Gradually I cooled down and started to think more calmly about my situation.

I hadn't just lost Robert, I felt I'd also lost Jen. I was still angry at her for not confiding in me about her brother. And for setting me up as the object of Michael's groping, never-satisfied sexual hunger—at least for as long as Michael wanted me. And for using me to deflect suspicion from what she'd done to Michael. I was a fool for having believed everything Jen told me. But today, I didn't care about any of this, after what she had suffered. I just felt sad and alone.

Suddenly, I needed to be cleansed and purified by the freezing cold air, so I went for a walk in the park. The world around me was covered in snow, and the trees were nothing but dark branches under white blankets. The world had been stripped bare—emptied out by the winter cold; and I wanted the same experience. I wanted to die from the cold and be reborn—innocent, hopeful, worthy of love. But soon, I just couldn't stand the cold any longer, so I came home again and cried for an hour.

Nothing made sense to me anymore; and in my new state of confusion, I found everything ridiculous. Fundraising was especially ridiculous. And frankly, I didn't care if Daniel kept on gambling, or settled down with Rusty in Picton, or both.

I checked in with Megan, to hear her voice and let her know how I was doing. And this time, I finally told her about my feelings for Robert. Her reaction was kind but realistic. "I'm sorry to hear you lost someone you cared about, Rachel. I know you were attracted to Robert and he meant a lot to you. But honestly, it might not have turned out well if you two had gotten together. It might just have been a replay of your marriage to Michael—another bad boy, a lot of excitement in the beginning, then a lot of disappointment and heartbreak."

My first reaction was to argue back, but I knew Megan was right so I let it go. She could have also said "and be smarter the next time," but then, that wouldn't have been my sweet sister Megan.

And I vowed to myself there wouldn't be a "next time."

Two days later, I booked off the morning to attend Robert's funeral. It was small, just a few dozen people. At the brief and simple ceremony, only two people gave eulogies. The speeches were short but elegant, each in their own way.

I'd expected to hear Jen read a poem—perhaps that famous poem by W.H. Auden, *Funeral Blues*. You probably know the one I mean, the one that starts "Stop all the clocks, cut off the telephone." But Jen didn't speak that day. Only Martha and Gene spoke. Martha said Robert had been a good son and a man of many qualities. He was loyal and lived by his own code of duty and honour. She'd miss him terribly, she said, but knew he would live on in the minds of his friends.

Gene Tretnikov, dressed in elegant formal wear, said Robert

had been like a younger brother to him, even like a son. He'd loved Robert and respected him. More than that, he'd relied on Robert for help and advice. In those respects, Robert had never let him down. It had been a privilege and a pleasure to know Robert, and he didn't expect to meet another person like Robert during his lifetime.

As Gene finished, I silently remembered the rest of Auden's poem, especially the third stanza, and whispered it to myself. Of course, it was sentimental mush in my case. Robert and I had never gotten far enough for him to be "my talk, my song." But maybe we could have, if he had lived.

After the ceremony, men in black suits moved Robert's coffin to the crematorium. The rest of us left the sanctuary and passed into the Memory Room to shake hands with Martha and Gene, and then to share food, drink, and conversation. Gene himself had arranged the food and drink, so we sampled more Black Sea caviar and, once again, I got to pair it with good champagne and pomegranate seeds.

Another day had brought another funeral and another funeral banquet, and it was still just autumn. I looked around the Memory Room and, once again, saw familiar faces. I chatted briefly with Gene about his business. He'd told me he'd just hired Trish McCormack to run his investment properties in Picton. My father was there too, out of respect for Gene, and briefly said hello. Over in a corner, I saw Matt Carling chatting with Bradley Wong, smiling and, occasionally, laughing. I'd heard from Beth that the deal with Jupiter Pharmaceuticals was going ahead. Matt had even hired Preston McCormack as his personal assistant and the two got along well.

Jen was wearing a pearl-white silk pantsuit and heavy gold necklace, not the black suit she'd worn to Michael's funeral. She strolled around the room with her Pentax, taking photographs of everyone. As always, she was the permanent outsider, documenting people's oddities and strange relationships. I waved to her, and she took a photo of me waving.

Jen, I came to learn, had always favoured doing business with Jupiter Pharmaceuticals, even though the company employed Guzman, that psychopathic monster. At first, I was surprised when Jen cited Jupiter's "pursuit of something good" (meaning, saving lives with medicine) to excuse Guzman's violence. But Jen might have had another reason to excuse Guzman's violent behaviour. Like her, J-C had suffered violent injustices that scarred his youth—injustices and humiliations similar, at least in degree, to those she had suffered. Maybe when Jen talked about Guzman, she was remembering her own terrible past, her own rage, and her own violence.

Daniel was stuck at home with a tube dripping antibiotic into his arm, and I'd persuaded Ellie to come to the funeral with me instead. She was wearing a new black dress that looked magnificent, and Martha and Gene were both bowled over by her beauty and good manners. Gene said if Ellie ever needed a summer job, or something longer term, she should let him know. He always had something that needed doing, he said. She smiled and said she would do that.

Some of Robert's friends from the Calypso were there too. I greeted a few of them, including Rusty Wagner—even more than before, a vivacious red-haired woman with more poise and charm than I would have imagined in a casino greeter. She was pleased to hear Daniel was on the mend. We agreed that Daniel was a character when he got enthusiastic about something (or someone). At that moment, I might have been discussing an ex-husband, or even a stranger, with his new wife. Once again, my feelings of detachment from Daniel surprised me.

After half an hour, I hugged Martha and Gene and left the gathering. Ellie could find her own way home, of that I was certain. It was cold now and I realized there would be a great many days of winter to come. On the other hand, spring would arrive in only four or five months—just like it did every other year.

When I got home, I poured myself a weak scotch on the rocks and spent a long time sniffing it. I loved the smell. And I thought about Robert and Gene and our lunch at Grazie—all our jokes and toasts and good feelings. I sipped the scotch once or twice, then poured it down the sink.

36

Her friendly wave at Robert's funeral told me Jen might be open to having an honest conversation. She'd lied to me this past year—in fact, had been lying to me ever since we'd first met. But she must have been in terrible pain all these years, because of what Michael had done to her. Since childhood, she'd led a secret life that she allowed none of us to see. So Jen and I had unfinished business we needed to wrap up.

The next morning I phoned Jen and suggested we meet at a place we'd never met before—a public recreation centre in North Toronto with an indoor swimming pool. We were, supposedly, going to combine some exercise with catching up. She played along by ignoring this was something we'd never done before—in fact, would never have done before. A public swimming pool? Come on.

And through most of our conversation that day, we sat on a bench beside the pool shivering in our bathing suits. It was a miserable place to meet but I wanted to be in a public setting where she couldn't hurt me. And where she could see I wasn't wearing a wire to record our conversation.

"I'm not sure how to start this conversation, Jen," I said quietly. "I'm mad at you for tricking me and lying to me all these years. But I also feel awful about what Michael did to you, and that you felt you had to keep it secret from me, your best friend. Why didn't you tell me?"

"I *did* tell you, in a thousand ways. Or at least, I tried to tell you. But you never heard me. You were always listening to the voices inside your own head."

"What do you mean, I never heard you? Help me understand what you're saying."

"It's like you once said—I speak through my art. I thought the message of those photos I showed you—the ones from the Tate Galley and the *Spoon River Anthology*—couldn't have been clearer. And that book I sent you about Loki: that was to tell you to watch out for my tricks. I'm not who I seem. I am a person of many disguises. And what I told you about my intern: that was you I was talking about, no one else. And then there was that poem I read out at Michael's funeral. What did you think that poem was about? I was telling you, and everyone else, what I thought of Michael."

"What part did Robert play in all this?"

"I wanted you to know Robert, and to love him too, as I did. I thought you'd be an even better influence on Robert than Gene. So, I planned the tennis match at the Granite Club with that in mind. Your meeting with Robert wasn't accidental. I figured things would just develop from there, and they did."

"Why are you so roundabout in everything you do, Jen? Why can't you just talk plainly to me?"

"It hurts too much to say plainly, out loud, the terrible things I've seen and experienced, Rachel. The terrible things Michael did to me. And the terrible things I've done to myself. You don't know the half of it."

"I just learned recently that you tried to take your own life by jumping on to the subway tracks. And that you were an in-patient at the Clarke Hospital for months after that. Why didn't you tell me about that either?"

"For one thing, you were away in Massachusetts, living with my horrible brother—who you thought was so wonderful. For another thing, you never seemed to notice when I tried starving myself to death two other times. Or started cutting myself. The cutting went on for years and you never even noticed. You just didn't care enough to notice."

I thought for a moment about those "signs" I'd missed. She was right—I couldn't recall any of them and felt deeply ashamed. "Of course I cared, Jen. I've always cared," I said, meekly.

"I figured Michael must have told you about all the fun he'd had with me, and you thought I was worthless. Like he did."

I was horrified to hear her say this. But Jen was right about one thing: she'd scarcely existed for either of us when we were off at graduate school in Massachusetts. Oh sure, I exchanged a few emails with Jen, but mostly, I'd started a new life. Michael and I might just as well have moved to Pluto. I was ashamed of what I'd done—shutting her out for all those years—and wondered how I could make it right. It wasn't going to be easy, I knew that much.

"Here's the problem, Rachel. You can't hear a lot of things, especially things you don't want to hear. That's why you couldn't see what Michael was about. That's also why you married Daniel—Mr. Beige—even though you prefer bad boys like Michael and Robert, and Gene Tretnikoff."

"And I get that," Jen continued. "You grew up in a comfortable home with two loving and dedicated parents. They gave you everything and just wanted you to be perfect—as perfect as you could be. I grew up in a crazy home with two drunken parents and an abusive brother. No one was there to protect me or even listen to me. I had nothing and you had everything, so it's not surprising that you see the world through rose-colored glasses. And that you can't see me through those glasses."

Was I really the person she was describing? Was Daniel really a Mr. Beige, another Matt? Had I really been attracted to Gene Tretnikoff? And was I just too blind to see what was happening to Jen? Was I as deaf and blind as Jen was saying? I was supposed to be all-seeing, all-hearing Heimdall to Jen's Loki.

"Okay, suppose I can't see these things," I said. "I still think that if you had told me, in plain words, what was happening to you, I would have tried to help you. I wish you had shouted into my ears until I finally heard you and understood you," I said, trying to regain the moral high ground.

"I was too ashamed, Rachel. And I'm just not someone who shouts into people's ears. I let my pictures do the shouting and, if you take the trouble to look at my pictures and think about them, they shout plenty loud. People say pictures are worth a thousand words, right? Well, I'm never going to shout into your ear. So if you want to be friends with me, you're going to have to listen better. You're going to have to find my wavelength and listen carefully."

"I don't know how to do that, Jen, or even if I can learn how," I told her. And that was the pure, honest truth. If I had been so blind and deaf for the last thirty years as to ignore Jen's warning signs, how could I expect to do any better in the future?

"I guess we'll have to wait and see," she answered. "By the way, here's something else I'm sure you never figured out."

Jen paused for effect.

"I was the one who told Michael to offer you twenty million for a program on international crime. Of course, I was surprised when he went ahead with that idea. I mean, to the extent that he went ahead with it at all."

"Why did you tell Michael to do that?" I asked her.

"Why do you think?" she asked me. "You should chew on that for a while, Rachel."

We stared at each other for a minute, two minutes, five minutes. There wasn't anything more to say. Either we were going to develop the skills we needed to hear each other, or we weren't. Meanwhile I was freezing—my skin was turning blue and my nipples were so hard they looked like they were trying to stage an escape from my bathing suit. It was time to go.

But before we parted, Jen finally asked me a question she'd probably been wanting to ask me the whole time, perhaps her real reason for getting together that day. "So," she said. "Have you shared your theories about me and Michael's murder with your police friend? Roxy, isn't it?"

"No. Not yet."

"Not yet?"

"Don't push me. That's the best I can give you right now."

We left it at that. Jen and I weren't enemies and we weren't exactly friends either. We were acquaintances or maybe even strangers; at least Jen was a stranger to me. Would we remain strangers or develop the friendship I'd always imagined we already had? We'd have to think on that, then continue this conversation at another time. Maybe.

The problem is, I loved Jen like a sister. She was my best friend, though I had scarcely known her before. Turning her over to the police would be like gnawing off my own arm. Naturally, I recognized a duty to uphold the law. But I recognized another duty as well—a duty of love and mercy, if there is such a thing.

That night, I dreamed about Jen as she might have been before I first knew her, when she was about twelve or thirteen, when Michael first started raping her. She must have cried and screamed and then, like Hera in that picture she showed me, stared into empty space. Her eyes must have been popping out of her head, begging for someone to protect her and rescue her. And that was never going to be me. I was never going to be the hero of her story. I was Heimdall, ignorant of everything except the way things were—the status quo, the old ways.

The winter passed faster than I had expected and, finally, spring arrived, then summer, and then fall again. But the year had been far from uneventful. During the winter I had gradually discovered myself. I had thought about my addiction to "bad boys," and why I always made such bad choices in men. And I had brought my alcohol addiction under control.

After Daniel lost six of Empire's trucks gambling, Peter had bought out Daniel's share in the business, so Daniel was now a man of leisure. He didn't fit into my life anymore, so we separated, on the way to getting a divorce. He moved down to Picton, where he shares a little love nest with Rusty Wagner, just like Megan had foreshadowed. He comes up to town every other weekend to spend time with the kids, and they're handling the split just fine. They also enjoy visiting Daniel in Picton now and then and tell me Rusty is nice.

I wonder if Daniel's paid off his $110,000 gambling debt yet, or if he's continued to build it up. Either way, that's not my problem any more.

Beth Coale seems to be doing fine now too. She's living with her lover Susan at the family home in Forest Hill, and they travel a lot. Beth's beauty cream is doing well and from what I hear, she's come to terms with Will's death. Melissa is finishing university and has a new boyfriend. I haven't met him yet but I hear he's nice—not a bit like Michael.

Dean Grabol has left our university. After being head-hunted last year, he took the provost position at a large university in western Canada. The last I heard, he was raising large sums of money for their science and medical programs. Our new dean is much nicer: slightly less manic about fundraising than Sandor had been. But she's still under orders from our own provost to raise millions, just like Sandor had been.

My research assistant Connie Newton has continued to write her doctoral dissertation. Her topic is the role of rage in domestic violence, with a focus on men's anxiety about failure and disrespect. I have tried not to bug her with emergency requests any more.

My mom has written a new book, this one about the role of grandparents in raising "perfect" grandchildren. It's on the best-seller list in the US and Mom's making the circuit of talk shows again, correcting people's misbeliefs. Her message is that, in a world of precarious marriages, working mothers, and single parents, grandparents have an ever-larger part to play in raising a new generation of perfect children. But she hasn't made much of an effort to perfect my own children or Megan's, and maybe that's for the best.

Dad is playing a lot of golf and still promoting the development of Prince Edward County. Construction is already underway for a new hotel, a clinic, a restaurant/entertainment complex, and three six-storey harborside condos. Gene has flown "across the pond" a few times to see Dad and make sure everything is moving along smoothly. On one visit, Gene and I got together for dinner and chatted into the early hours. He raved about Irina's success at our university, and praised me for my own accomplishments, all as usual. Trish McCormack now runs the Calypso's loan business and will manage Gene's new condos and other Picton businesses when they're up and running.

Megan has opened new design shops in Montreal, Calgary, and Vancouver. From what I hear, they're all going well. She spent the past year jetting from one shop to another, hiring and training people and consulting on major projects. So Megan is becoming rich and famous, but she remains herself: full of fun, a doting wife and mother.

My own health is much better, I'm glad to say. I almost never have panic attacks any more, and haven't thrown up for two months now. Actually, two months and seven days. I'm still taking medication to help me keep calm, but mostly I'm doing well without it. My liver is recuperating too. Al K. Hall and I are still friends but we don't see each nearly as often as we used to. The blackouts have ended too. Goodbye darkness, my old friend. I've learned to fix my life.

After all that's happened, I'm still fascinated by legends and fables and theories. They all seem more real to me, and more important, than most of the stuff that goes on in "real life." You may think that's crazy, but that's what I believe, for all sorts of reasons. Through legends and fables, I connect with my cultural roots and feel like I belong to something bigger than myself.

More than that, fables—even fables that feature animals or gods with human traits—teach me moral lessons. They remind me of what is right and wrong, and the consequences of making bad choices. In the world that existed before modern science, many hundreds of years ago, legends and myths helped people to understand the world of nature. Today, they still teach us—well, they teach me—about good and evil, the origins of the world, and human existence. They still help me make sense of the world around us. They also provide me with comfort in the face of things that are unknown and unexplainable.

For their part, the theories I love, whether they are scientific, philosophical, or speculative, stimulate my curiosity. They help me to explore the world in a deeper, more nuanced way. Even the legends and fables about Loki contain theories about the cosmos and the way the world works. And the legends of another culture help me think more clearly about the culture I live in. They also inspire my imagination.

Sometimes, I can relate to the characters in fables and legends even more than I can to people in "real life." They offer me insights into the personal challenges I am facing. And they help me reflect on my own life, so I can do a better job at solving the problems I face.

Seeing the world through the lens of theories—also, fables and legends—helps me make sense of reality. To be sure, it has its shortcomings. I'm not as attentive to the "real world" as some people I know—don't see and hear everything that's going on. Maybe that's why I didn't know so much of what I should have known about Jen, Michael, and Daniel. I was paying more attention to the stuff inside my head than to stuff that was in front of my eyes. Still, if I had the choice, if I could trade one kind of vision for the other, I don't think I would do it.

But that's just me. Maybe you do things differently.

And then there's the BIG QUESTION about Jen. (That's how Gene would have said it.) How did her story end? Did she get away with Michael's murder or go to prison? Well, you need to know there was a postscript to that frozen poolside conversation we had.

37

A few weeks after our get-together at the swimming pool, Jen contacted me again. By then I'd had enough time to miss her and to replay our last conversation in my head a million times. As the year came to an end, she sent me a card wishing me the best for 2023 and suggesting we get together. Inside she had printed a famous photo of Anne Sullivan with her prize pupil, the deaf and blind Helen Keller. The message read "Let's meet. Wish you could hear. Love, Annie."

So, I accepted her invitation and we arranged to meet for another meal at the Miller Tavern. I parked my car in the same spot as last time and found Jen inside at the same table as before, drinking the same drink as before. So, I followed suit and ordered the same drink as I had ordered the last time too.

Then I noticed Jen was wearing the same long-sleeved white blouse as Anne Sullivan had worn in that famous photo.

"Nice blouse," I said.

"Thank you," she answered. Then she beamed at me and I was glad I'd come. I felt her smile light up the room; then after a few brief pleasantries, she got right to it.

"I want to thank you, Rachel," she said.

"What for?"

"For the fact that no cops have come around to ask me about my alibi, or Michael's other diary, or my suicide attempt, or Robert's first gun. I assume all that's your doing. Or not doing."

I pointed to her blouse and said, "I can hear you now, Jen. And I'm sorry it took me so long to realize what you went through. It's just that, I can hear you but I still can't process it. I always thought there's no excuse for murder but… I mean, how am I supposed to judge what it feels like to go through … what he did to you? The point is, I can't tell the police what I know about you. They'll have to work it out for themselves."

"I see your difficulty," Jen said, looking around the room—everywhere except at me.

"I'm embarrassed at how naïve I was to think I could judge, or even understand, the kind of rage you must have felt. I know nothing about rage, really."

"Does that mean you're amping up your rage research?" Jen asked, smiling.

"No. Actually, I'm dropping it. I want to learn more about a non-violent crime like tax evasion or money laundering. Robert's specialties."

"He'd be honored," Jen said, just a bit ironically.

"Actually, a lot of my life feels fraudulent. I'm ditching my marriage because it feels done. Daniel and I were never soulmates, and we never will be. And I can't do fundraising anymore. Dean Grabol chewed me out for failing to bring in the Coale donation and I just don't care. I don't want to raise money to memorialize creeps anymore. So I'm putting that behind me too."

"Your dean is an ass-face for not appreciating how hard you worked for him," Jen said.

"Thanks for saying that," I told her. "You're right, he was. And I'm glad to say he's soon going to be my ex-dean."

"Rachel, that's one of the reasons I wanted to meet. I can't help you with Daniel or your crime research. But I can help with your fundraising if you'll let me. Quit fundraising if you're done, but there's no need to slink away. You can still land two of the biggest donations your unappreciative ass-faced soon-to-be ex-dean has ever seen."

"What are you talking about?"

"I've convinced Beth to donate twenty million to your school for a program on domestic violence. And Gene and Martha want to donate another twenty million to honour Robert with a program on international crime."

Instinctively, I started thinking how pleased my new dean would be. And how happy my parents would be. This would be the perfect accomplishment my mother had been waiting forty years to witness, and Dad would see it as a shrewd bit of business. Then I stopped myself. I realized I couldn't do this. Anita would agree—this was a no-brainer.

"Sorry, Jen. It won't work for me."

From the look on her face, Jen was either genuinely puzzled or a great actor. "What's the matter? Do you think I'm trying to trick you?" she asked. "I'm not really Loki, you know. Every now and then, when I'm with my best friend, I let my guard down and speak honestly. Don't you even know that, Rachel?"

Then she added, "I guess this means you still haven't figured out why I asked Michael to give you that donation in the first place."

"Tell me."

"Because it was part of my own personal odyssey—my way of recovering from what Michael had done to me as a girl. I wanted some good to come from all his wealth and all the suffering he had caused me. The donation I pushed him to give you was my apology for introducing you to Michael. So if you accept the Coale donation, it will be like accepting my apology."

I didn't know—still don't know—if Jen the trickster was telling the truth or just trying to manipulate me for the hundredth time in our lives. But I wasn't going to take credit for either of the donations Jen had secured. I was out of the fundraising business. My life and sanity depended on that.

"I'll put you in touch with Dean Grabol, and he'll deal with those donations. That way, I can stay out of fundraising, and you and I can work on just telling each other the truth. But I need some truth from you right now: Who was I to you, during this long journey of yours towards revenge? Why did you want me around?"

"You were my safe harbour, Rachel, the loyal friend who was waiting for me, if I could ever make it home. You were my kind and wise and reliable helper."

In that moment, I finally understood our connection. It was flawed, as all human connections are, but it was our own. Despite all our arguments, deceptions and betrayals, I knew there was a bond of love between Jen and me. It had been battered and bruised, but it was still there, still intact. And that made me very happy. If Jen needed to be Loki, I would be her loving friend and partner, Sigyn. If Jen needed to be Ulysses, on an endless mission to god-knows-where, I would be her Penelope. And then I thought, if I sometimes needed to be Ulysses, Jen would be *my* Penelope. And if I sometimes needed to be Loki—hard to imagine, but possible I guess –Jen could be *my* Sigyn. I liked that idea.

We sat together, lost in our thoughts and connected by our shared history. Here we were, two friends trying to make sense of the world, of each other, and of our place in the grand scheme of things. Jen shrugged, acknowledging the craziness of our situation, and I came over to her side of the table. We sat next to each other, held each other's' hand, and for a long time we were quiet together. What would happen next, I wondered.

In the Norse myths, one of the nicest things Loki did was to save the goddess Idunn. Idunn was the keeper of the apples of youth, which the gods needed to eat to remain young. According to this myth, Loki initially helped a giant to kidnap Idunn. However, realizing the gods were aging without the apples, Loki felt remorse. Or maybe, he just wanted to avoid the wrath of the other gods for his role in Idunn's disappearance. To fix the problem, Loki transformed himself into a falcon, flew to the giant's realm and rescued Idunn. In fact, he transformed her into a nut to carry her easily, and flew her back to Asgard. By returning Idunn and her apples, Loki ensured that the gods would regain their youth and vitality.

This was the best Loki could do: his most virtuous act. But Loki's mere ability to do good on occasion, even when his actions were motivated by self-preservation, gave me the basis for hope. Someday, Jen would also do good for the sake of goodness alone, I thought. And when she did, I hoped she wouldn't turn me into a nut.

You may think that this account of how I finally solved the case of Michael Coale's murder was long and unlikely. Well, maybe it was, but it happened anyway. And as far as twisted, unlikely stories go, my story is simple as pie compared to the story of why Loki helped to kidnap Idunn.

According to the Norse myth, that incident began when Loki was traveling with Odin and Hœnir and they found themselves without food. They slaughtered an ox but found they couldn't cook the meat because a giant named Thjazi, using magic, had prevented it from cooking. Thjazi, in the form of a great eagle, offered to help them if they allowed him to eat from the ox too. The gods agreed, but Thjazi took a disproportionately large share of the meat. This made Loki so angry that he struck the giant with a stick. Thjazi, still in eagle form, flew away with Loki hanging on.

In exchange for his release, Loki had to promise to bring Thjazi Idunn and her apples of youth. So crafty Loki lured Idunn out of Asgard by telling her he had found some apples that he thought were as good as her own and that she should bring hers to compare them. Once they were away from Asgard, Thjazi, still in eagle form, took Idunn and flew away with her to his home, Thrymheim. And you know the rest of this story.

Well, here's what I make of that. First of all, tricksters seem to get themselves into unnecessary trouble all the time, and I don't plan to do that. I've had as much trouble as I will ever need or want. In fact, I promise to never try to solve another murder case—well, not unless I have to. Second of all, the cosmos is full of dangerous liars and shape-shifters. The worst of them are like Michael Coale, J-C Guzman, and Bobby Gupta, and deserve to die. But even the best of them—people like Gene Tretnikov or Bradley Wong—are dangerous. You can't really trust any of them, unless you are very lucky.

Third of all, everyone—even good people like Sigyn—is travelling through life in the midst of eight billion other sentient creatures who all have their own agenda. In the midst of all that traffic, you are sure to get bounced around now and then. If you're lucky, someone will come to your aid and, often, you can't guess where or when or how that will happen.

And I was lucky this time. Still at the Miller Tavern, Jen finally put her head on my shoulder and sighed. We were good friends again, in a tentative kind of way. I liked that feeling, though I had no idea what would happen tomorrow, or next week, or next year. With Jen, you could never predict the future.

But I found out the future sooner than expected.

Only a week later, I got an email from Jen. "I'm off on another mission, taking photos for a new book about the Global South. I'm not sure when I'll be back. So stay safe, Rachel, and be kind to yourself." When I phoned Matt to ask him about this, he said simply that Jen had left without any forwarding address, turning over to him the deed to their home and all their other shared property.

In the months that followed, I would get postcards from Jen every now and then, postmarked Rio di Janeiro, Cape Town, Mumbai, Fiji, and even Tierra del Fuego. They were always brief and cheerful, and always signed, "Love from your friend Jen."

Acknowledgments

This is a work of fiction and all the characters in it are fictional —figments of my imagination. That said, the book is intended to capture features of real life that I have found intriguing and, in some cases, disturbing. I hope the book will not seem merely fictional to you, the reader.

A first-time novelist has lots of people to thank for their help, so here goes.

First and most important, I want to thank my brother-in-law Al Wain for his continued support, suggestions, editorial work, and help animating and reorganizing my book. This novel never would have gotten anywhere near its intended destination without Al's imagination and skill. I also want to thank Les Butler, Al's partner, for her diligence in line-editing an earlier version of the novel.

Then I want to thank the people who read versions of this novel and gave me encouragement and suggestions for improvement. They included Michael Adams, Leah Brooker, Joy Fielding, Carl Korody, Nathan Ly, Nikki Meredith, Rachel Rosenberg, Diana Roy, David Stover, Joe Tepperman, Jack Veugelers, Wendy Wain, and Jeannette Wright.

Another group of people read the final version of the novel and provided useful reviews, some of which are excerpted on the cover of the book. They included Michael Adams, Rick Blechta, Rosemary Gartner, Neil Guppy, Bruce McGregor, Lars Osberg, Murray Pomerance, and Julian Tanner.

My wife, Sandra Wain, provided valuable advice and encouragement. She also showed a great deal of patience as I sequestered myself to write innumerable drafts of this book.

So thank you, Sandy, for putting up with this long but finally fruitful process.

My daughter-in-law Elena Tepperman set up a website for the book. Equally important, Elena created a cover for the book and captivating pictures of the novel's lead character, Rachel Tile.

Finally, I want to thank my friend and publisher, David Stover. David encouraged the preparation of this book and has, over several decades, encouraged me in the writing of non-fiction books. Some of these books were published by Rock's Mills Press, which David created. Others were published by Oxford University Press (Canada), which David previously headed. So thank you David for your continued support. Over the years, you have helped me immensely.

In the end, many people deserve credit for features of this book that are meritorious. Only I deserve blame for the features that are less-than-meritorious. With that in mind, I hope you enjoy the book.